A **NORMA** AND **BELLY** BOOK

DONUT
FEED THE

SQUIRRELS

This book was drawn with pencils, sumi brushes, sumi ink,
and watercolors on watercolor paper.

All rights reserved. Published in the United States by RH Graphic, an imprint of Random House Children's Books, a division of Penguin Random House LLC, New York.

RH Graphic with the book design is a trademark of Penguin Random House LLC.

Visit us on the Web! RHKidsGraphic.com • @RHKidsGraphic

Educators and librarians, for a variety of teaching tools, visit us at RHTeachersLibrarians.com

Library of Congress Cataloging-in-Publication Data
Names: Song, Mika, author, artist.
Title: Donut feed the squirrels / Mika Song.
Description: First edition. | New York : RH Graphic, [2020] | Audience:
Ages 5–7. | Audience: Grades K–1. | Summary: "Belly and Norma are the
best of squirrels . . . or so they think! After discovering donuts for
the first time, they are determined to get some for themselves, even if
they have to outsmart the food truck driver to do it!"— Provided by publisher.
Identifiers: LCCN 2019043727 | ISBN 978-1-9848-9583-7 (hardcover) | ISBN
978-0-593-12527-4 (library binding) | ISBN 978-1-9848-9584-4 (ebook)
Subjects: LCSH: Graphic novels. | CYAC: Graphic novels. |
Squirrels—Fiction. | Doughnuts—Fiction. | Humorous stories.
Classification: LCC PZ7.7.S6456 Do 2020 | DDC 741.5/973—dc23

Designed by Patrick Crotty

MANUFACTURED IN CHINA
10 9 8 7 6 5 4 3 2 1
First Edition

A comic on every bookshelf.

A **NORMA** AND **BELLY** BOOK

DONUT
FEED THE

SQUIRRELS

mika Song

Also by Mika Song

Tea with Oliver
Picnic with Oliver

To Jae

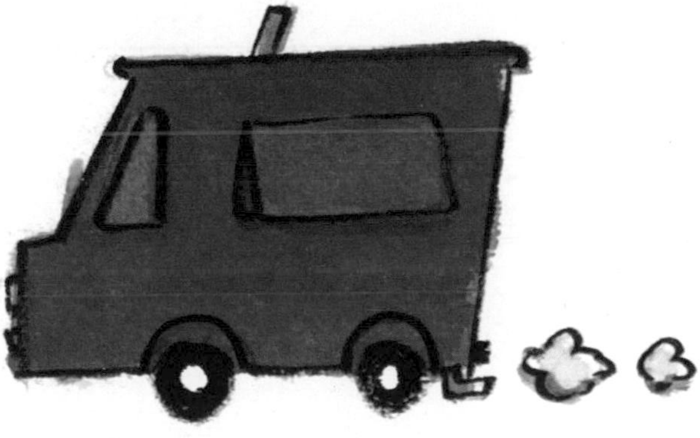

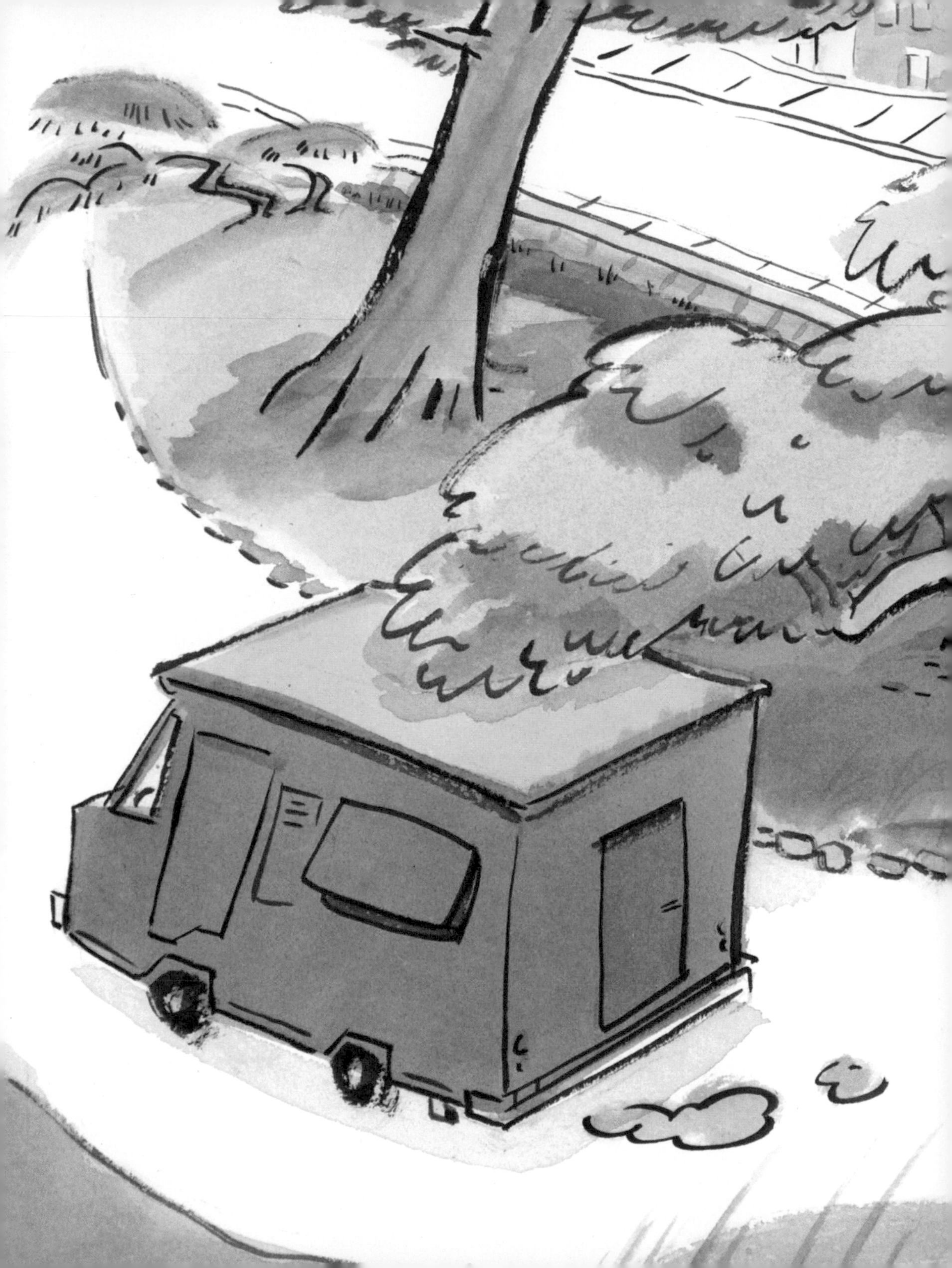

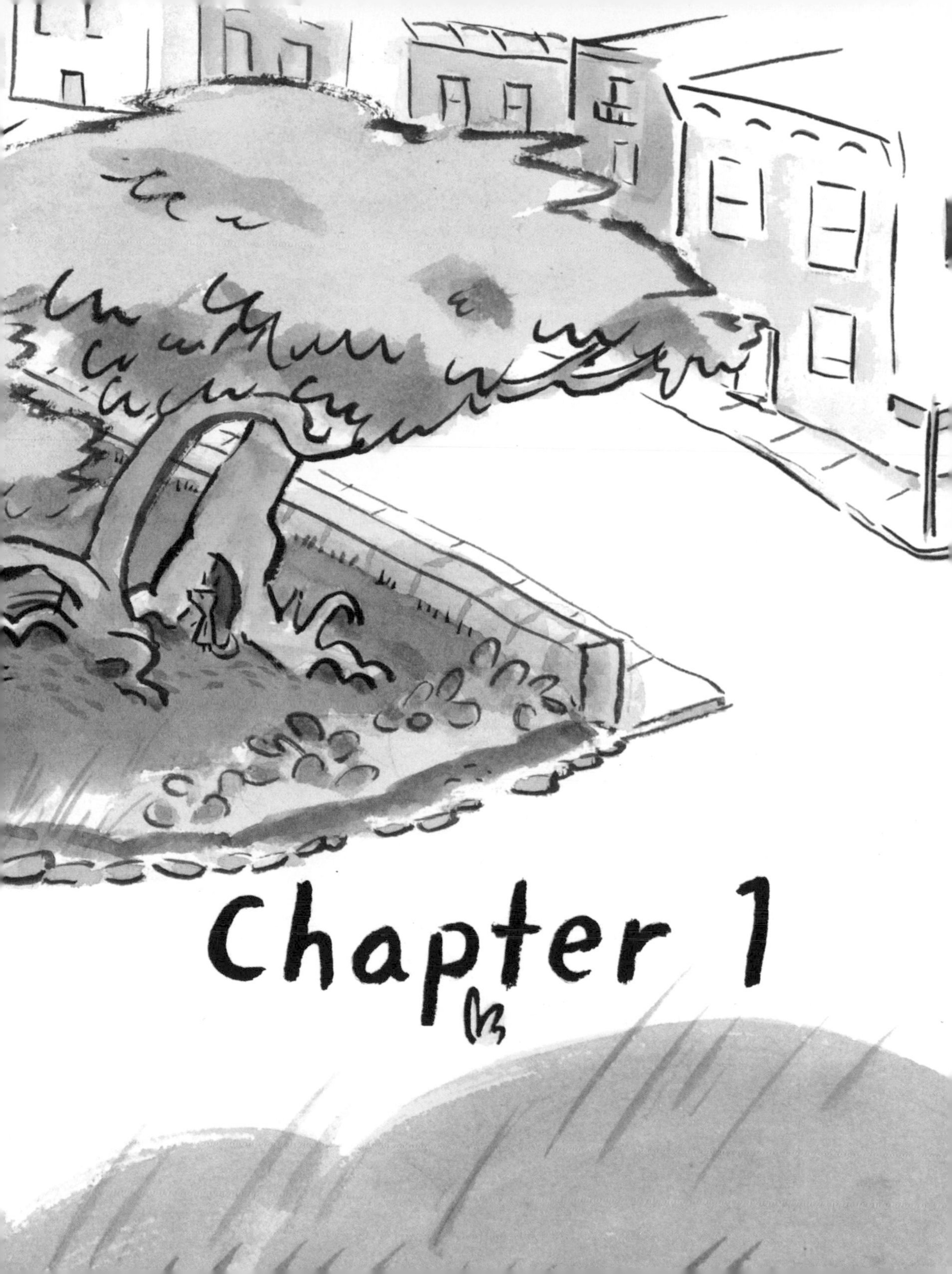

Chapter 1

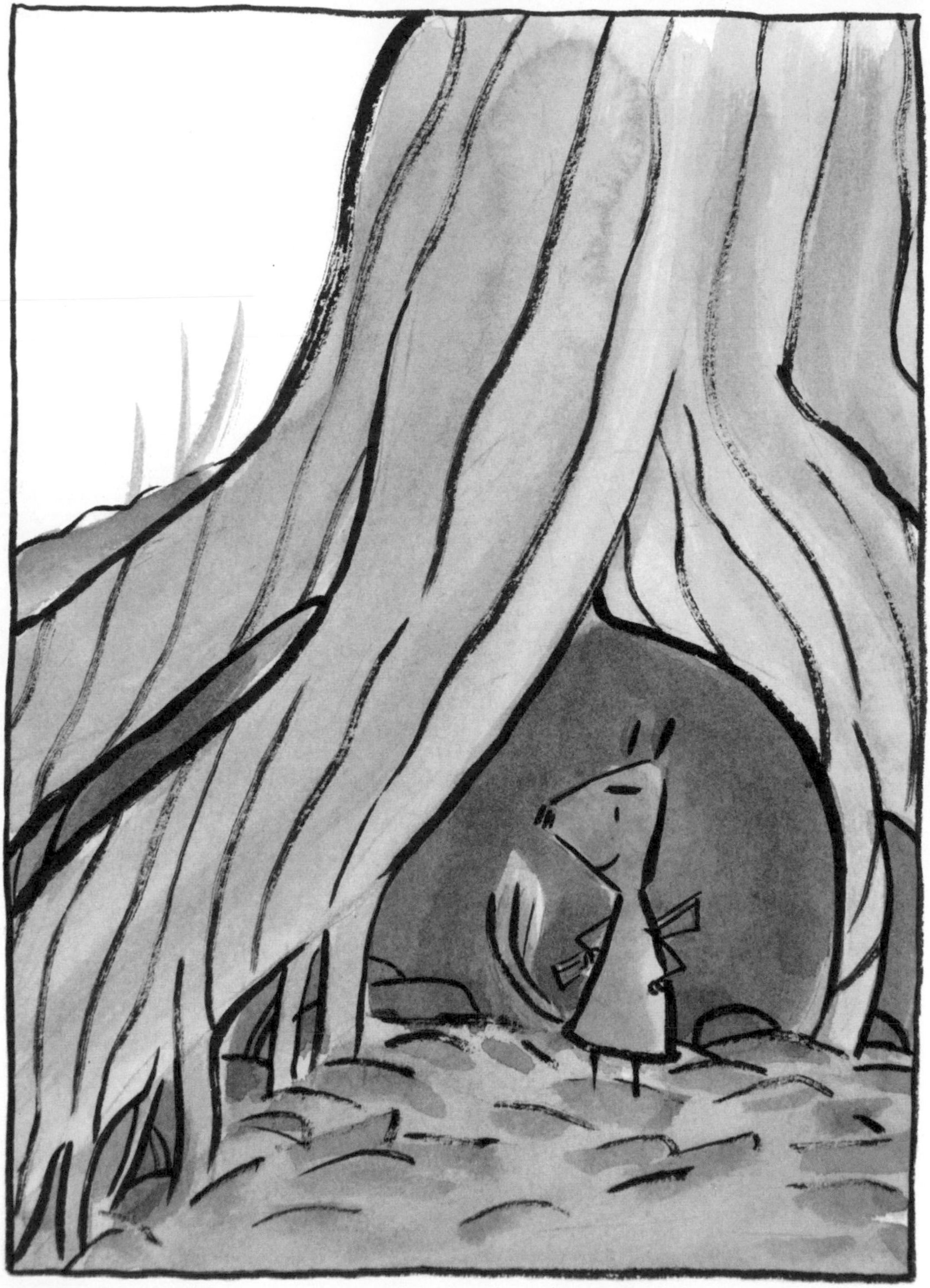

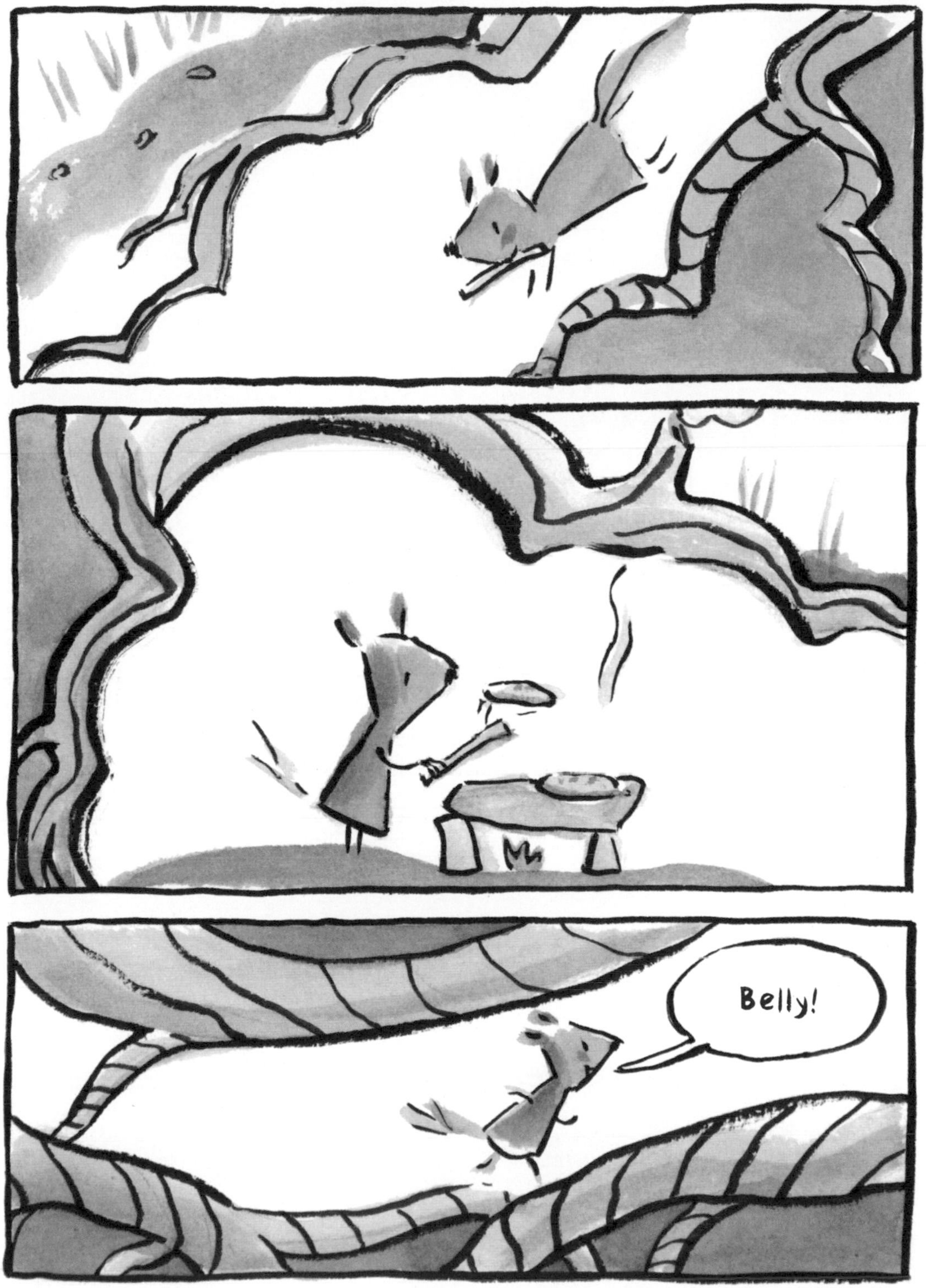
Belly!

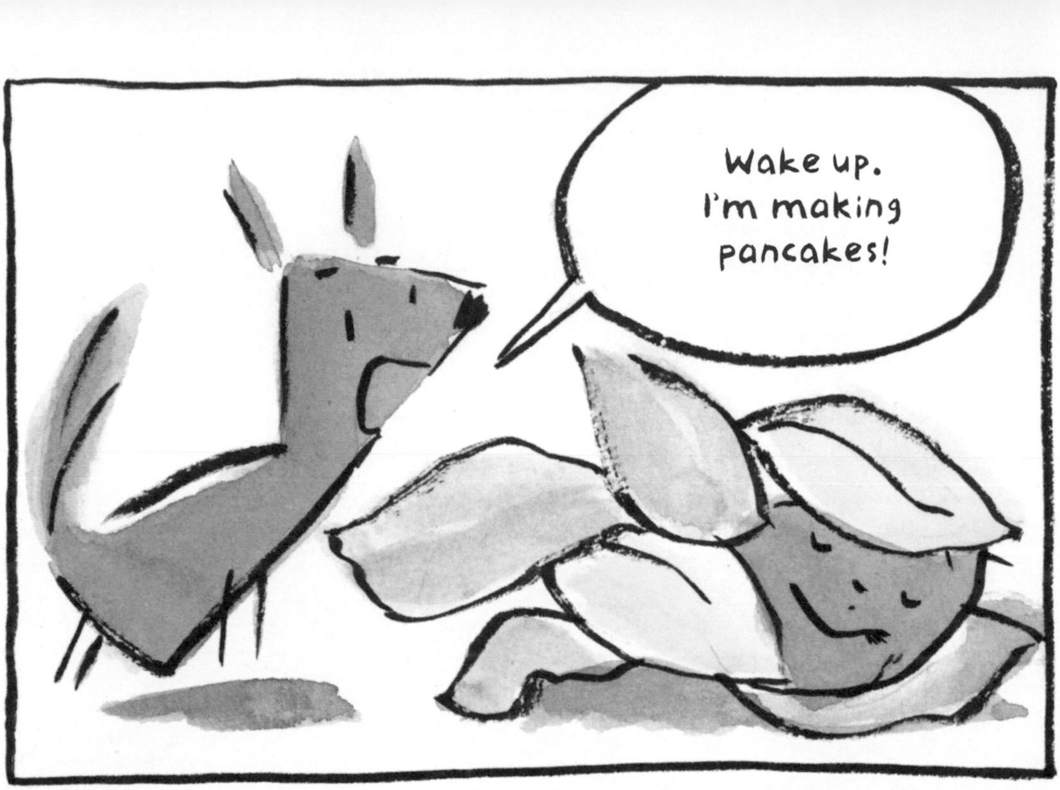
Wake up.
I'm making
pancakes!

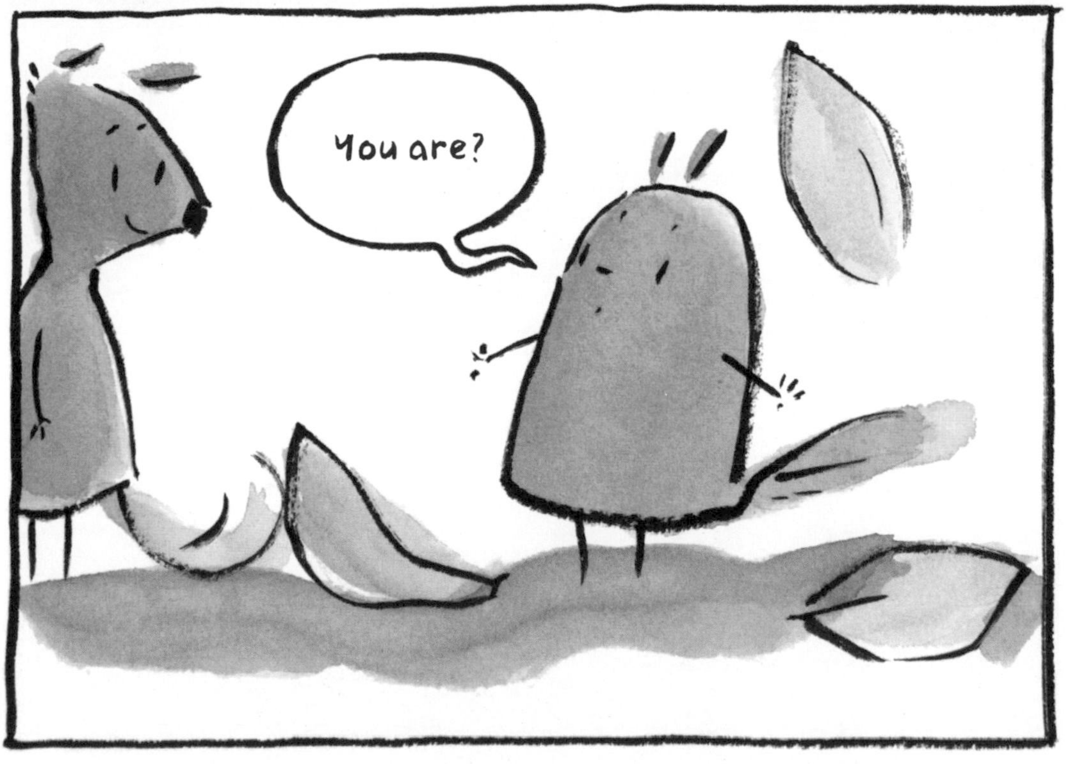
You are?

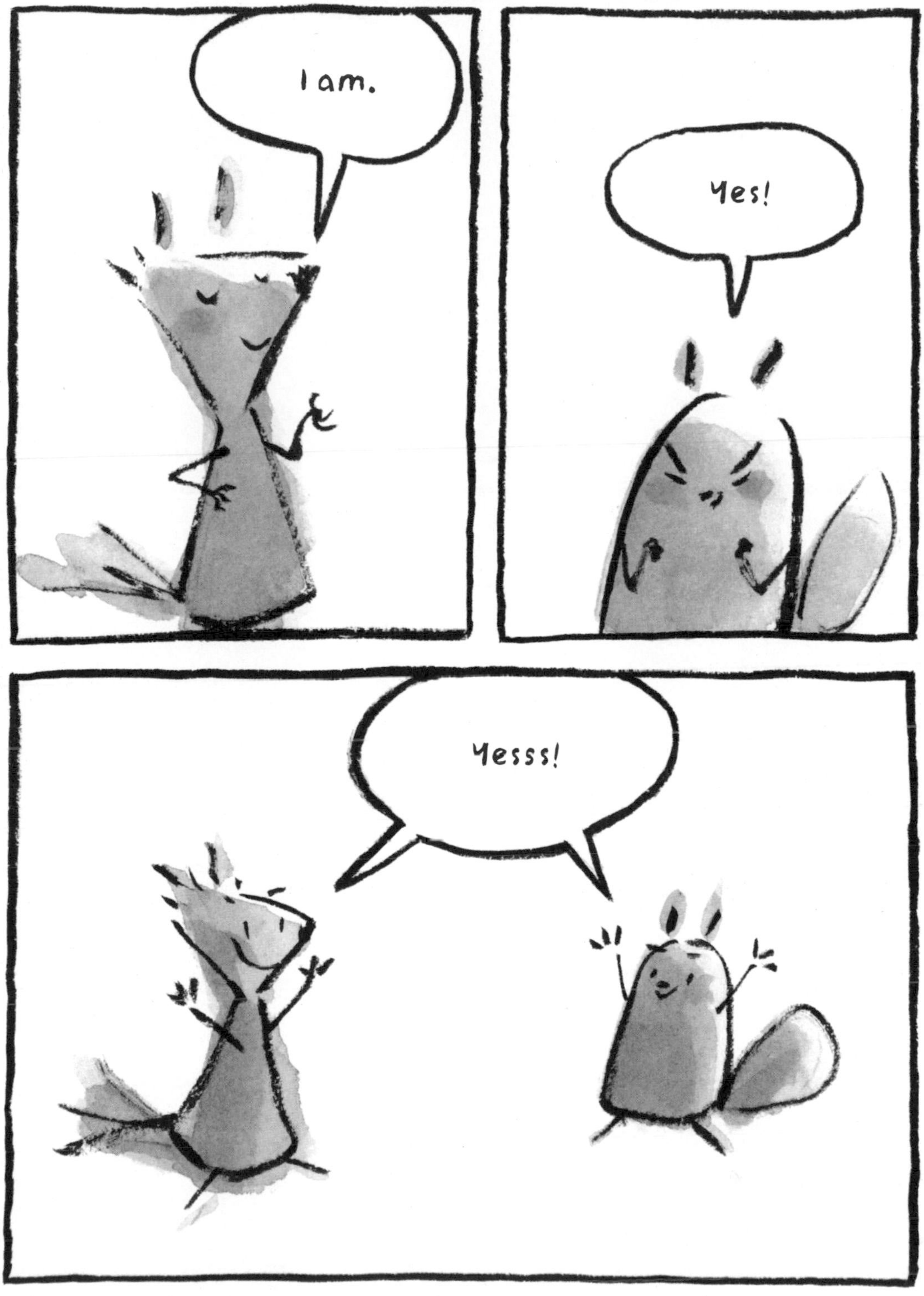
I am.
Yes!
Yesss!

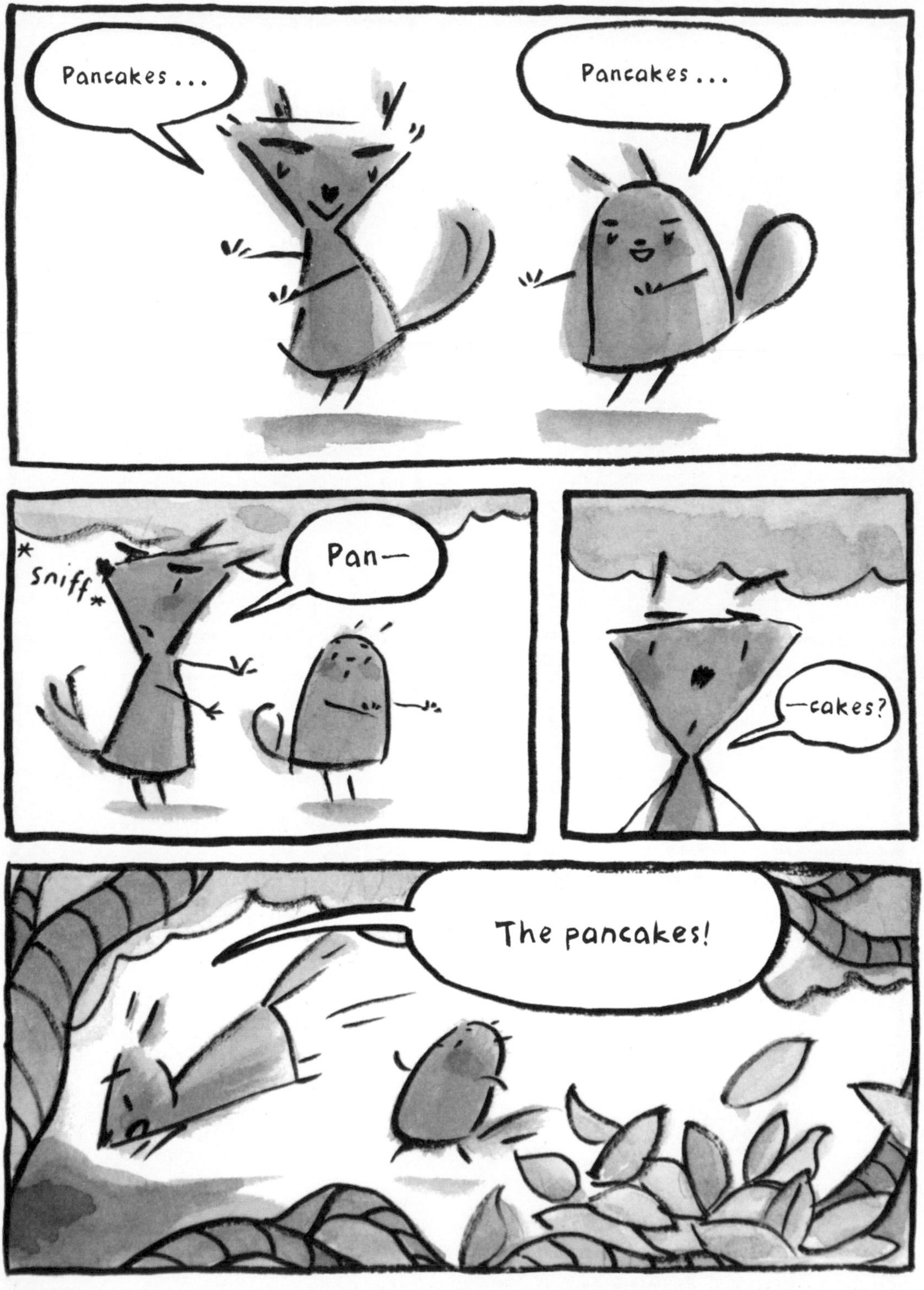
Pancakes . . .
Pancakes . . .
sniff
Pan—
—cakes?
The pancakes!

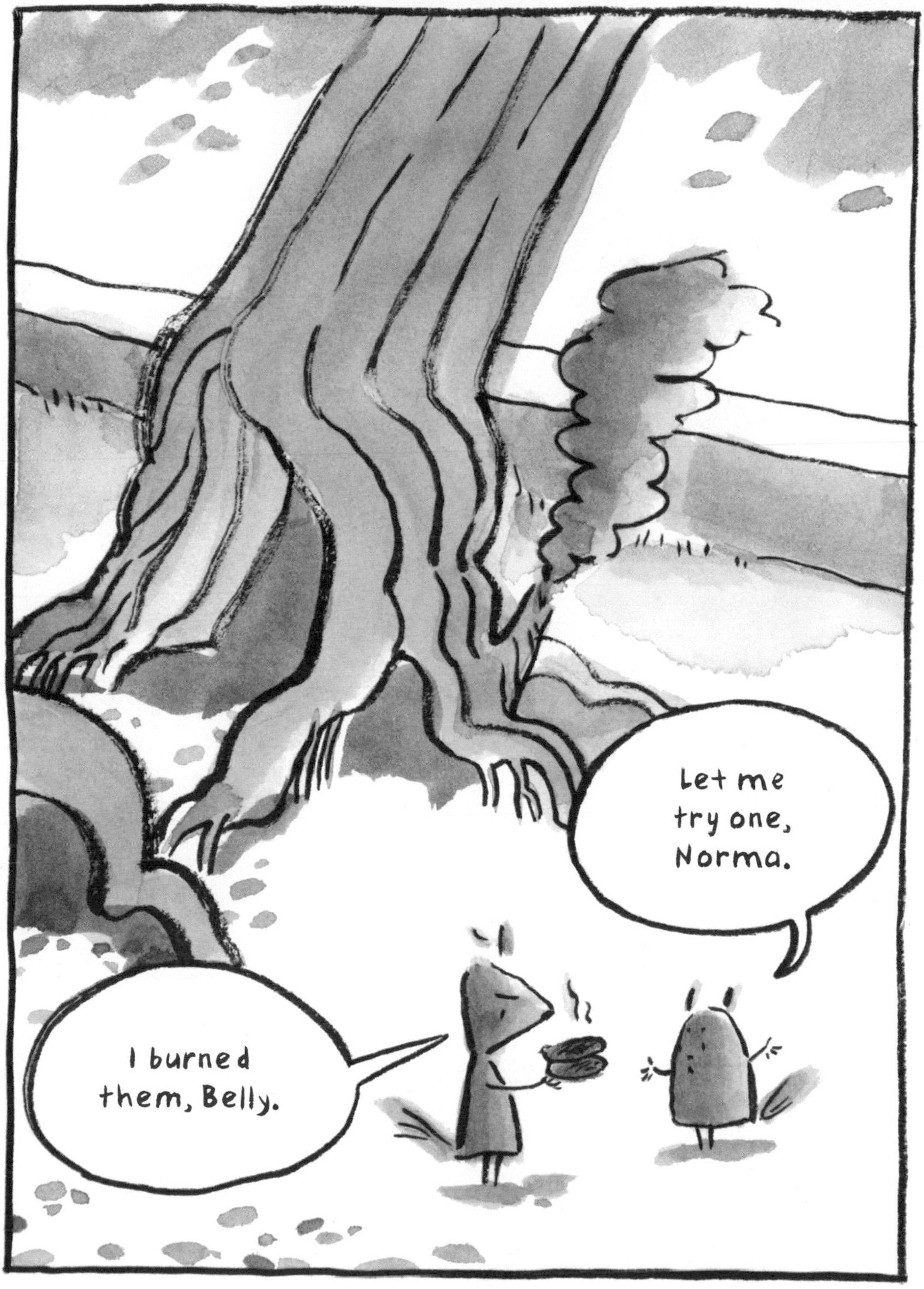
Let me try one, Norma.
I burned them, Belly.

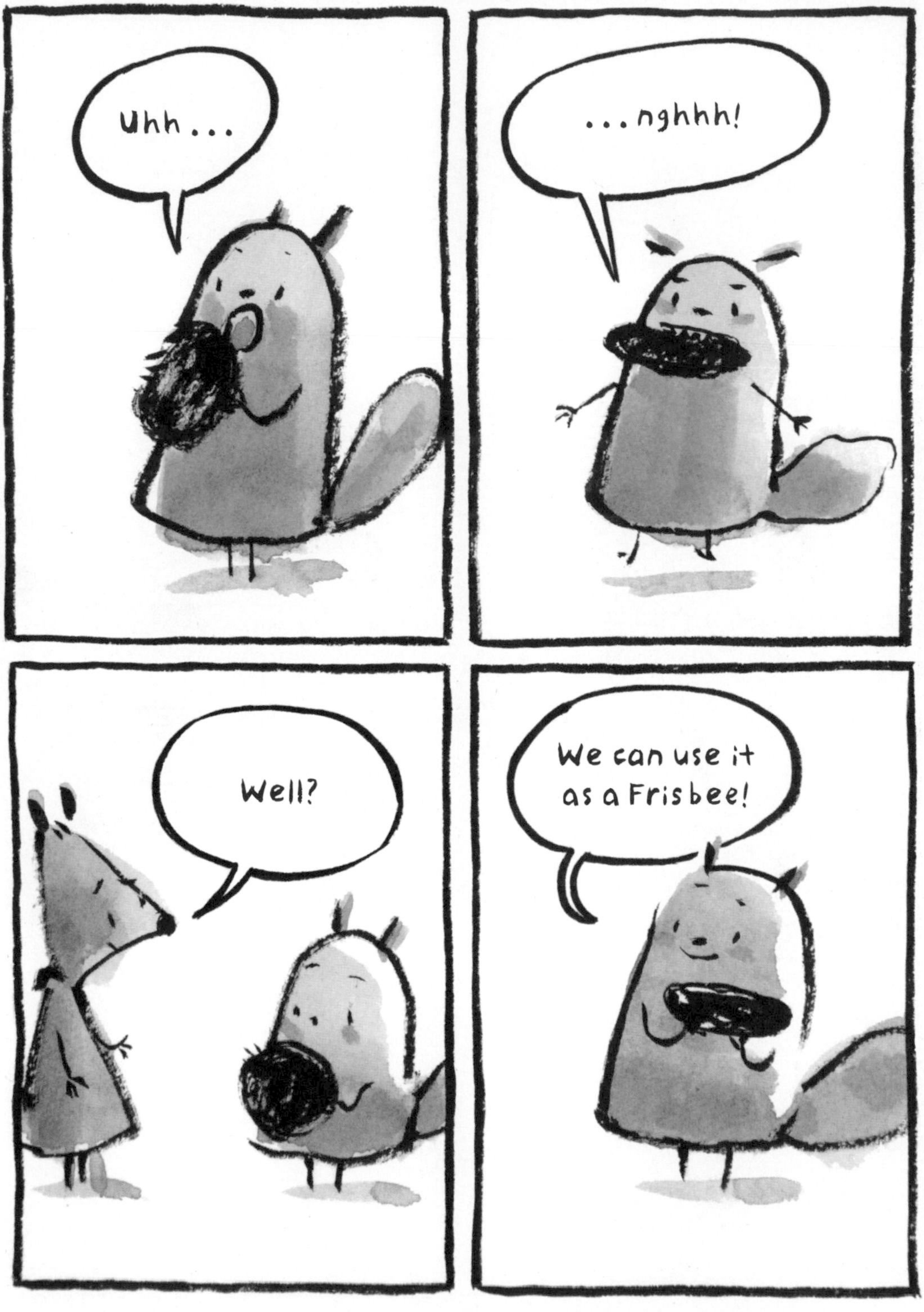
Uhh...
...nghhh!
Well?
We can use it as a Frisbee!

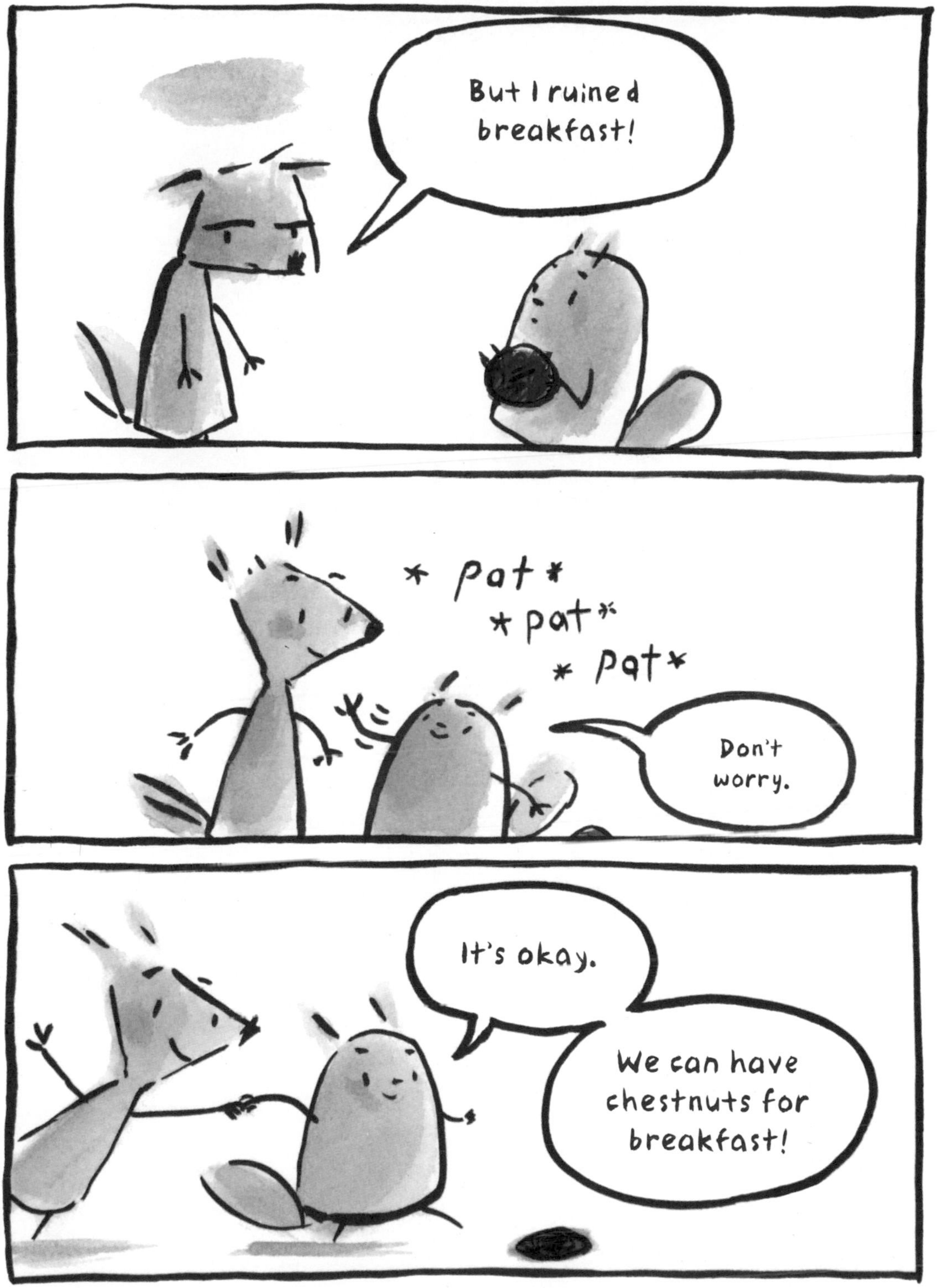
But I ruined breakfast!
pat
pat
pat
Don't worry.
It's okay.
We can have chestnuts for breakfast!

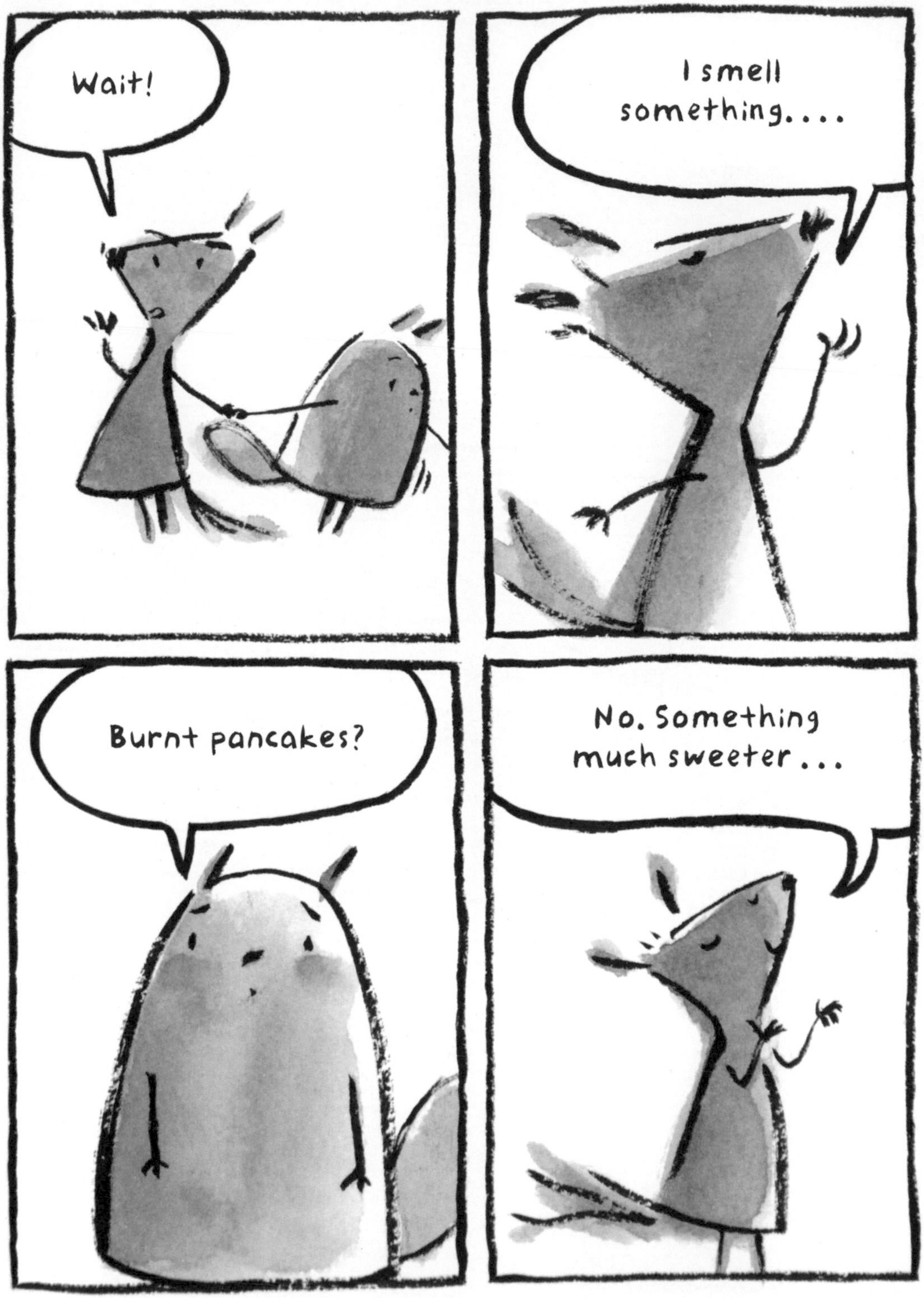
Wait!
I smell something....
Burnt pancakes?
No. Something much sweeter ...

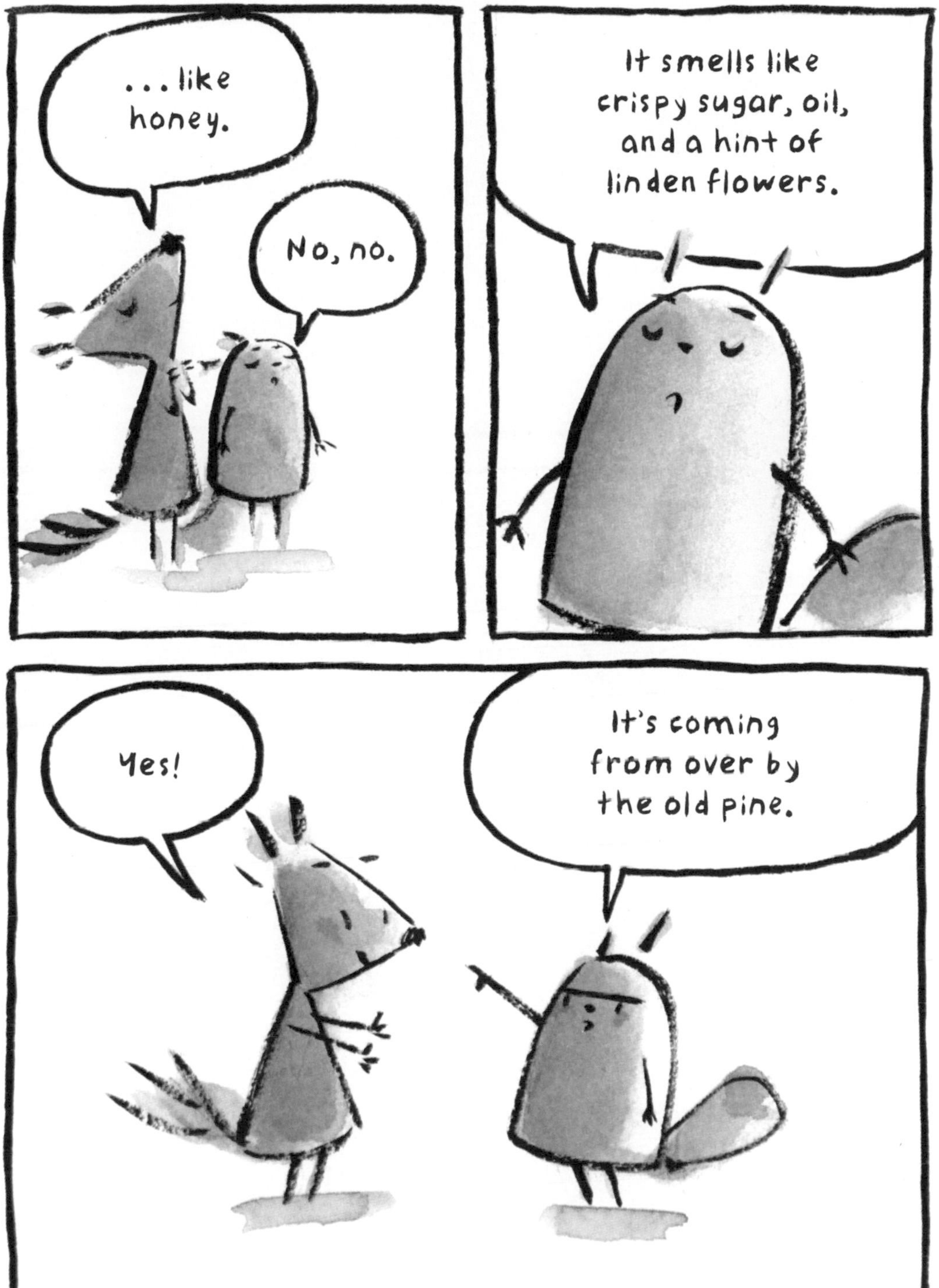
...like honey.
No, no.
It smells like crispy sugar, oil, and a hint of linden flowers.
Yes!
It's coming from over by the old pine.

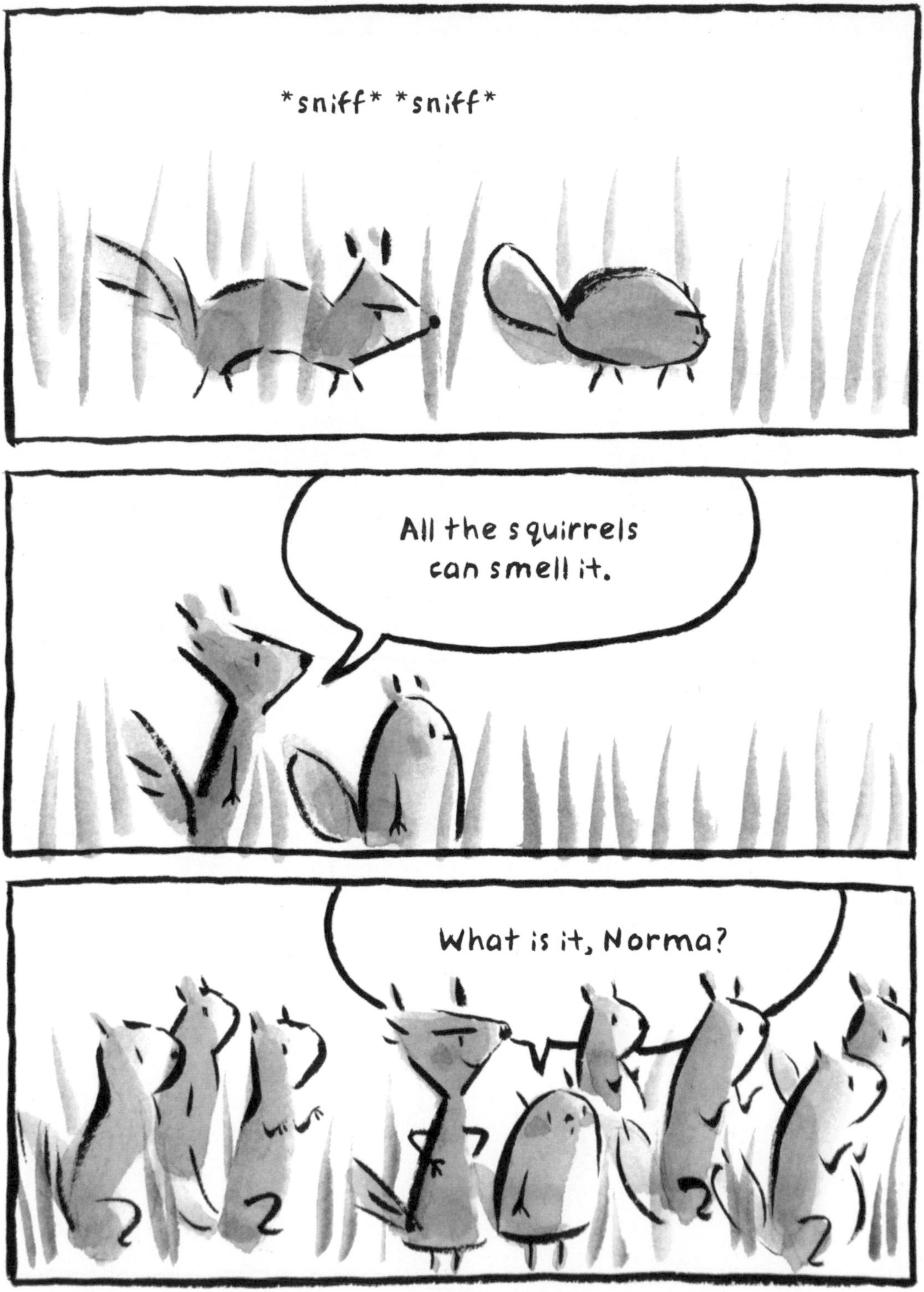
sniff *sniff*
All the squirrels can smell it.
What is it, Norma?

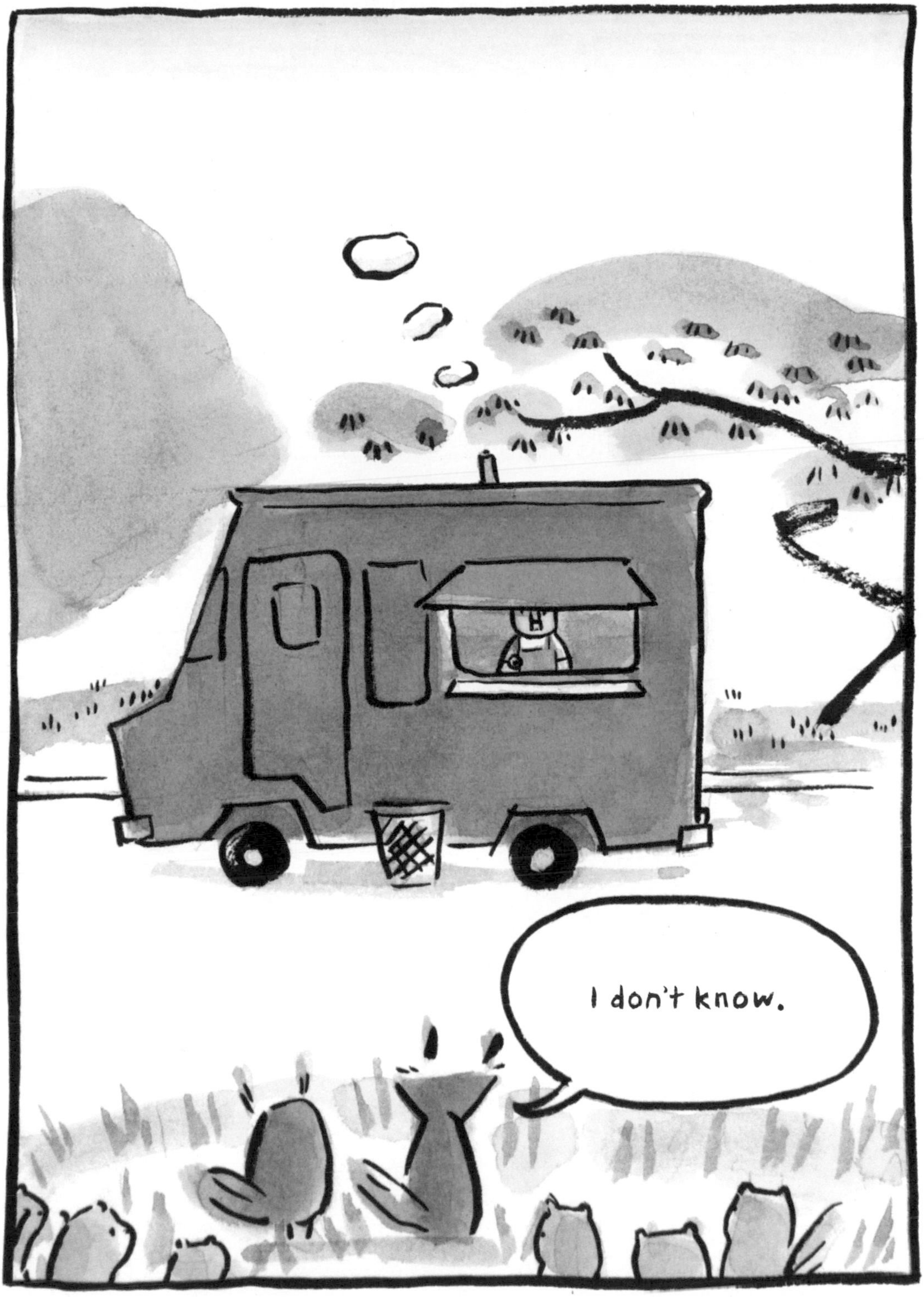
I don't know.

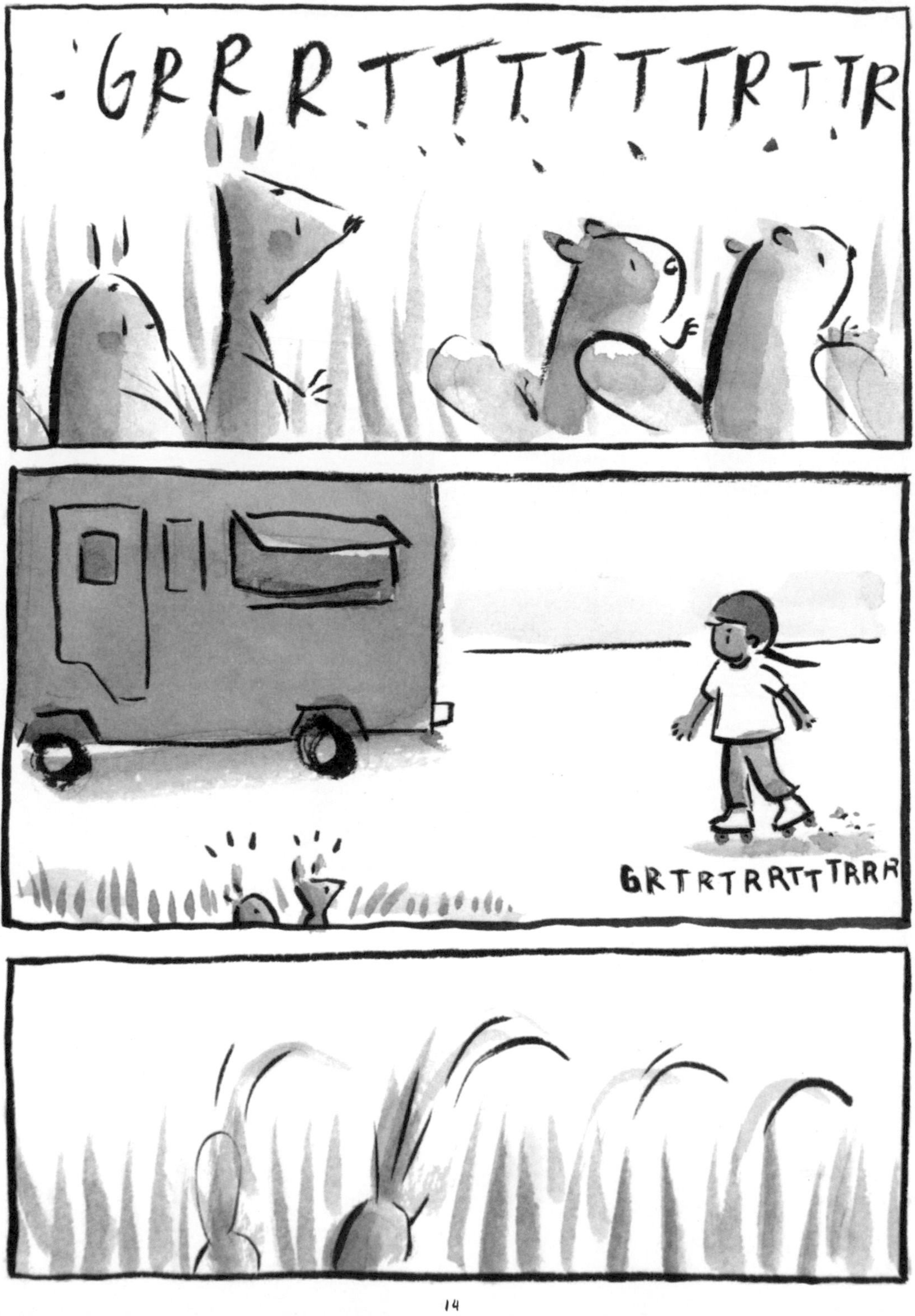
GRRRTTTTTTRTTR
GRTRTRRTTTRRR

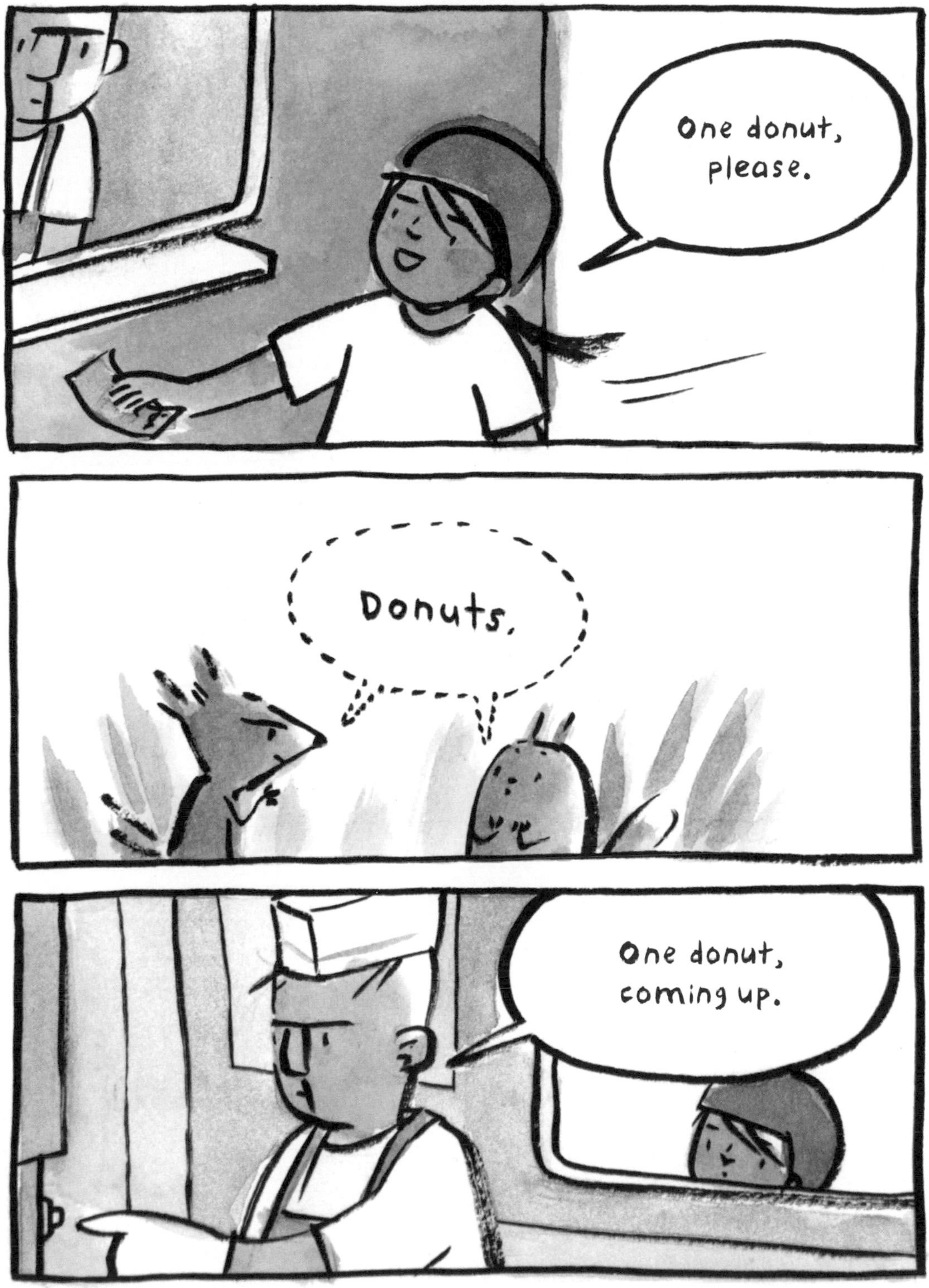

One donut, please.
Donuts.
One donut, coming up.

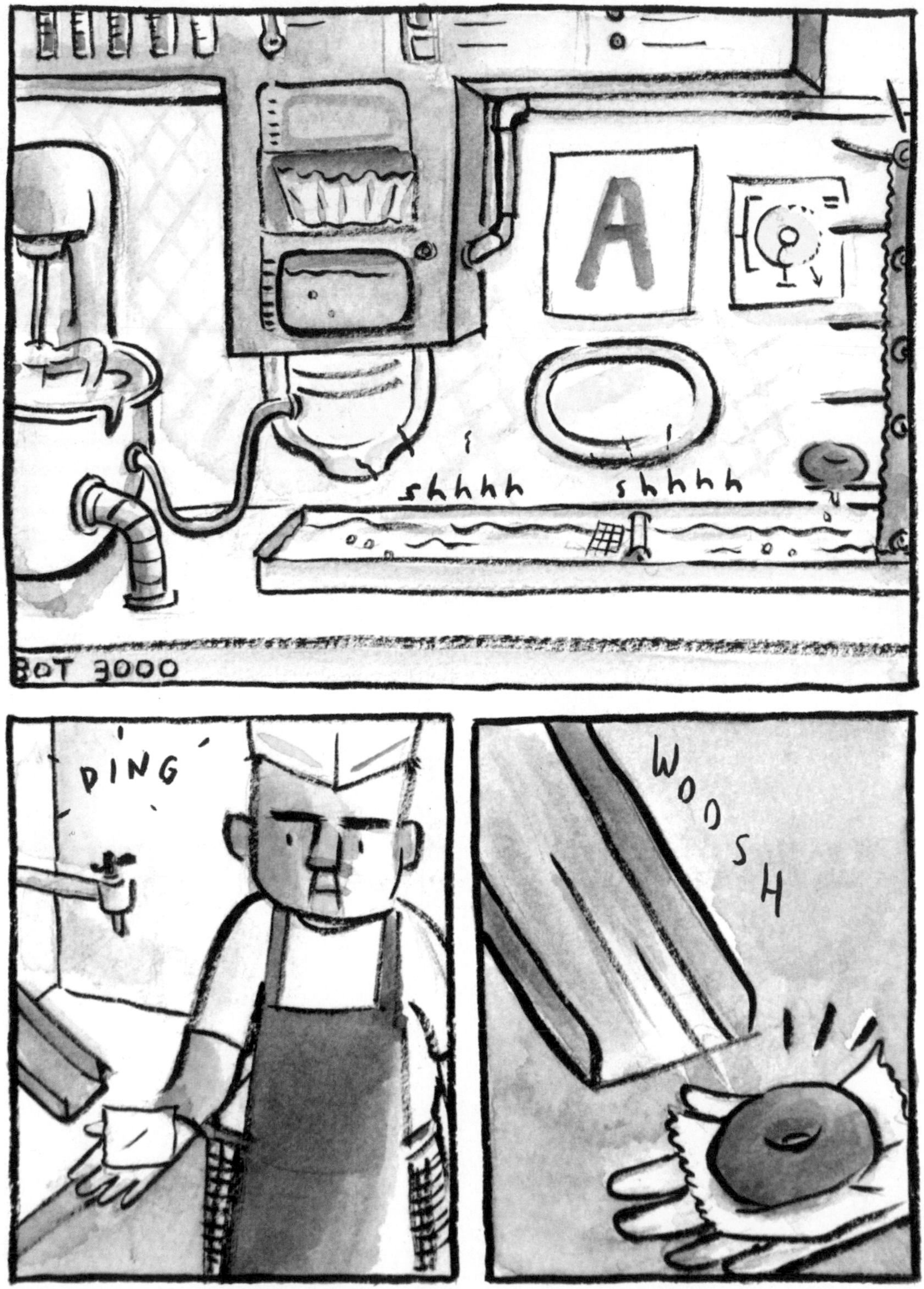
BOT 3000
shhhh shhhh
DING
WOOSH

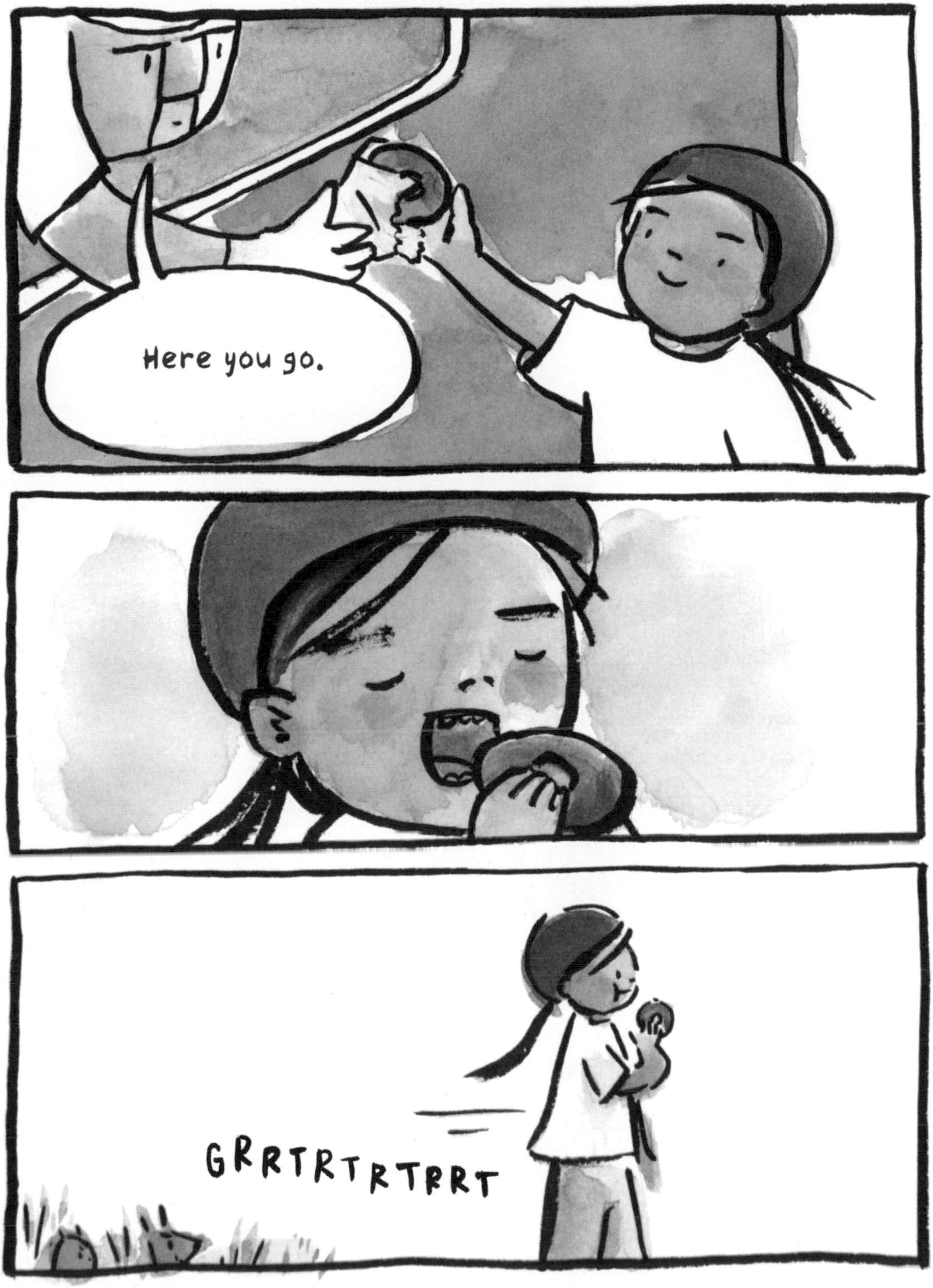
Here you go.
GRRTRTRTRRT

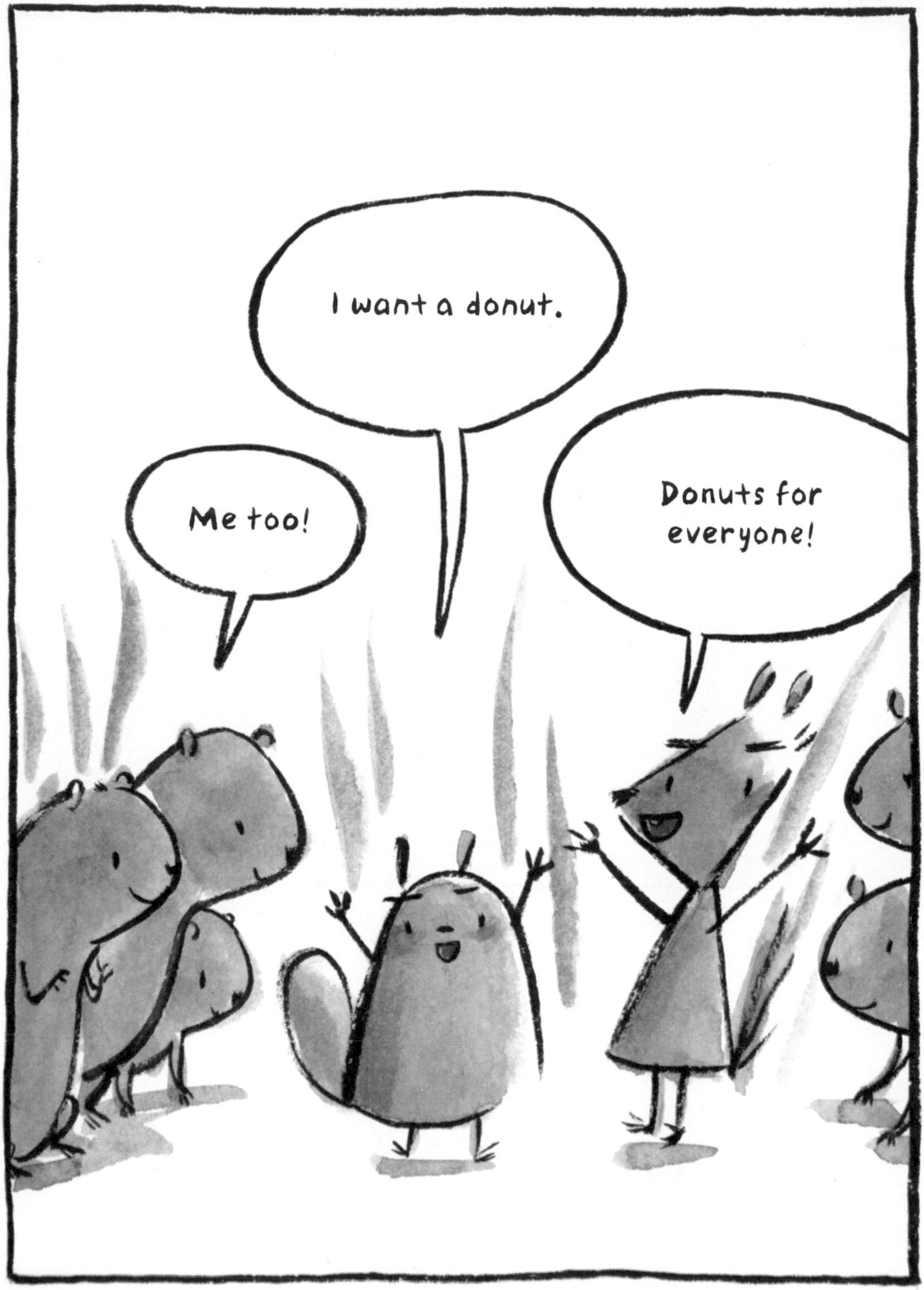
I want a donut.
Me too!
Donuts for everyone!

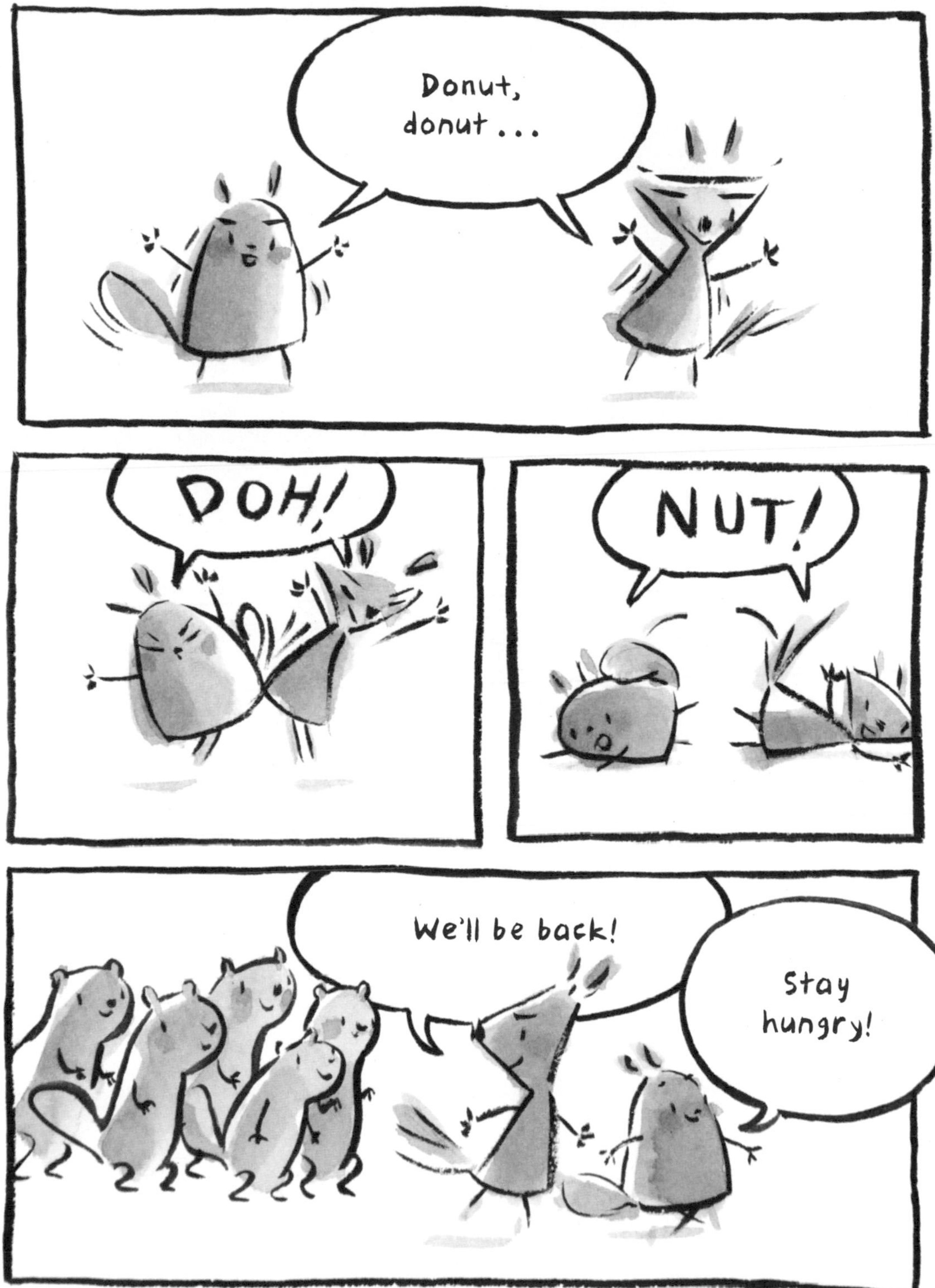
Donut,
donut . . .
DOH!
NUT!
We'll be back!
Stay
hungry!

Chapter 2

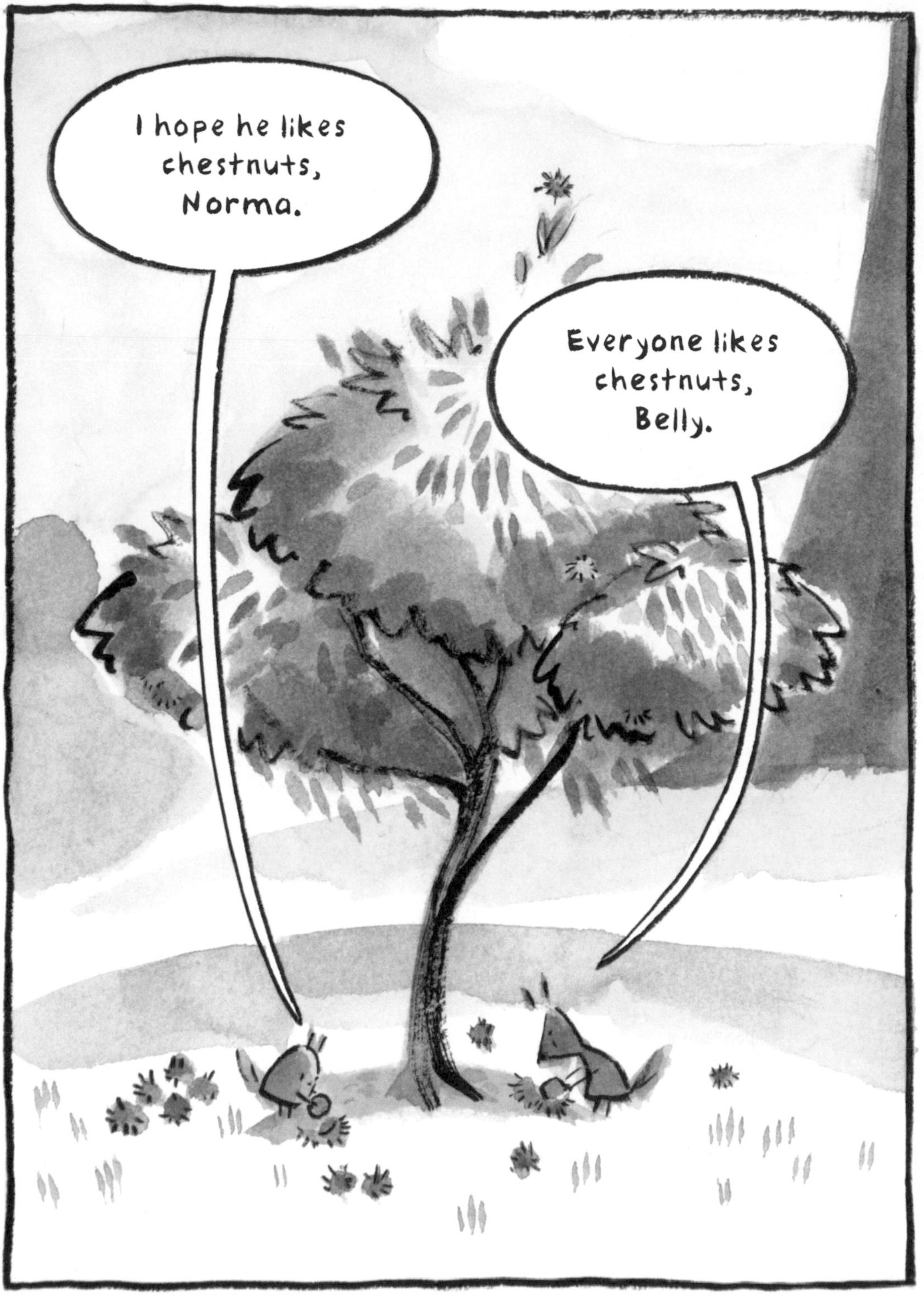
I hope he likes chestnuts, Norma.
Everyone likes chestnuts, Belly.

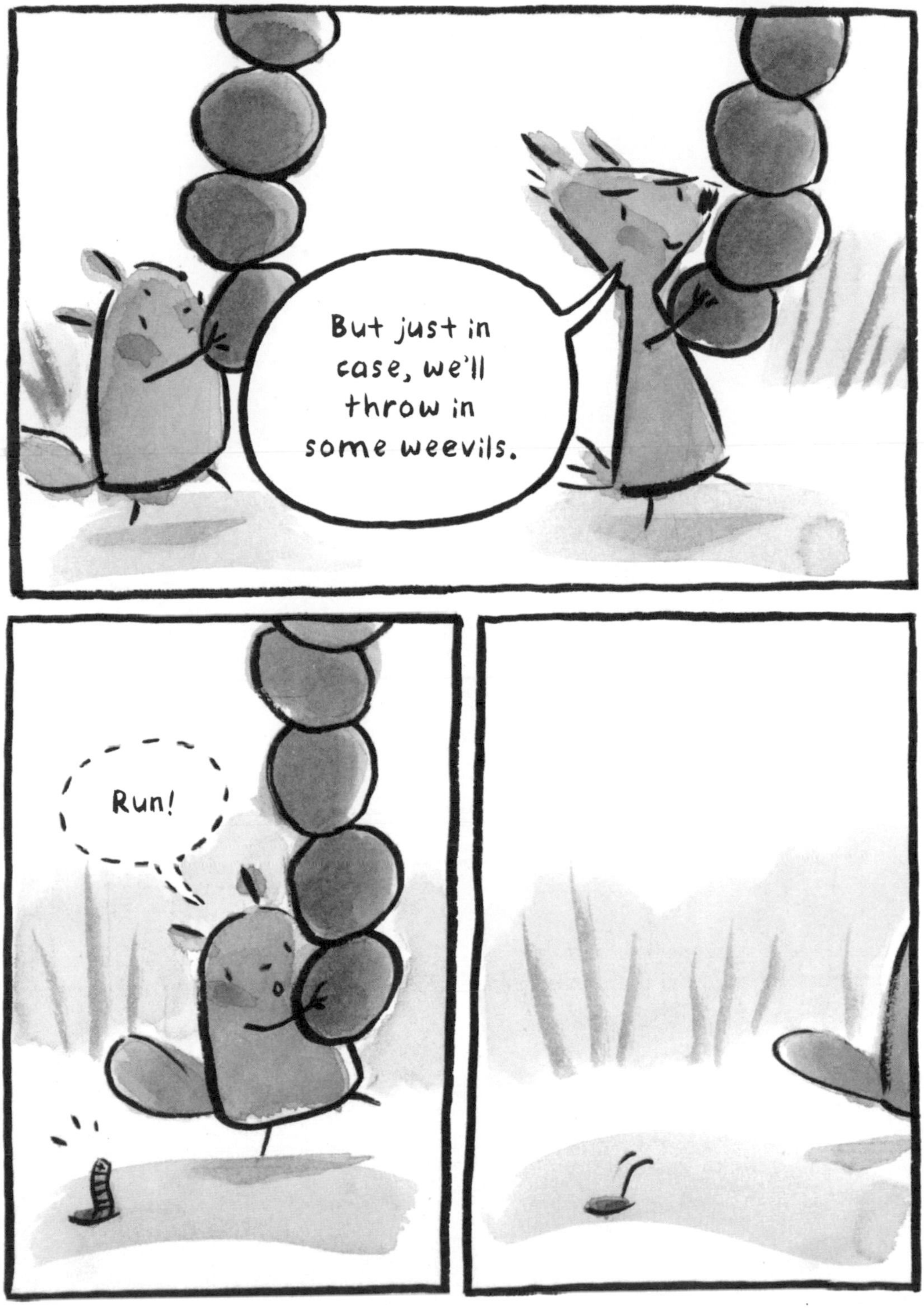
But just in case, we'll throw in some weevils.
Run!

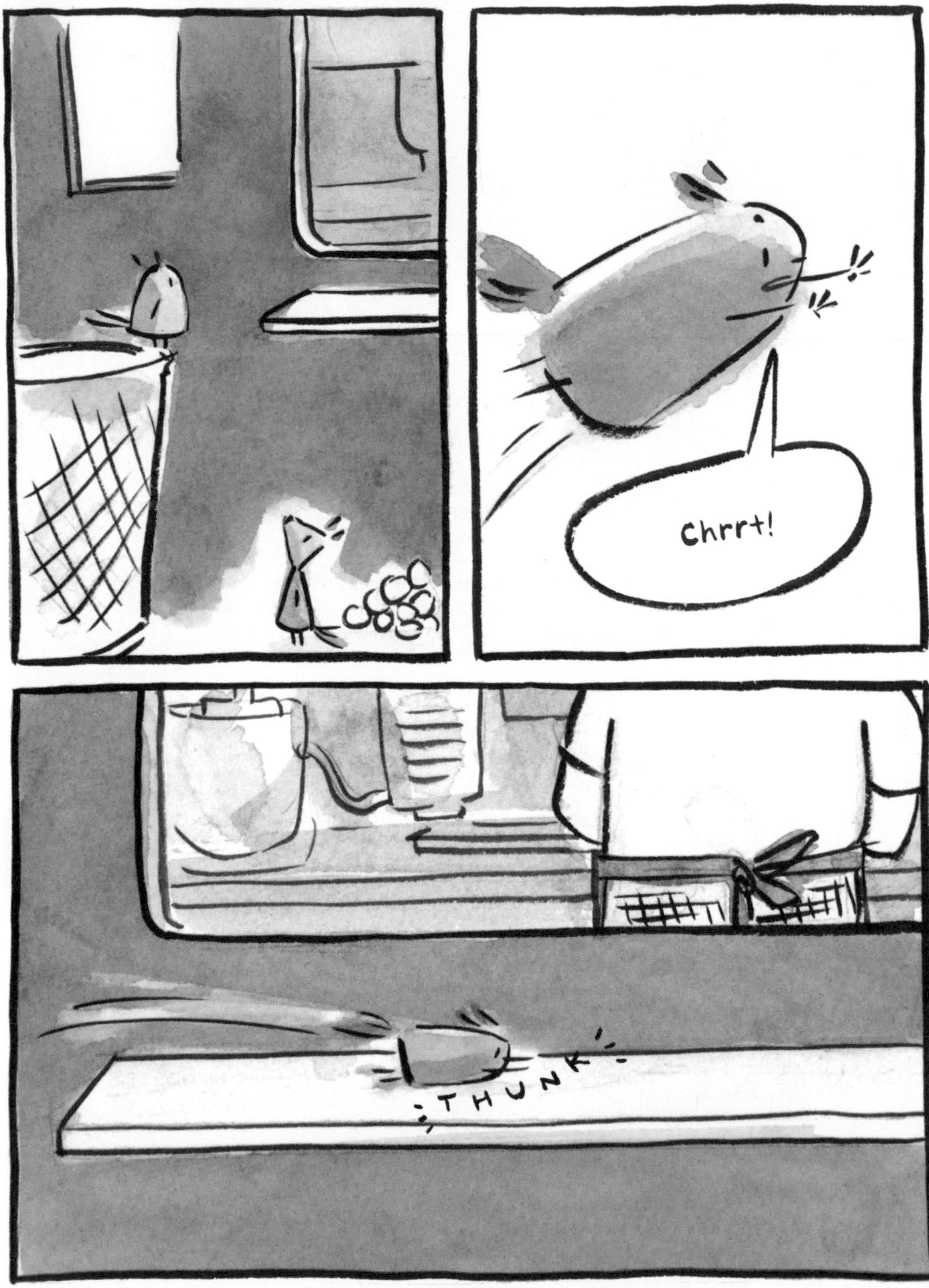
Chrrt!
THUNK

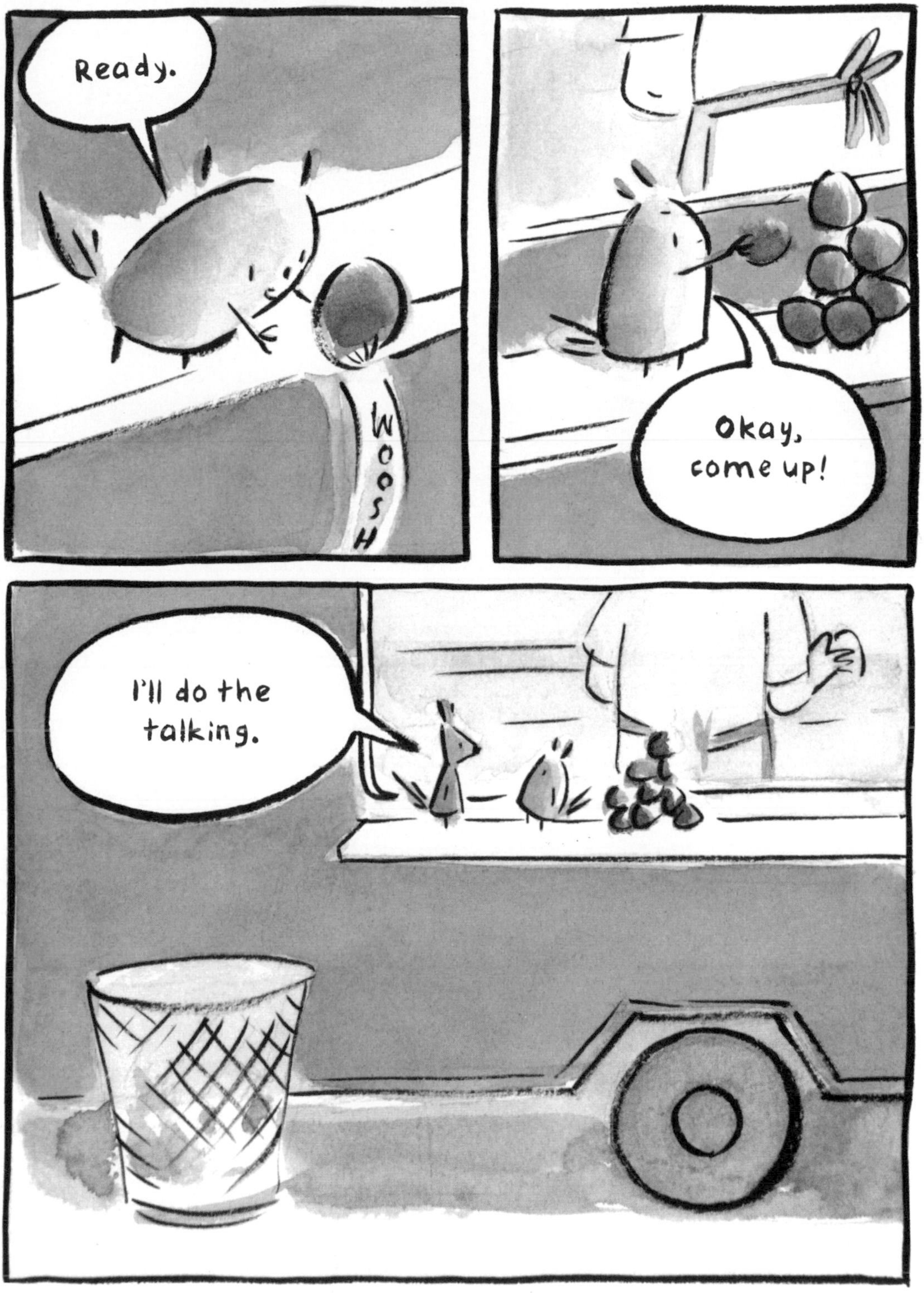
Ready.
WOOSH
Okay, come up!
I'll do the talking.

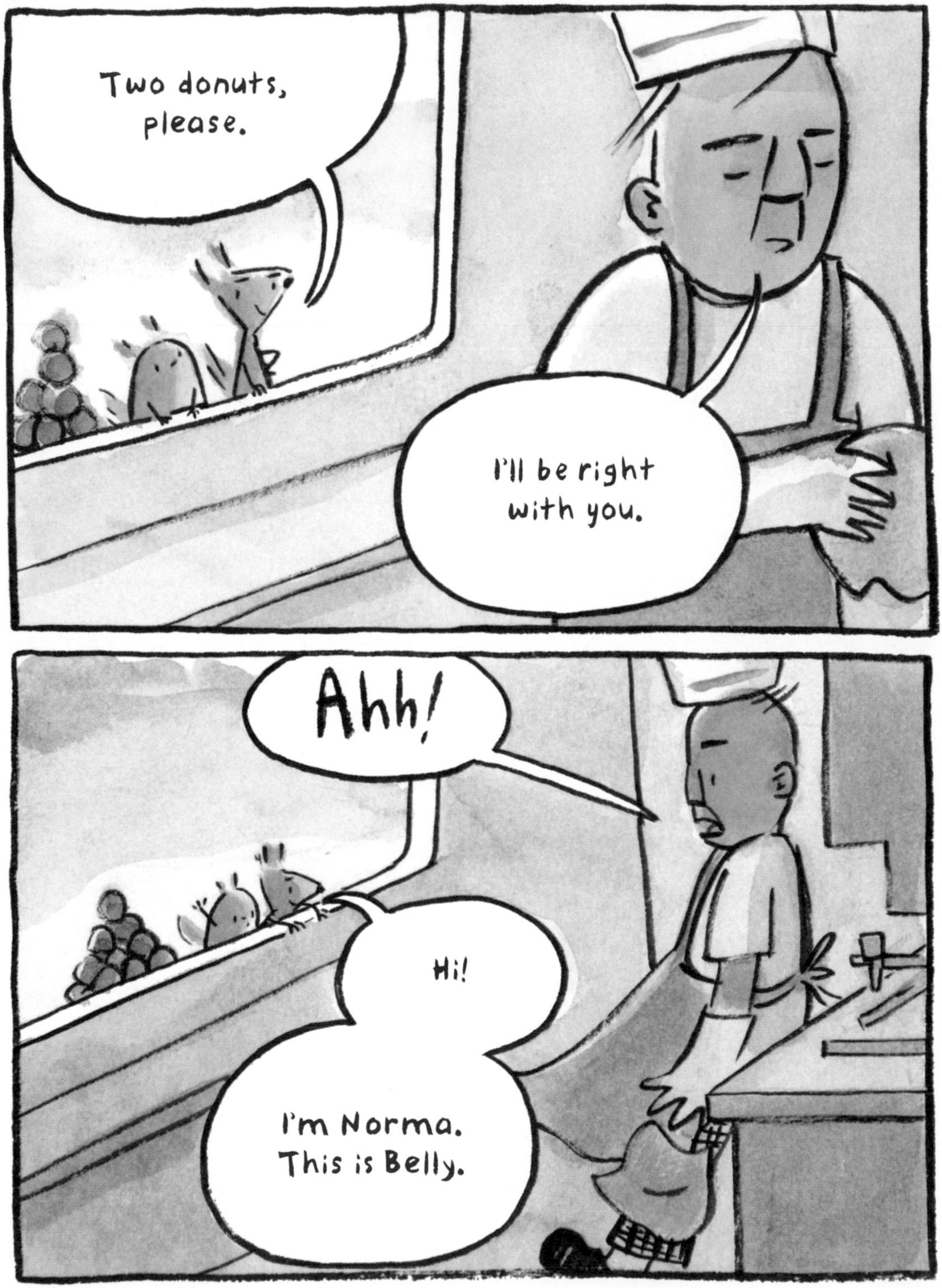
Two donuts, please.
I'll be right with you.
Ahh!
Hi!
I'm Norma. This is Belly.

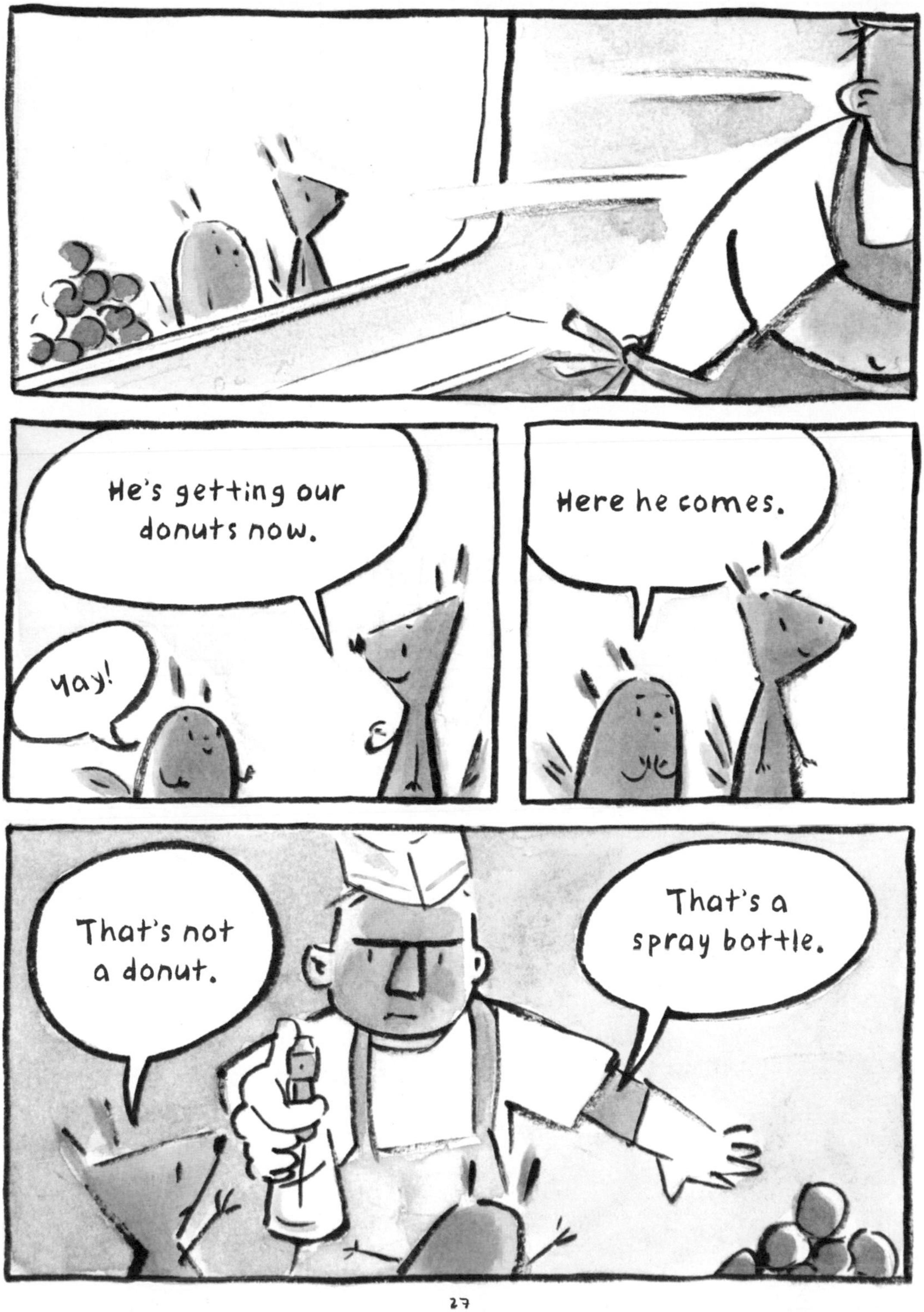
He's getting our donuts now.
Yay!
Here he comes.
That's not a donut.
That's a spray bottle.

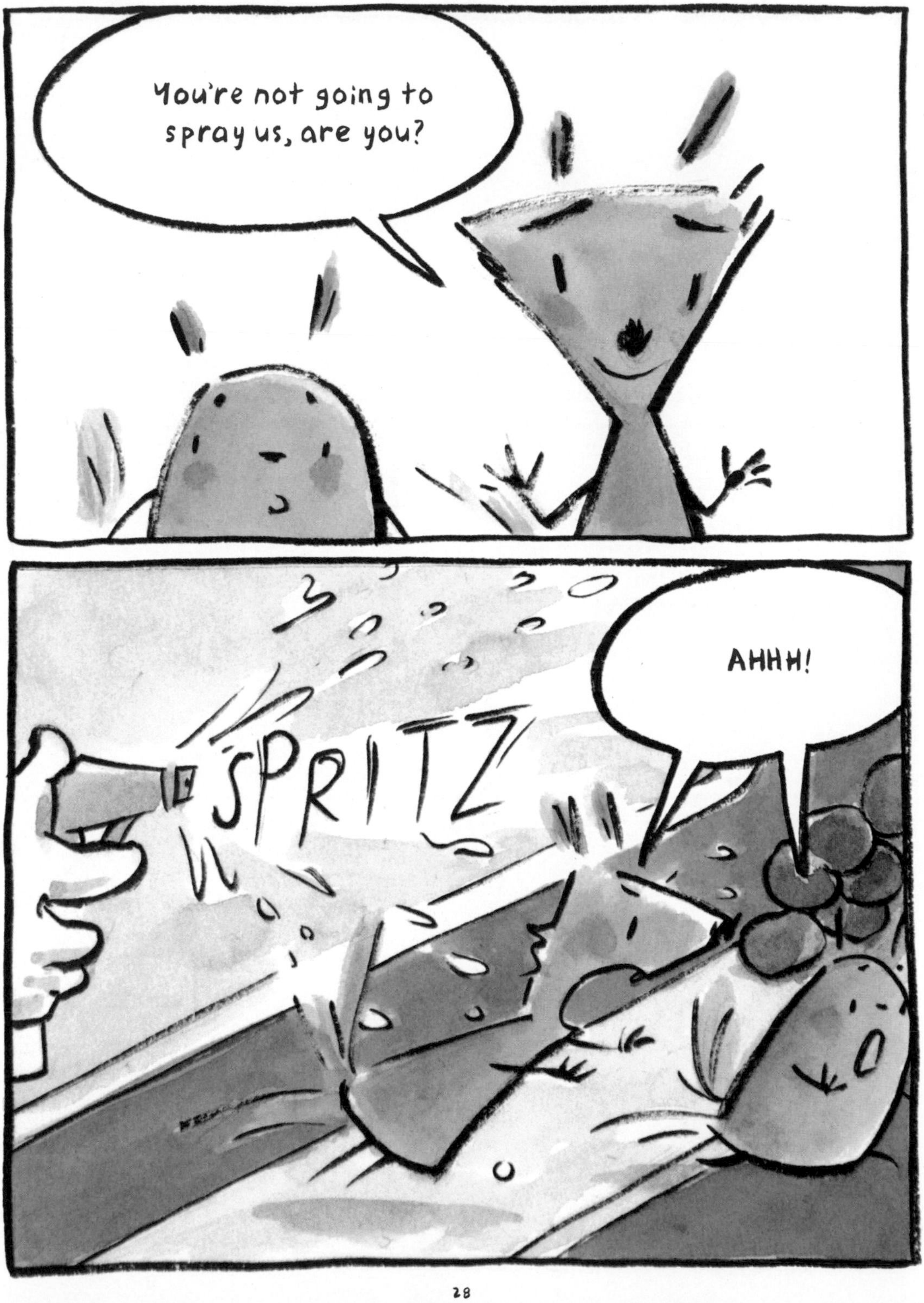
You're not going to spray us, are you?
SPRITZ
AHHH!

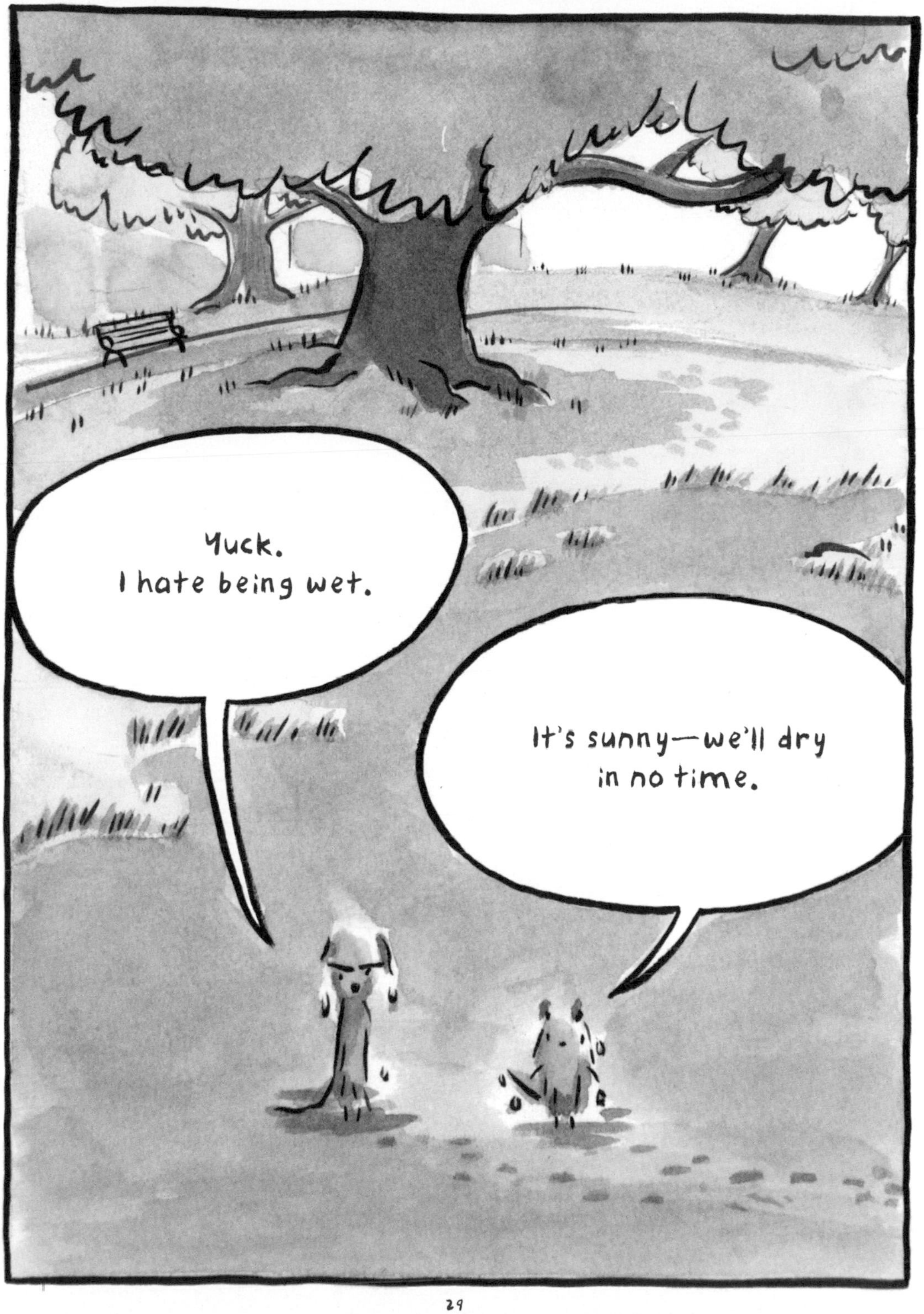
Yuck.
I hate being wet.
It's sunny—we'll dry in no time.

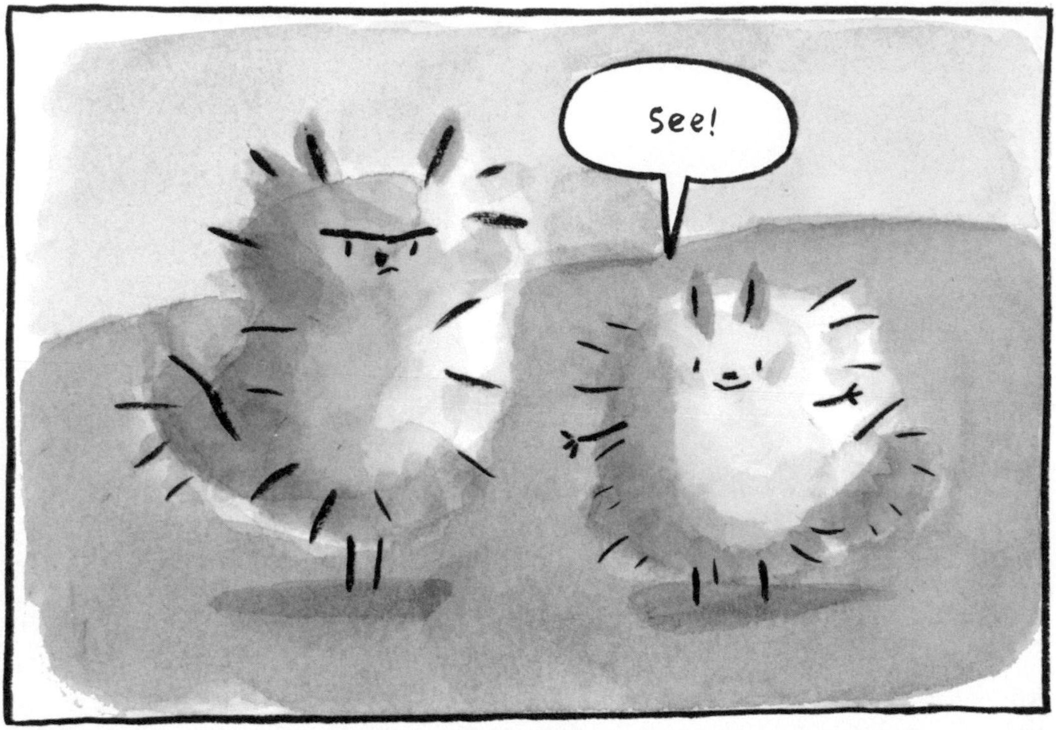
See!

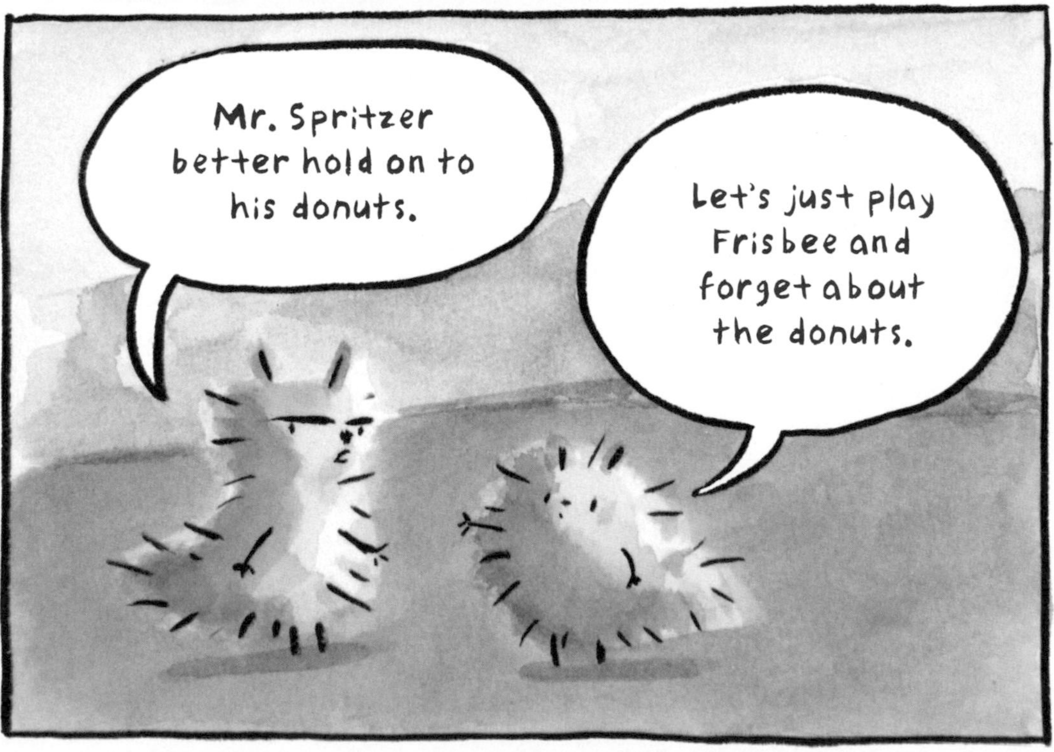
Mr. Spritzer better hold on to his donuts.
Let's just play Frisbee and forget about the donuts.

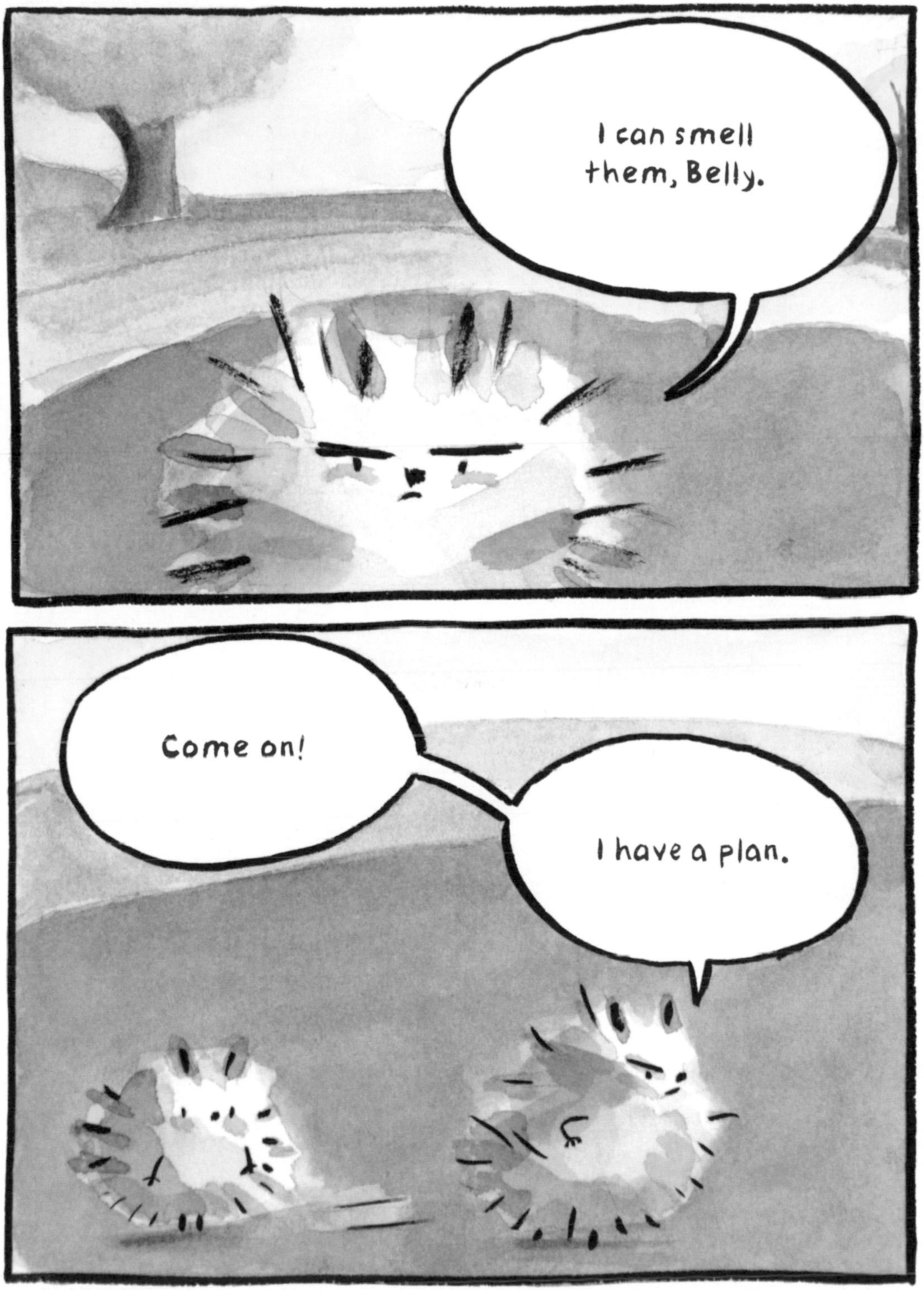
I can smell them, Belly.
Come on!
I have a plan.

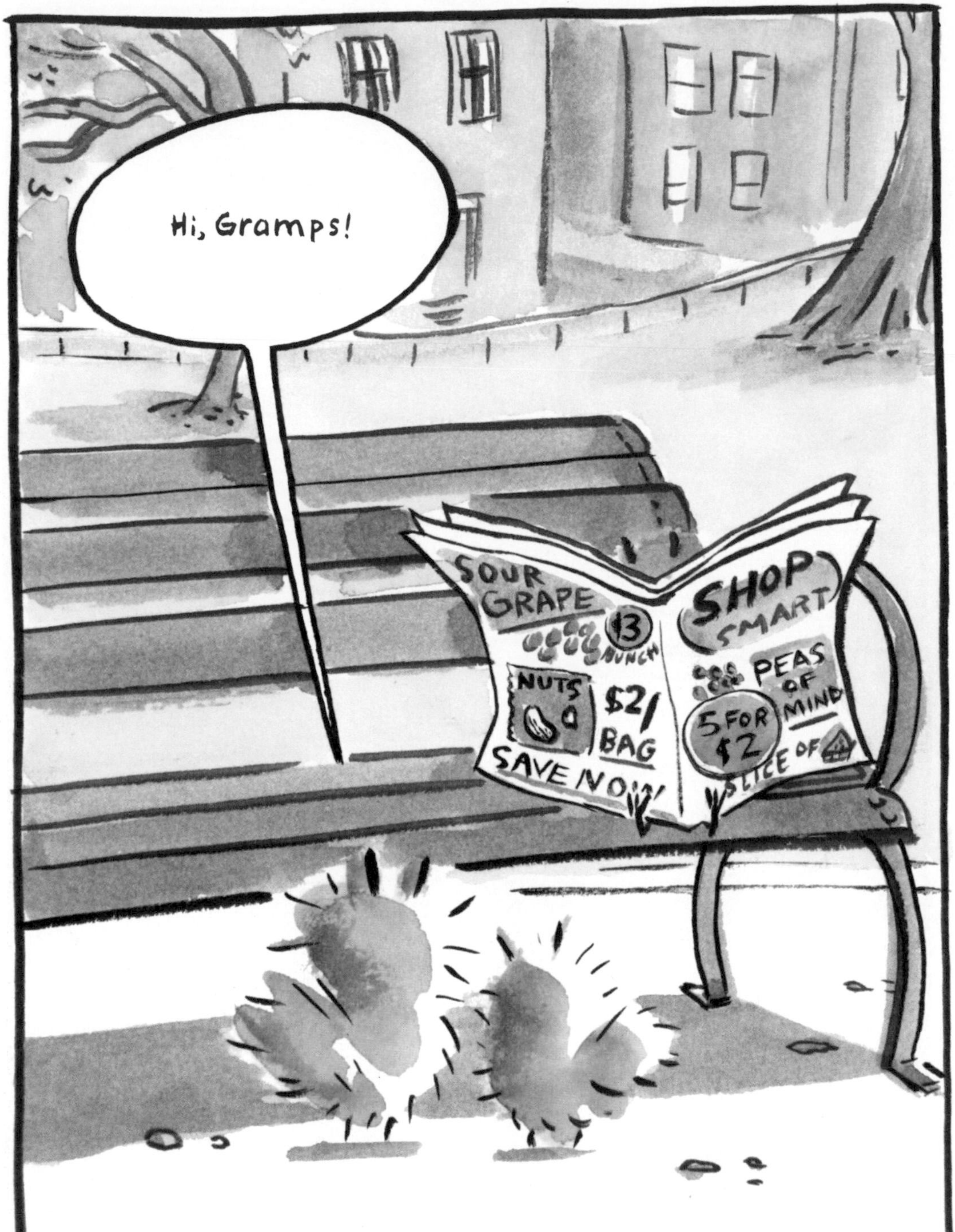
Hi, Gramps!
SOUR GRAPE
$3
SHOP SMART
NUTS
$2/ BAG
SAVE NOW!
PEAS OF MIND
5 FOR $2
SLICE OF

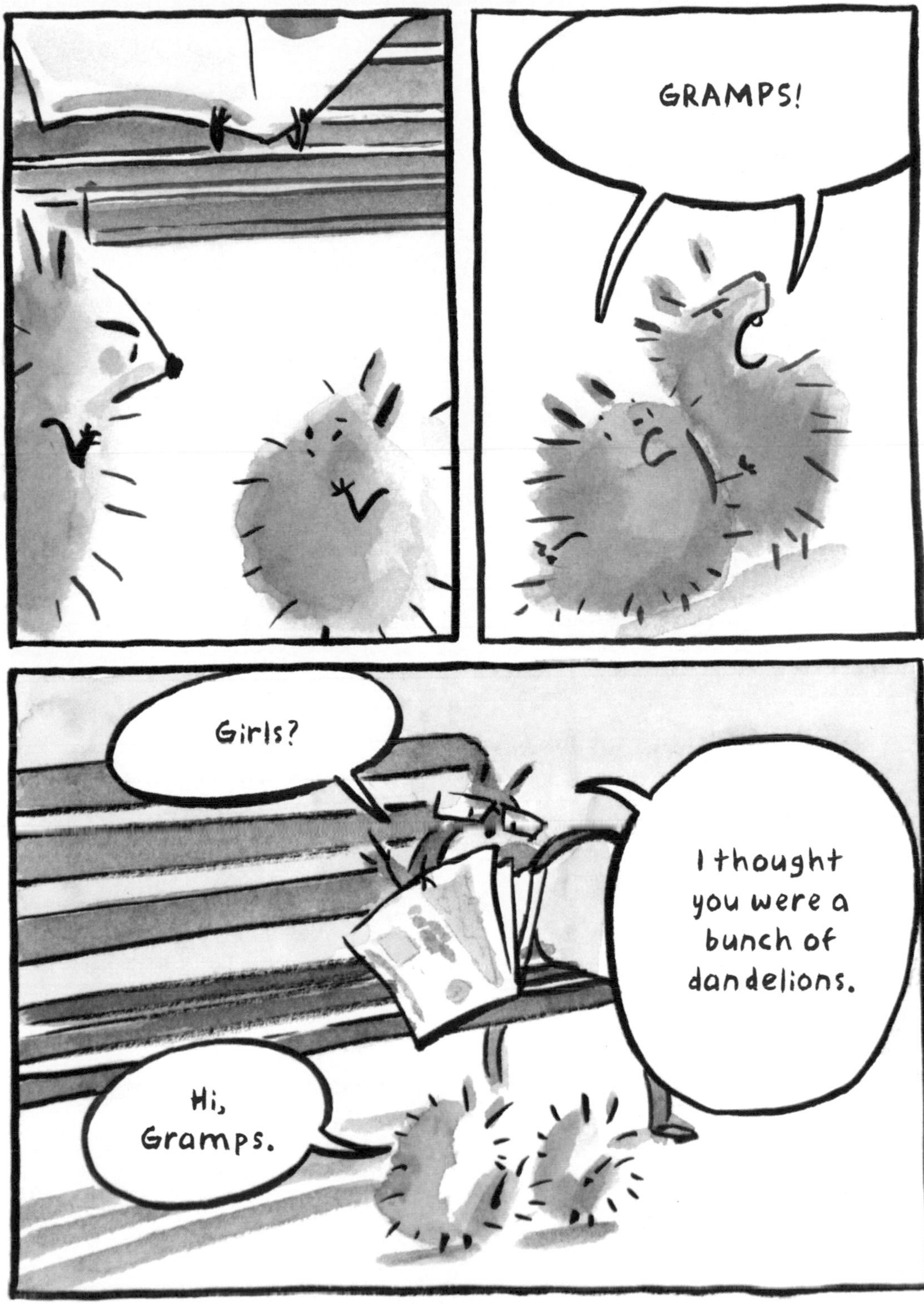
GRAMPS!
Girls?
I thought you were a bunch of dandelions.
Hi, Gramps.

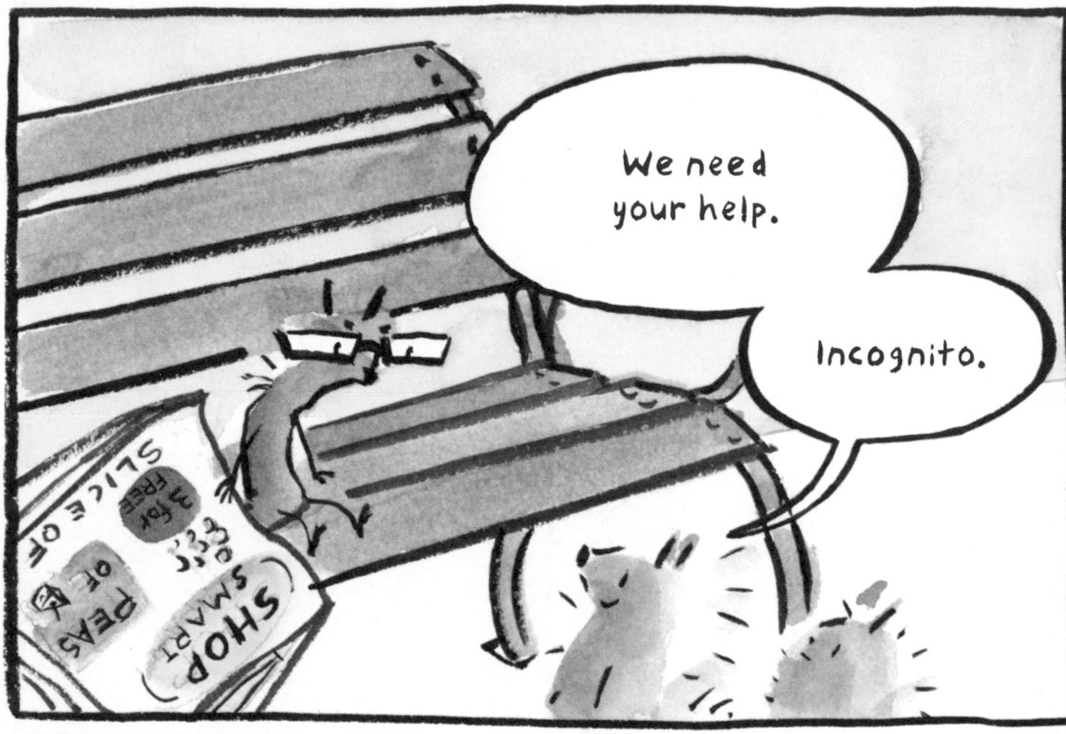
We need your help.
Incognito.

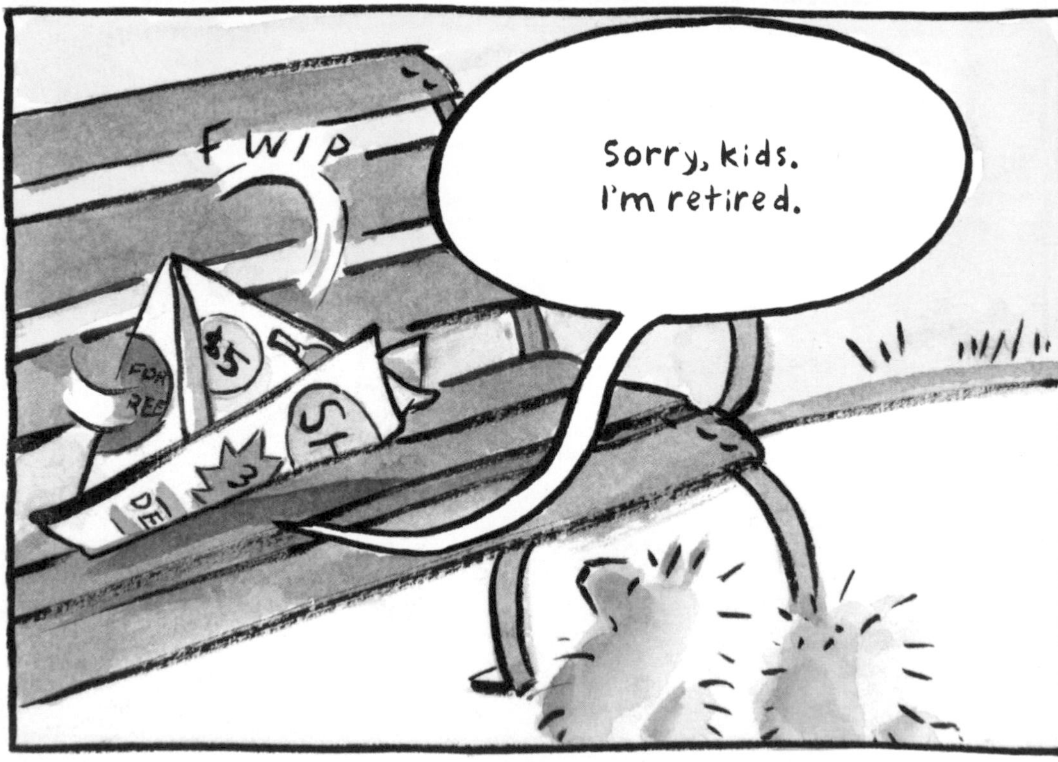
FWIP
Sorry, kids. I'm retired.

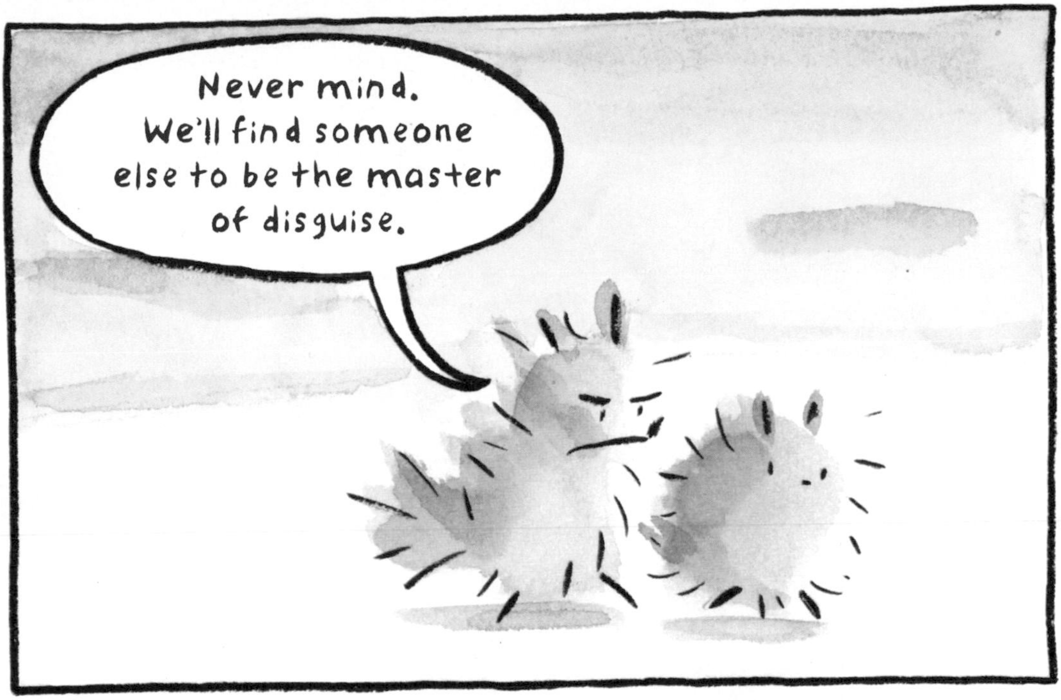
Never mind. We'll find someone else to be the master of disguise.

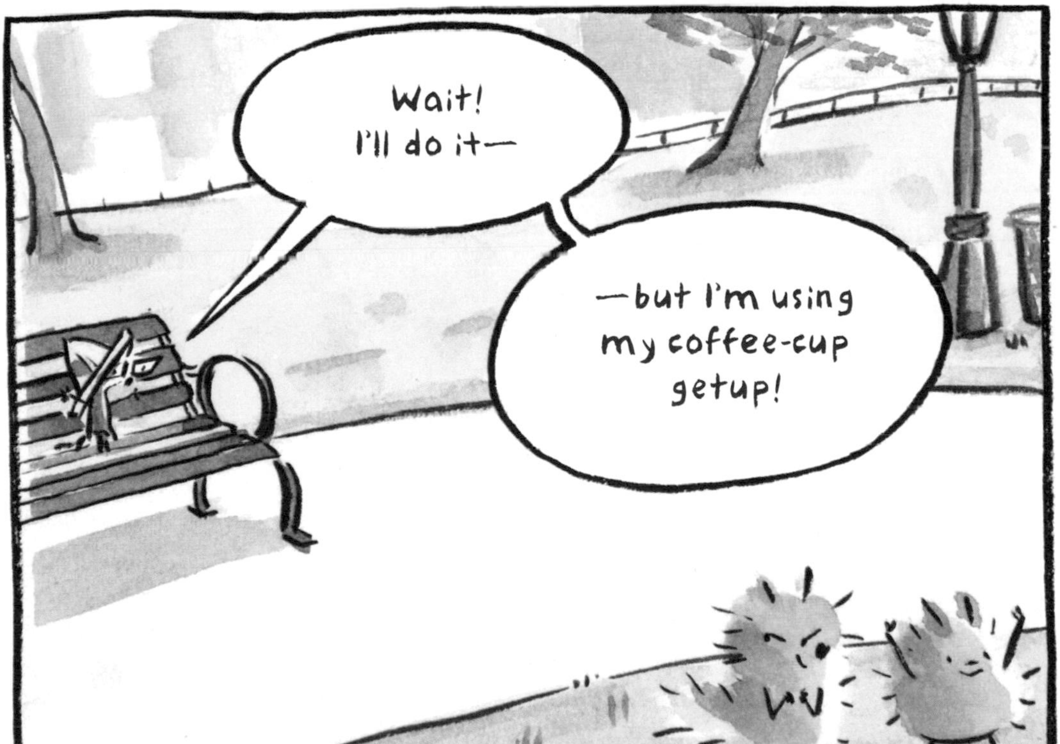
Wait! I'll do it—
—but I'm using my coffee-cup getup!

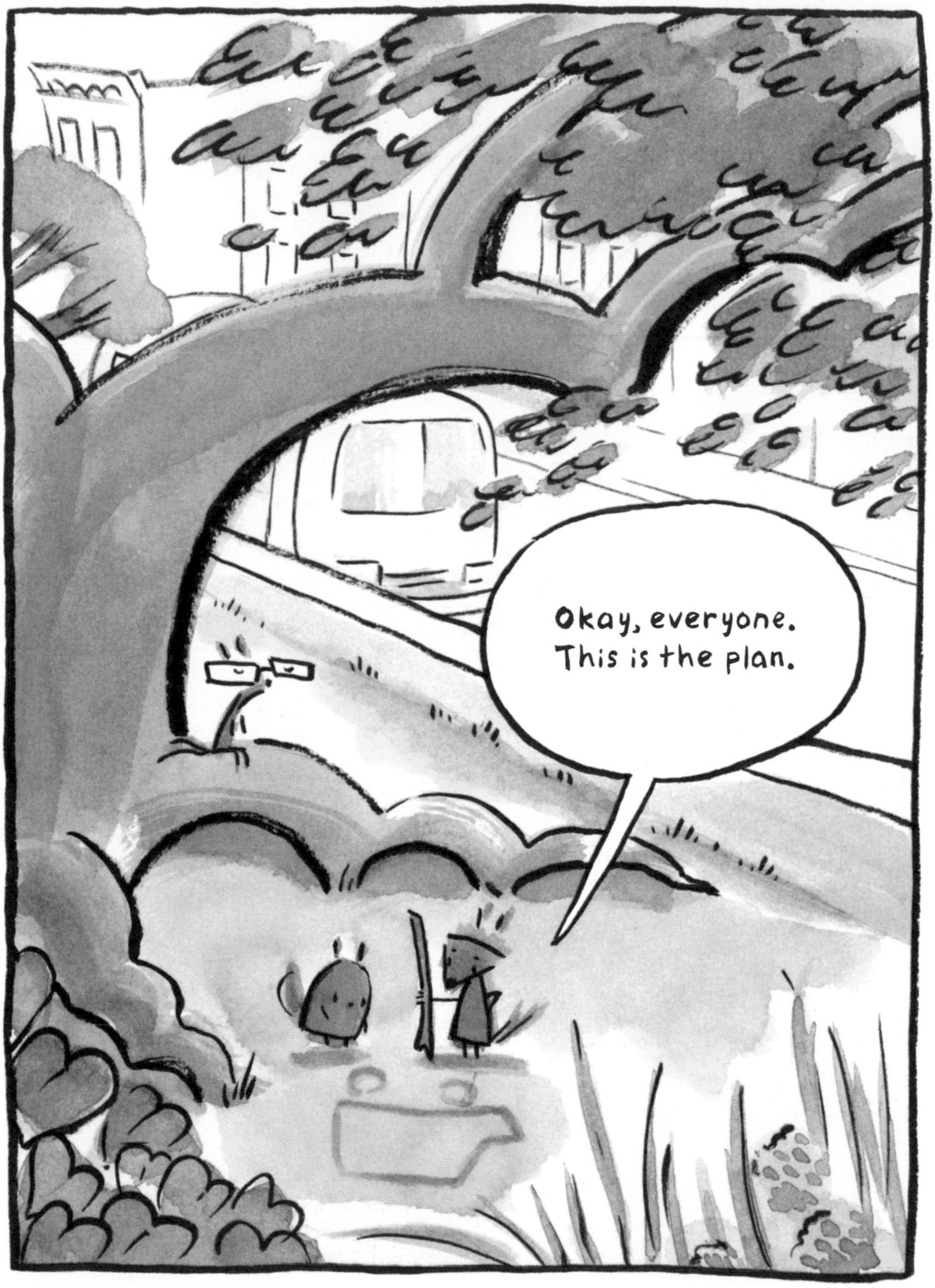
Okay, everyone. This is the plan.

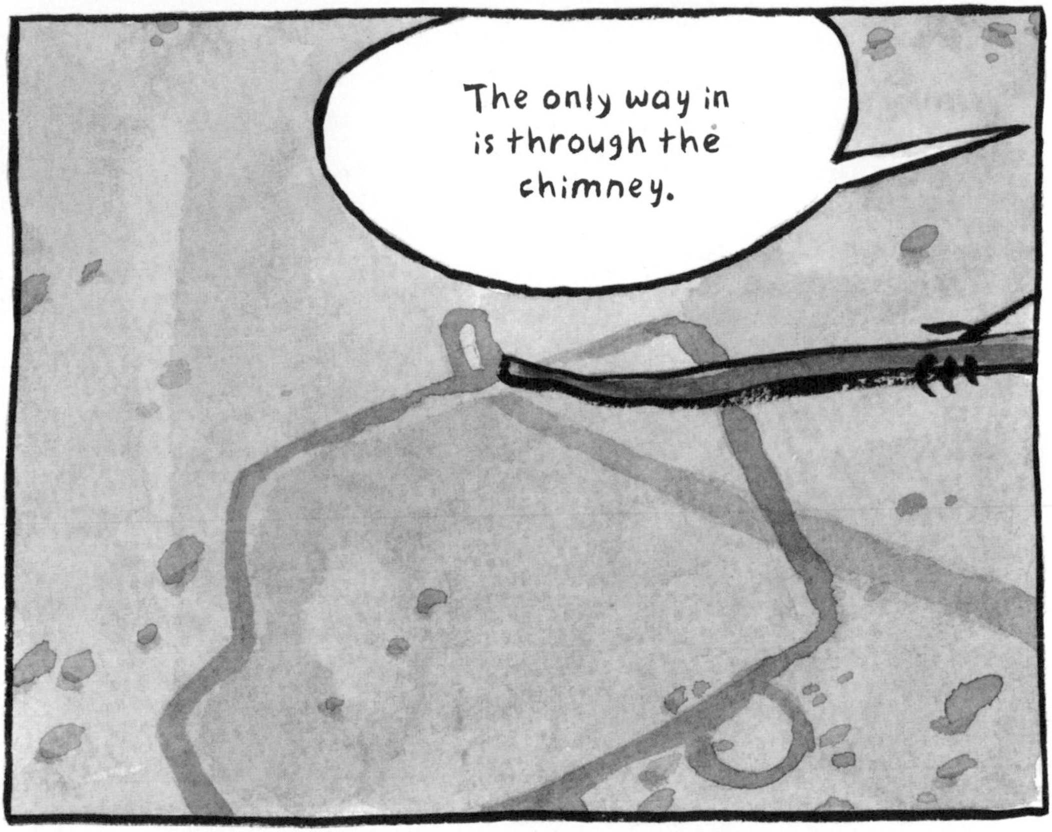
The only way in is through the chimney.

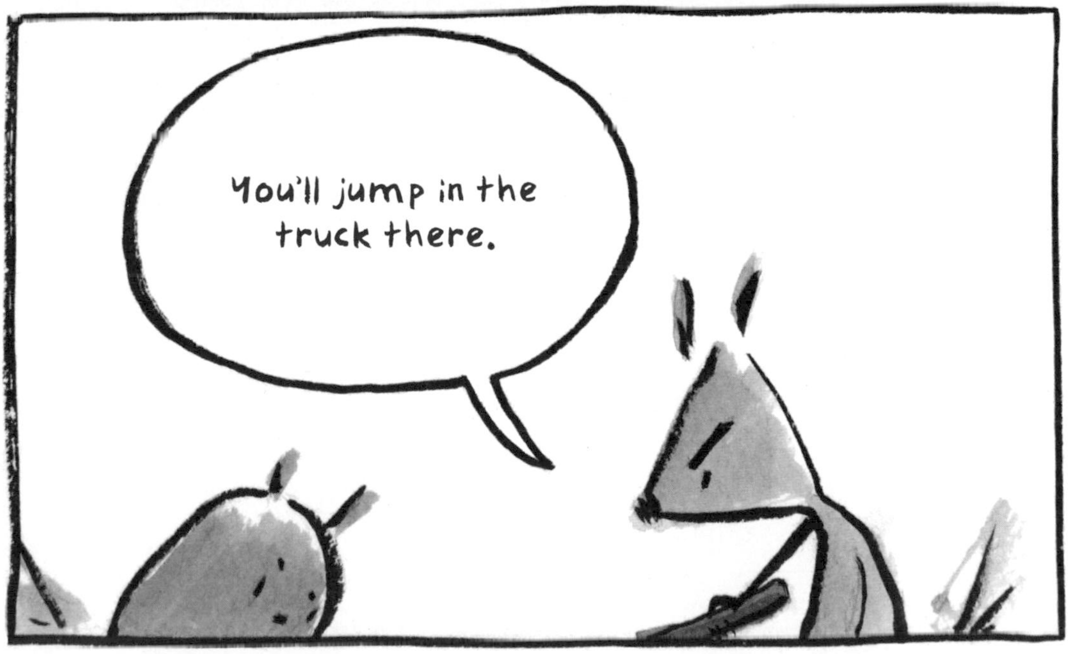
You'll jump in the truck there.

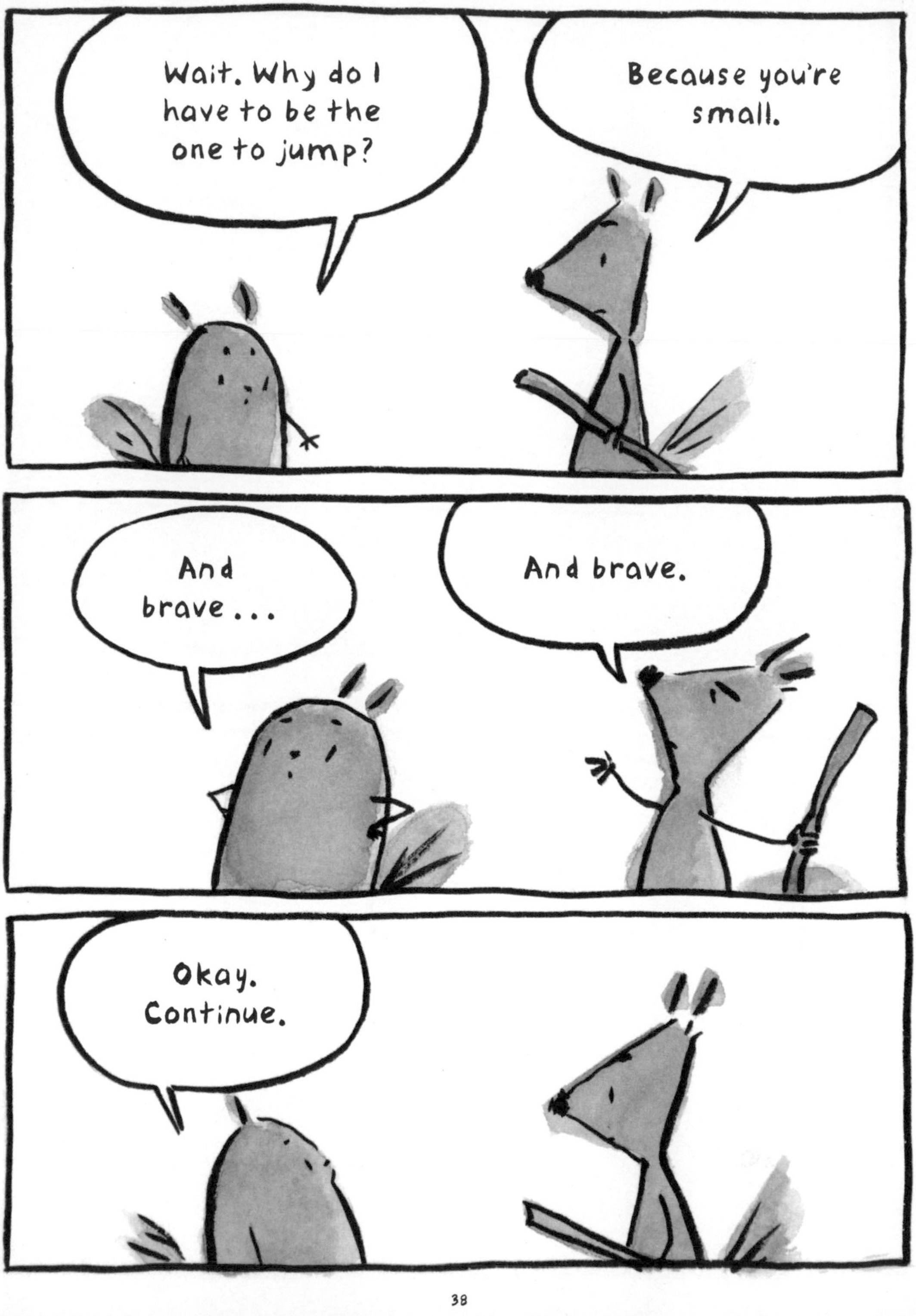
Wait. Why do I have to be the one to jump?
Because you're small.
And brave . . .
And brave.
Okay. Continue.

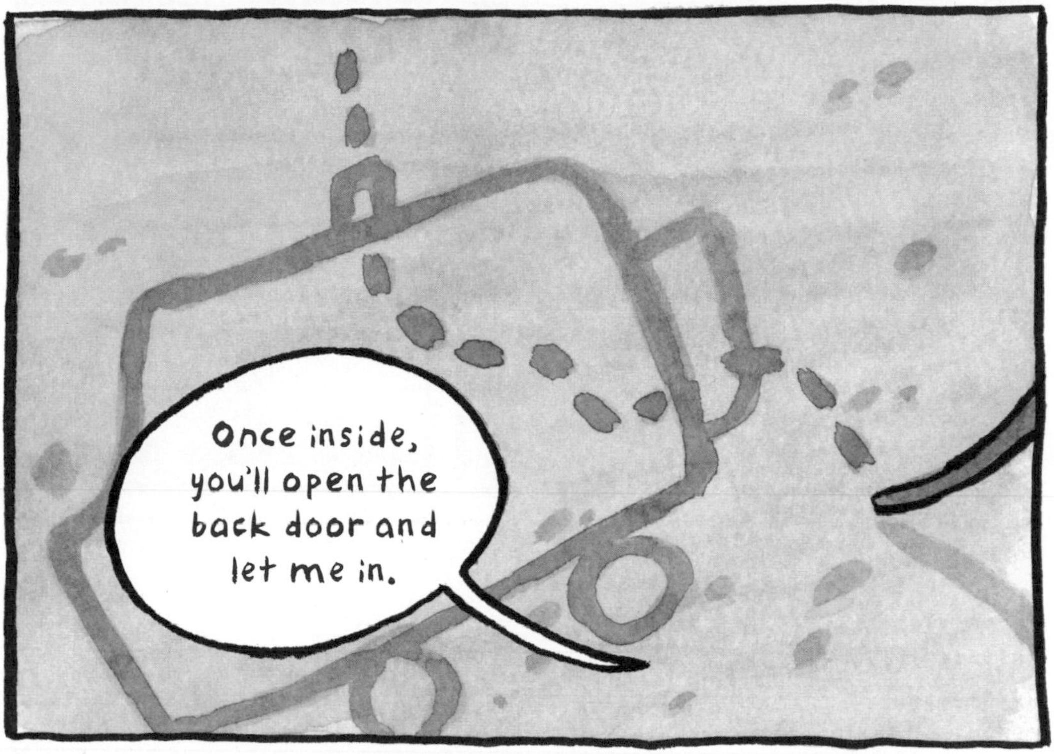
Once inside, you'll open the back door and let me in.

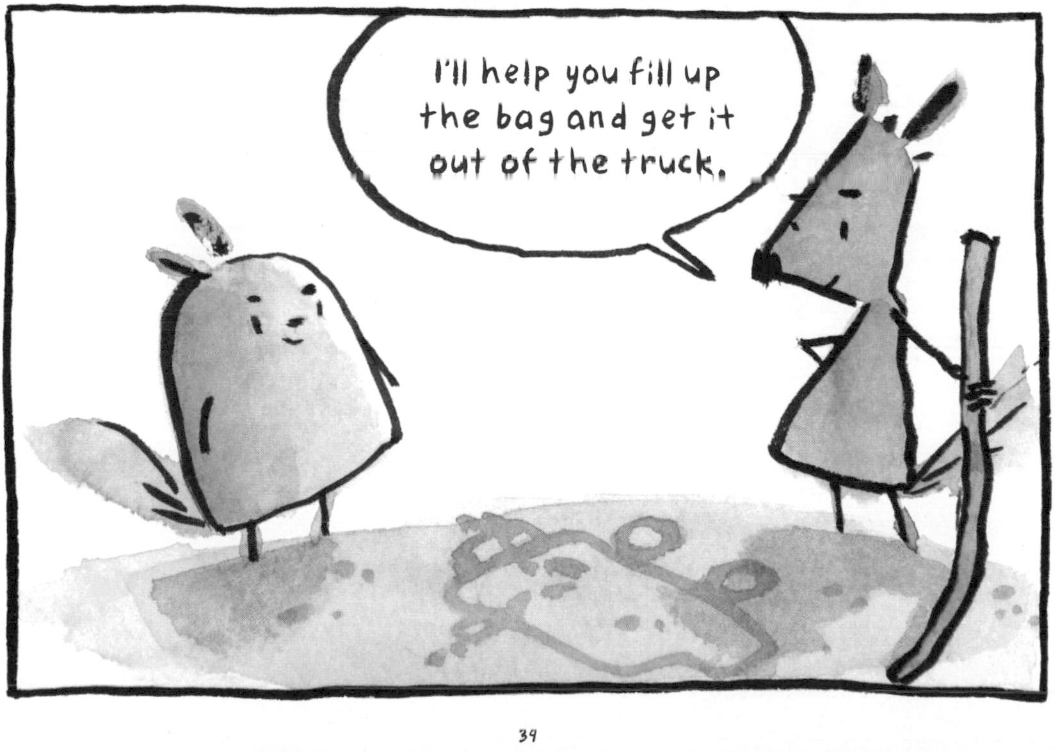
I'll help you fill up the bag and get it out of the truck.

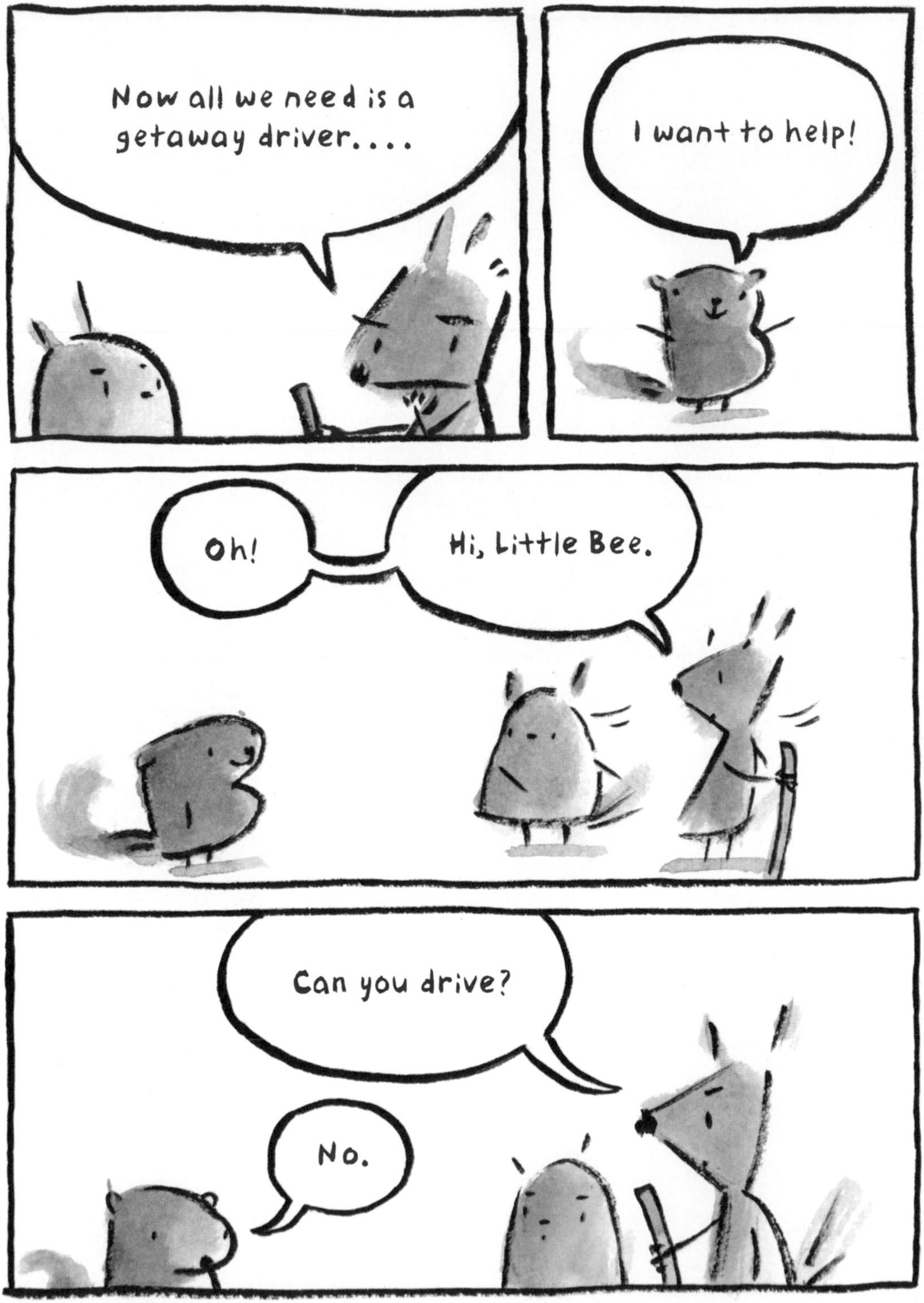
Now all we need is a getaway driver....
I want to help!
Oh!
Hi, Little Bee.
Can you drive?
No.

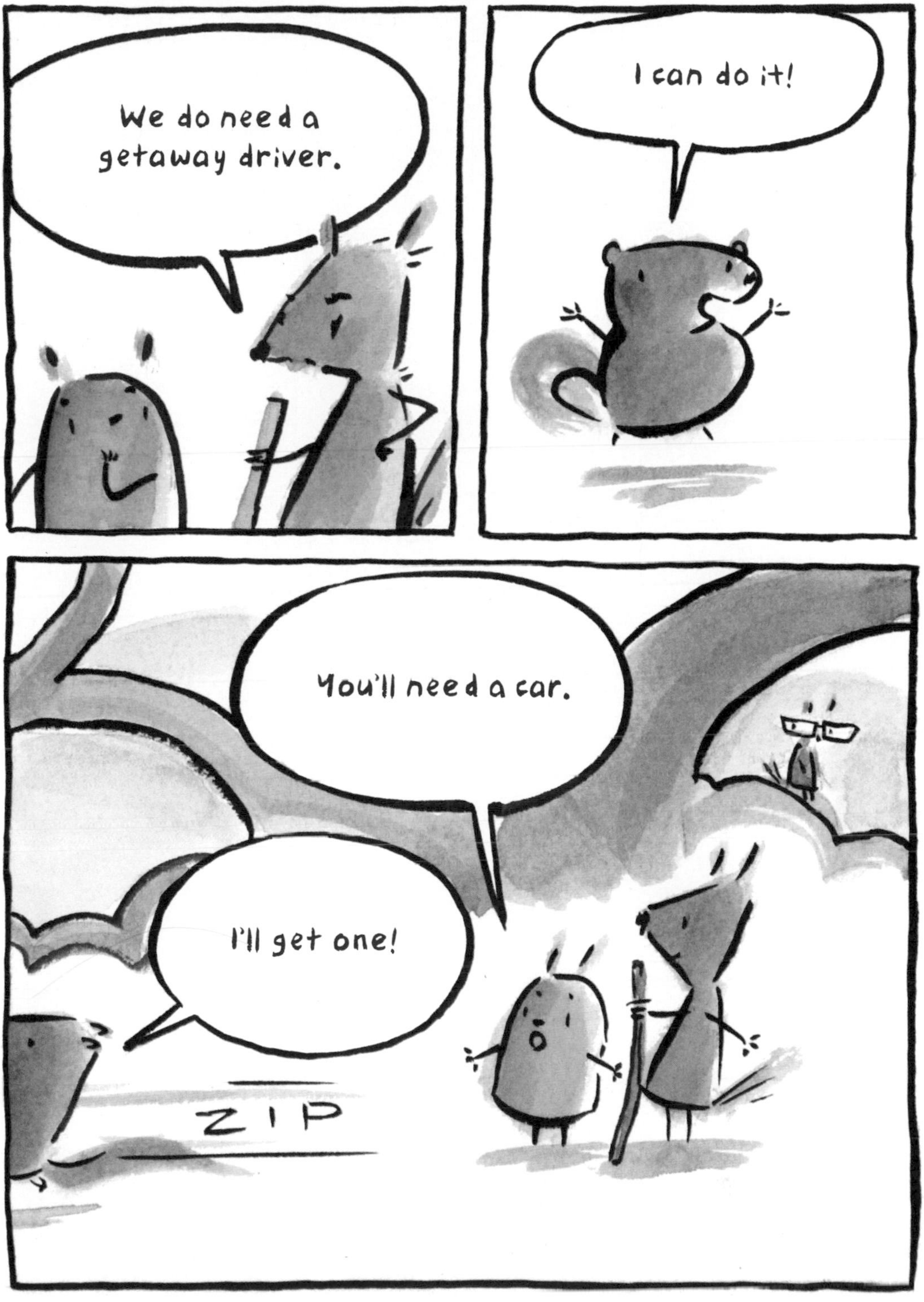
We do need a getaway driver.
I can do it!
You'll need a car.
I'll get one!
ZIP

Chapter 3

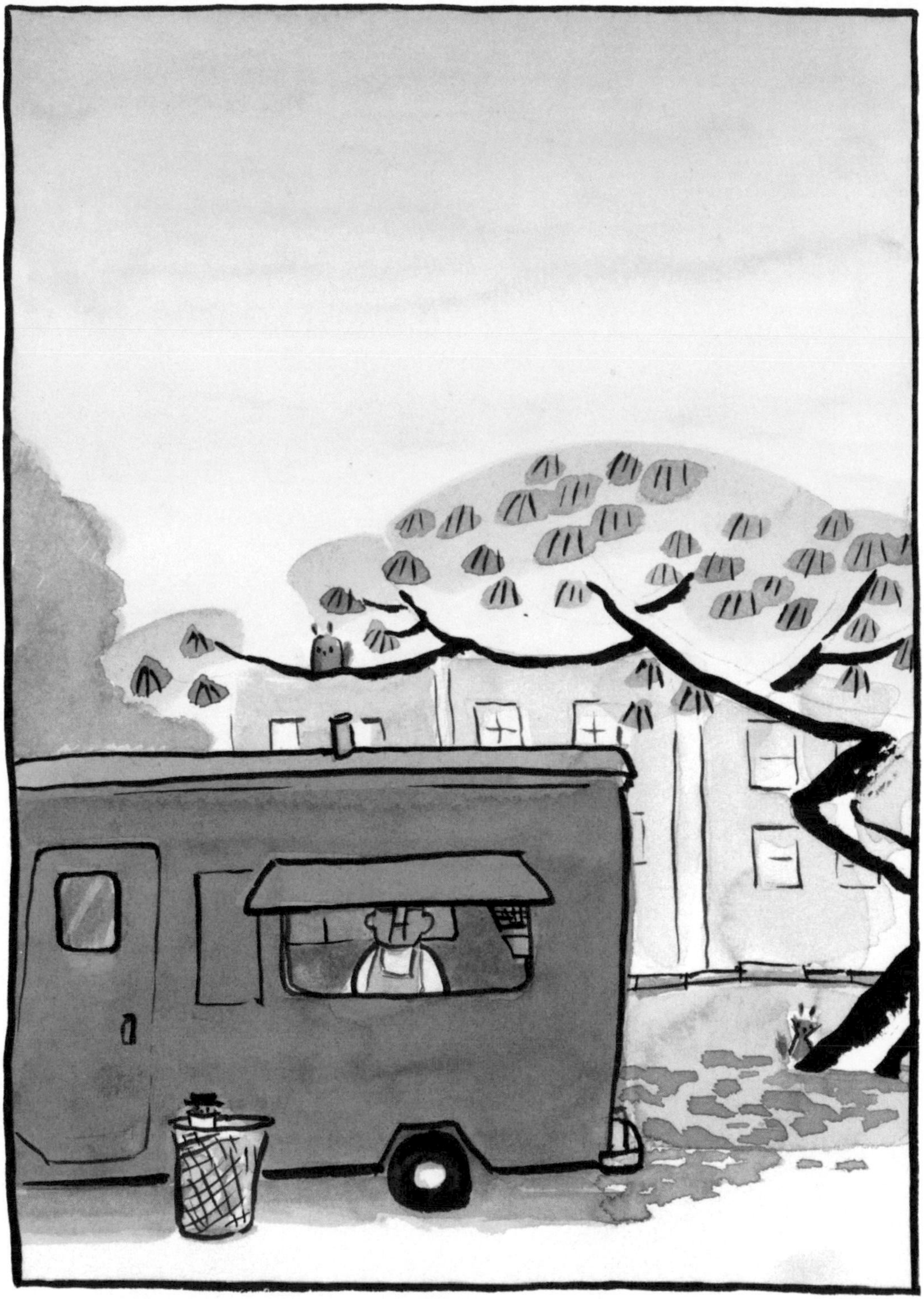

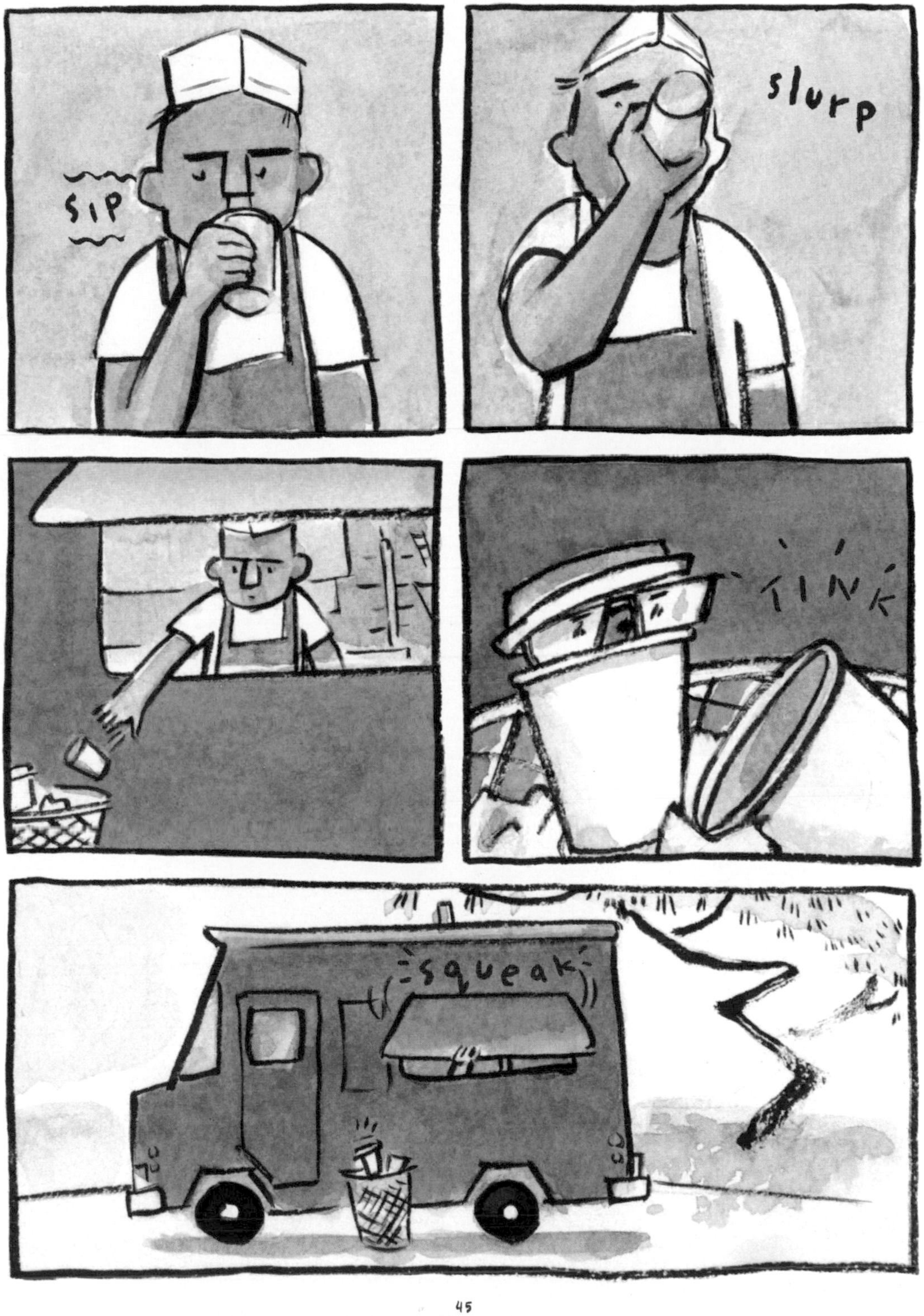
SIP
slurp
TINK
squeak

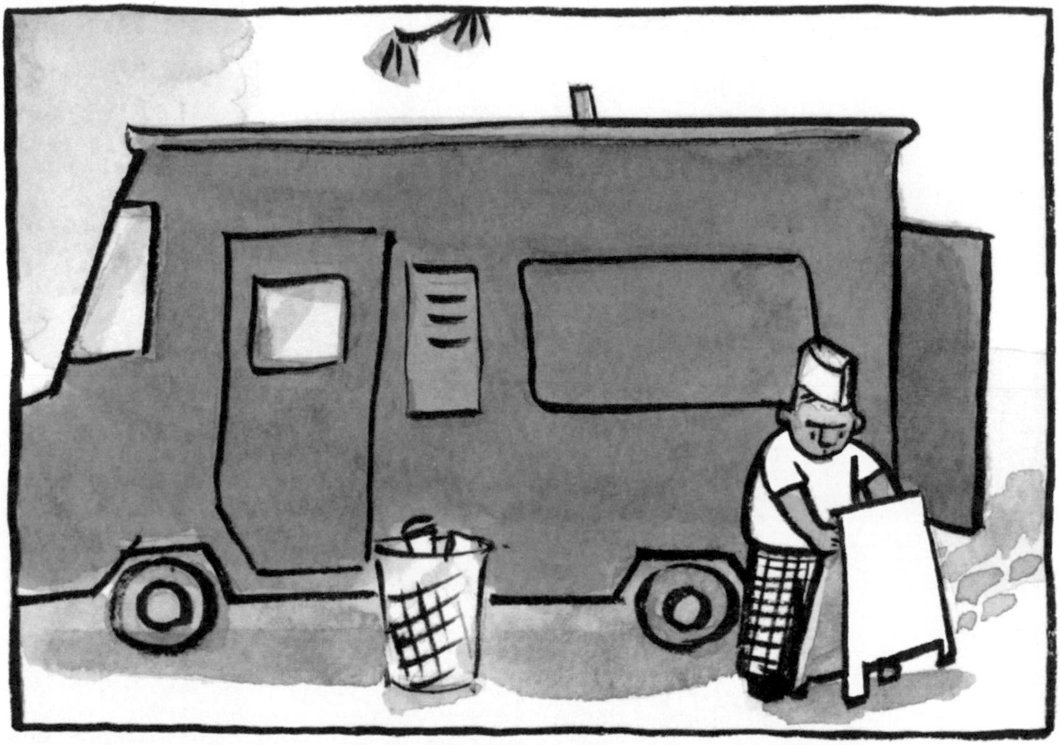

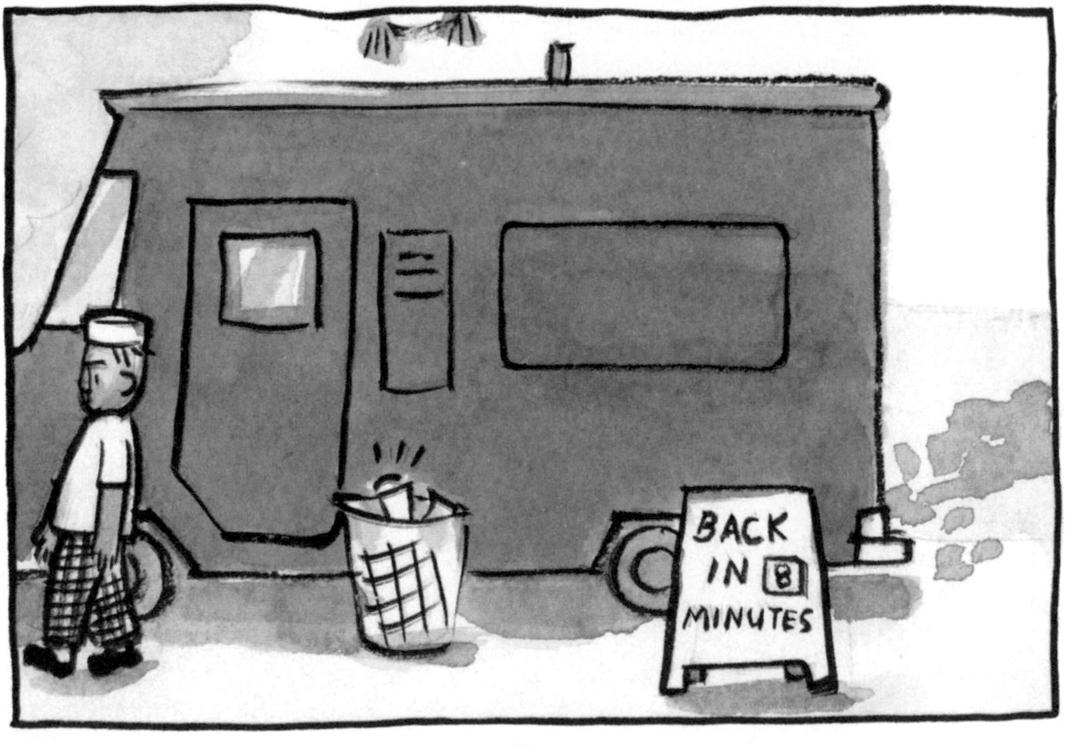
BACK IN 8 MINUTES

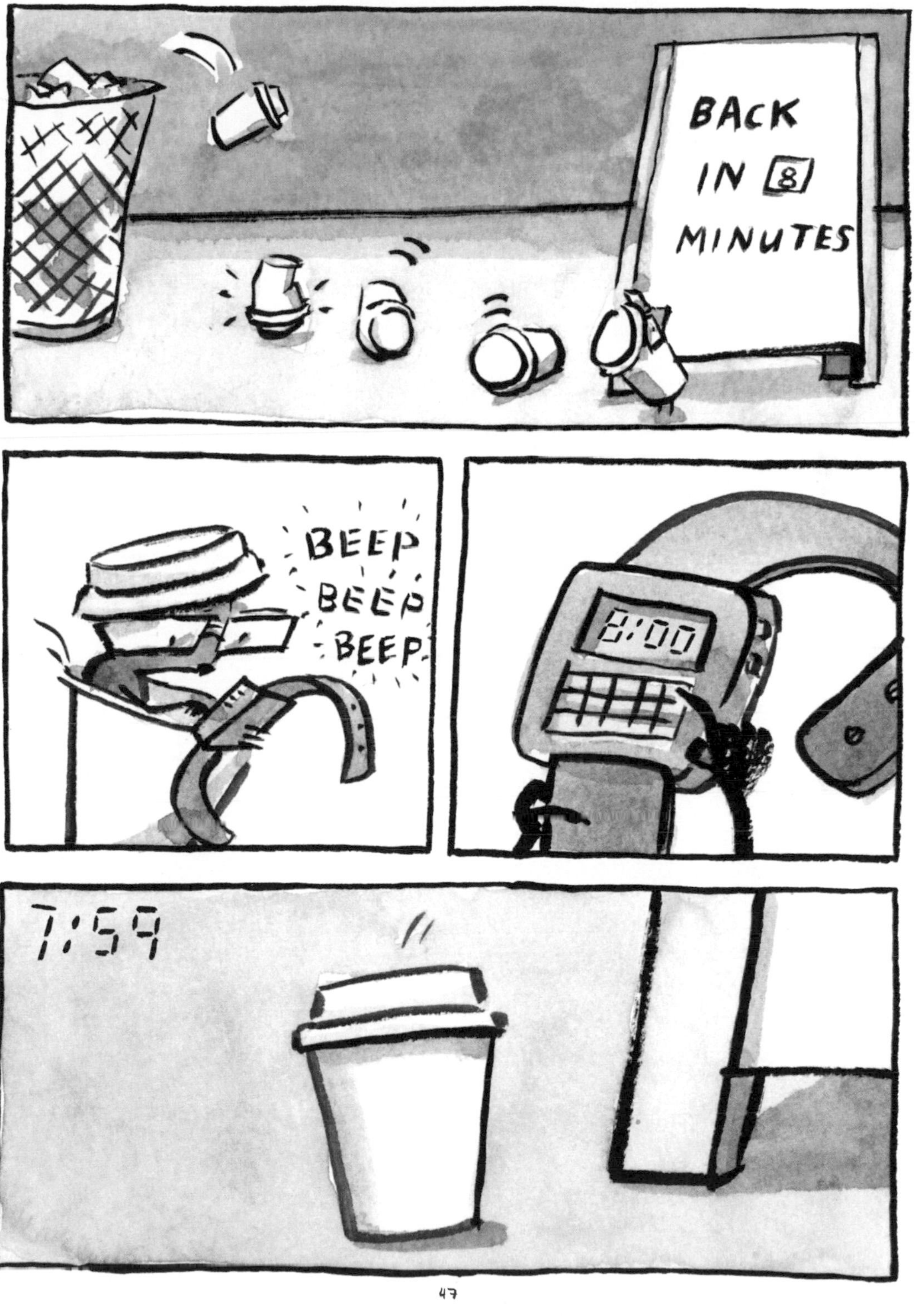
BACK IN 8 MINUTES
BEEP BEEP BEEP
8:00
7:59

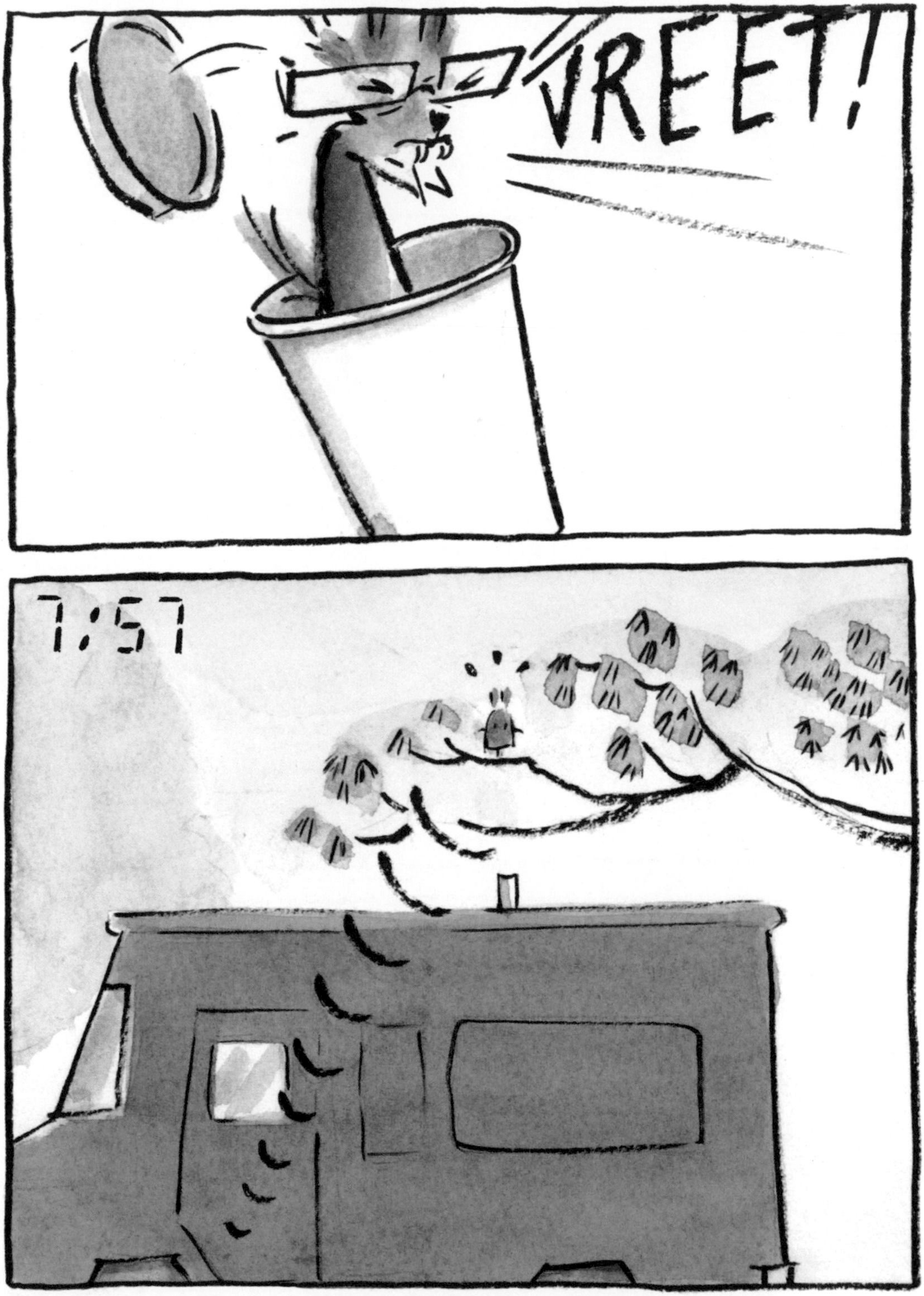
VREET!
7:57

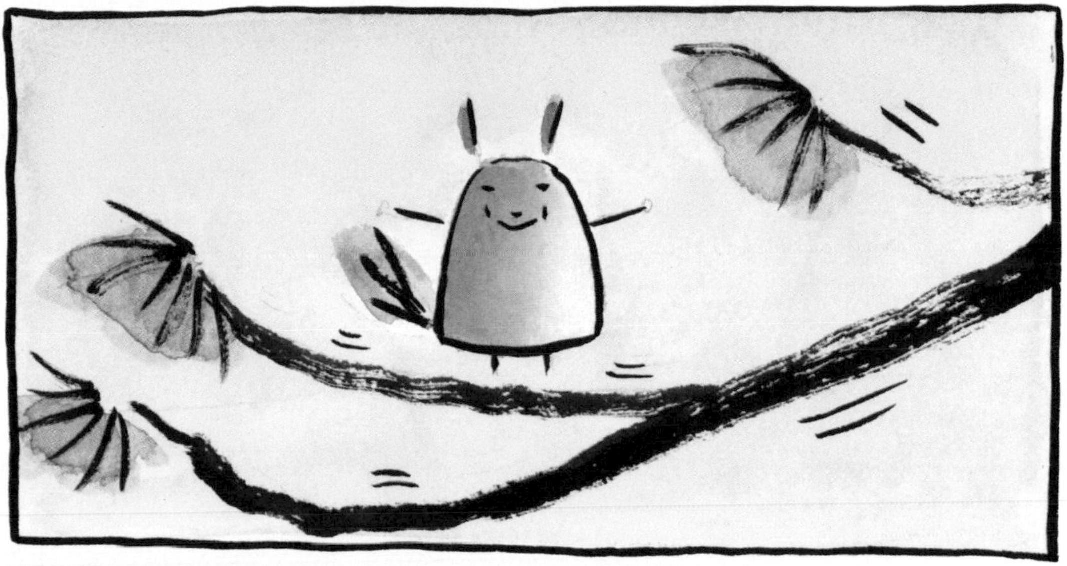

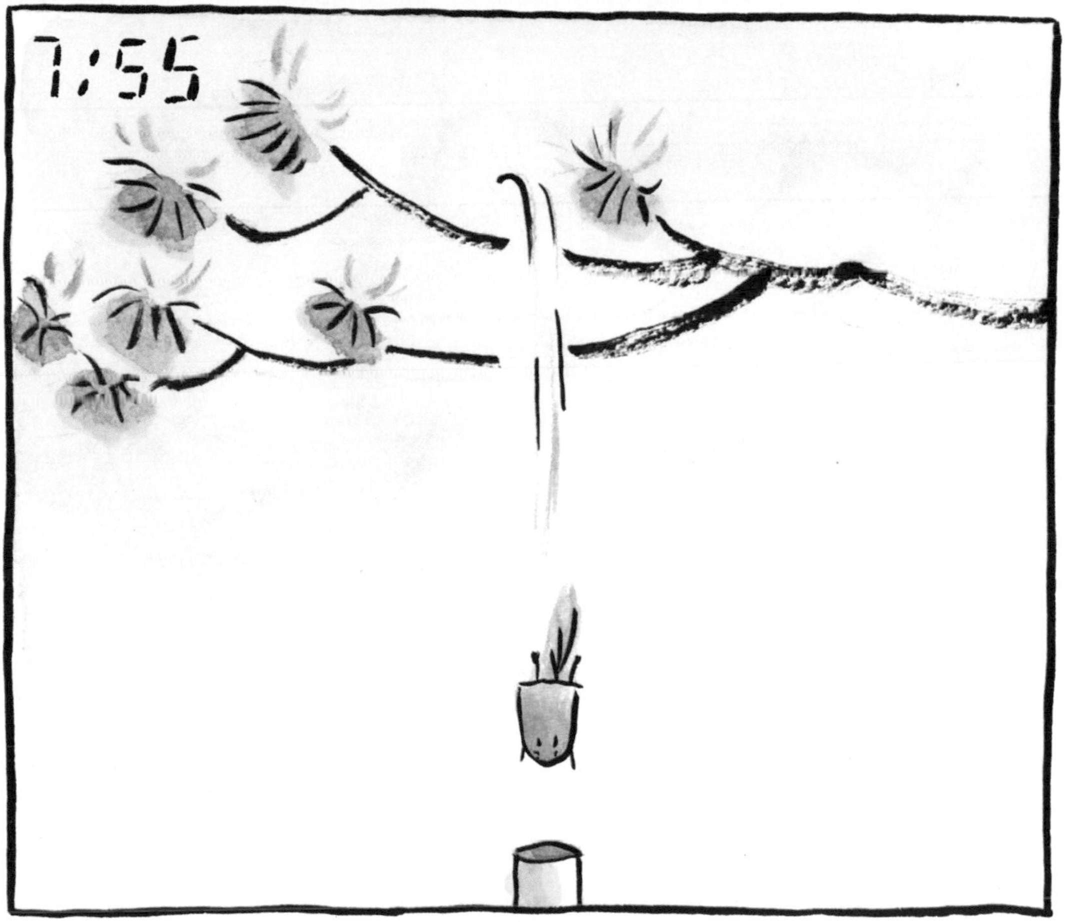
7:55

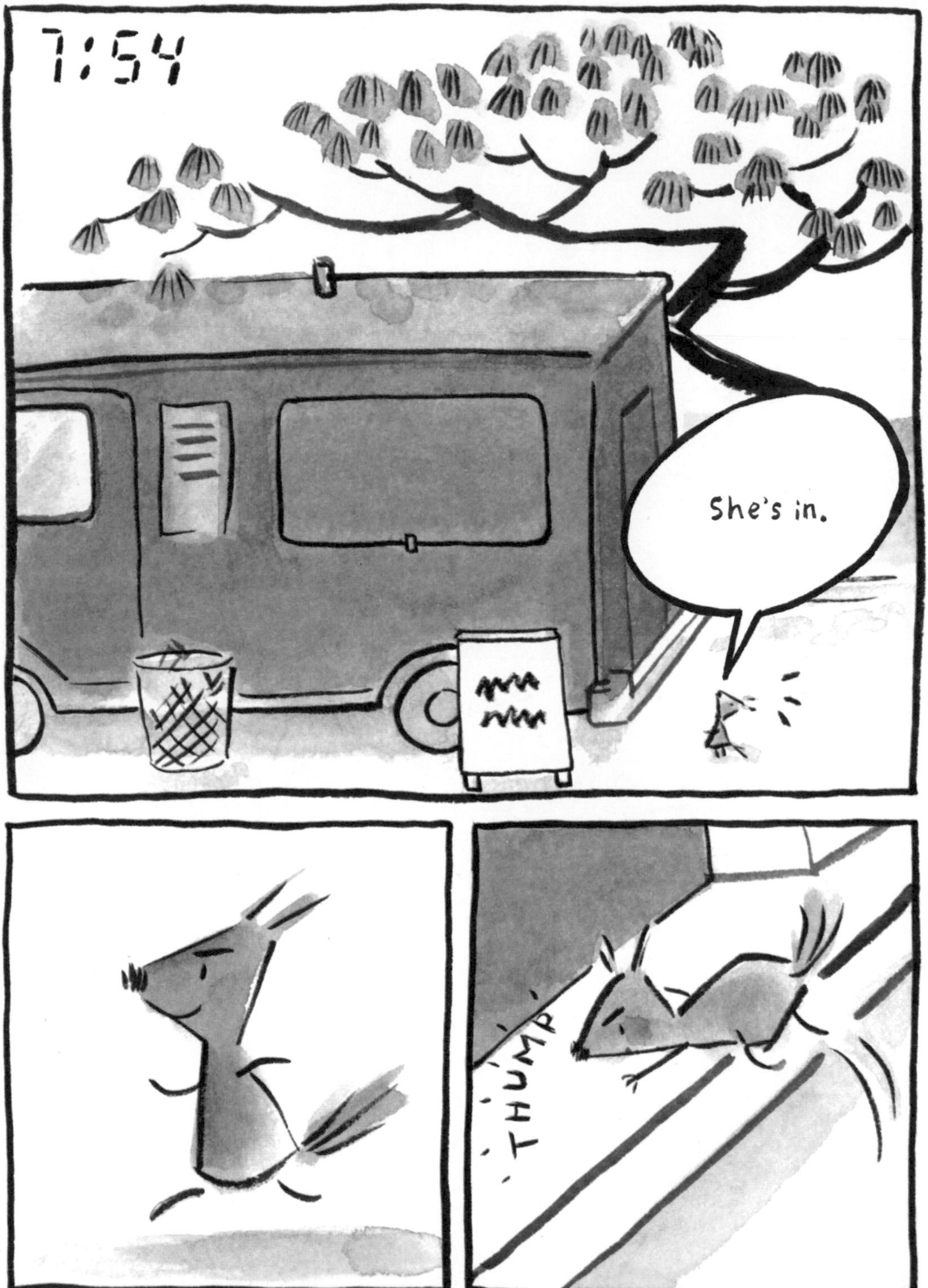
7:54
She's in.
THUMP

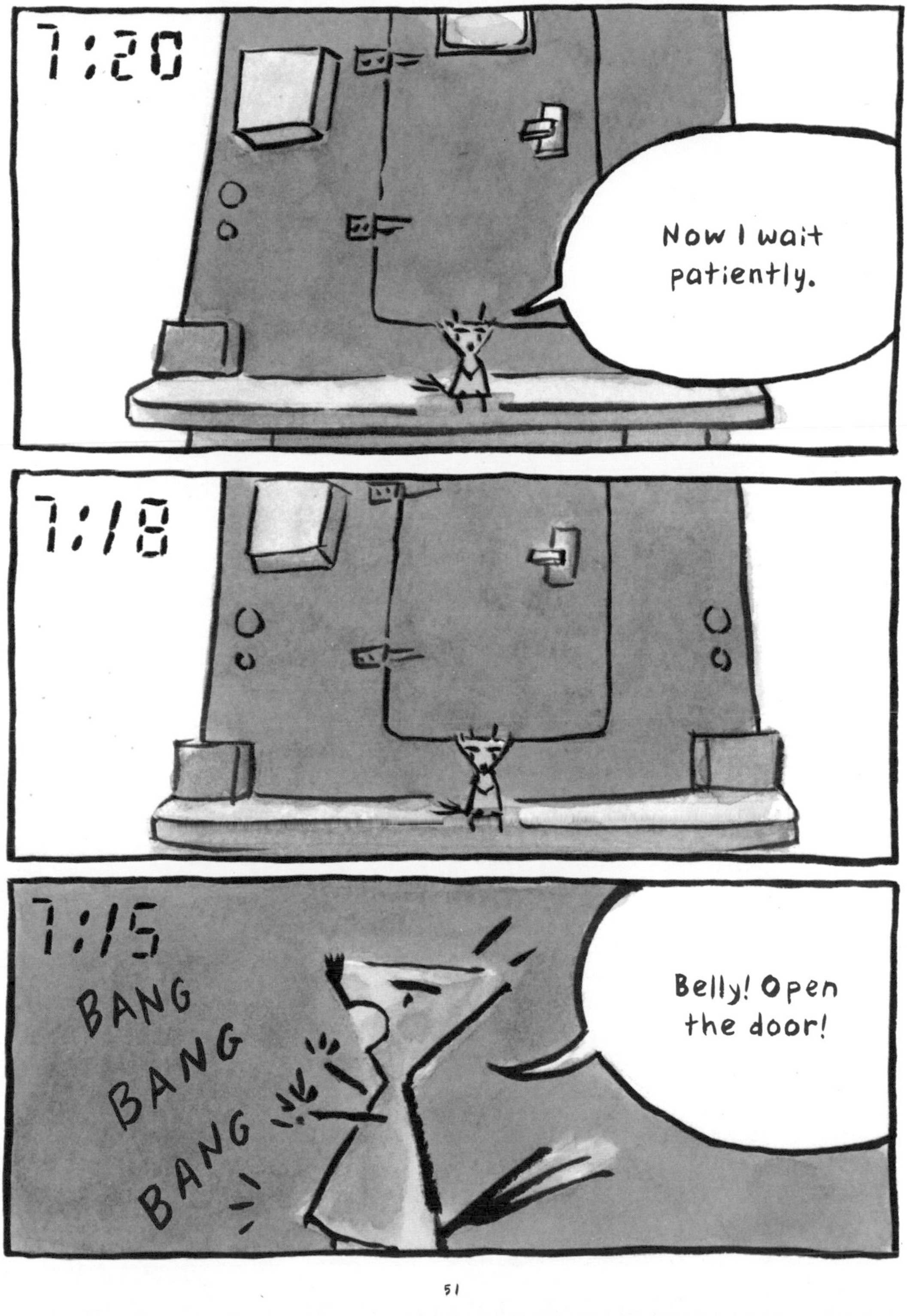
7:20
Now I wait patiently.
7:18
7:15
BANG
BANG
BANG
Belly! Open the door!

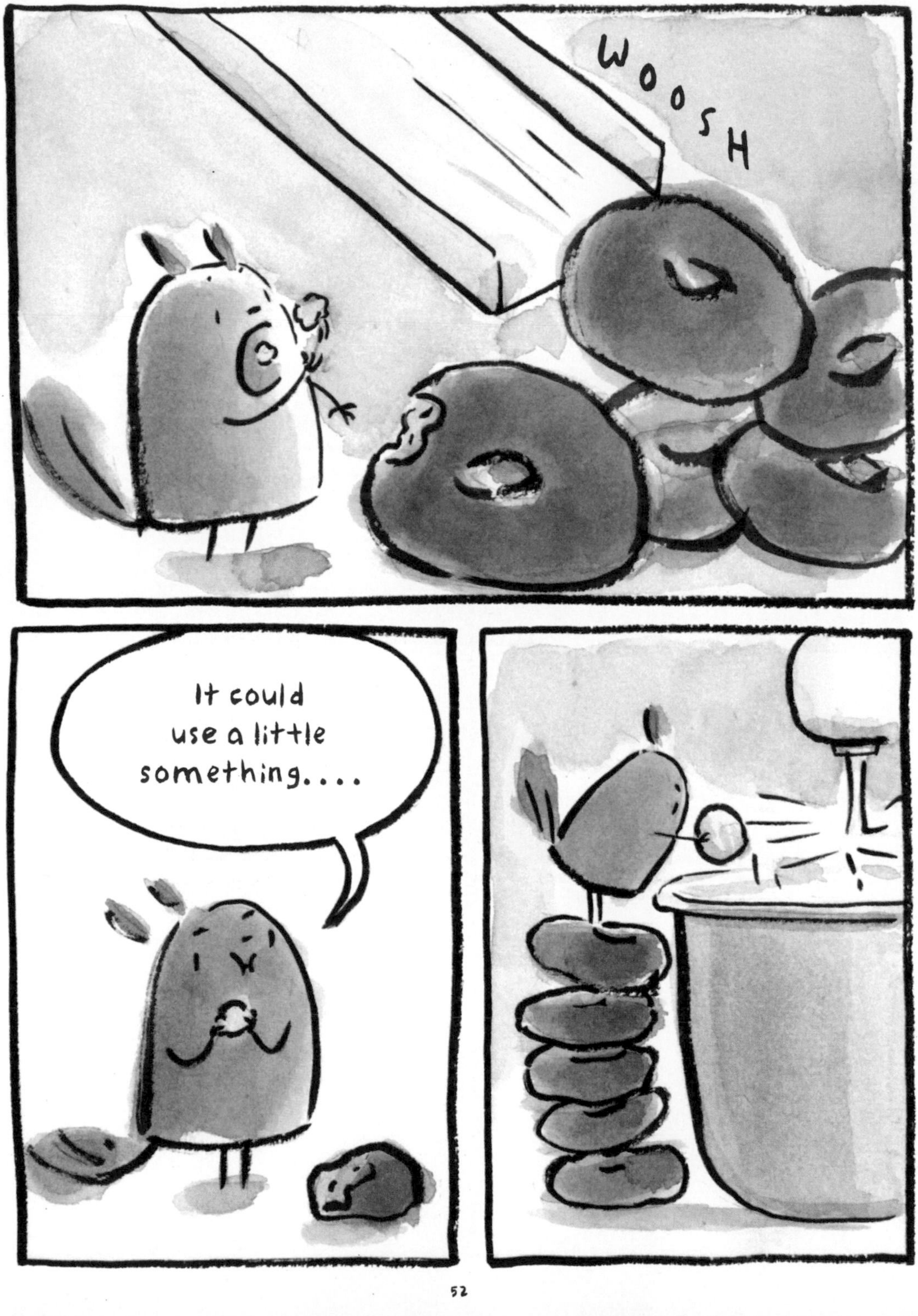
WOOSH
It could use a little something....

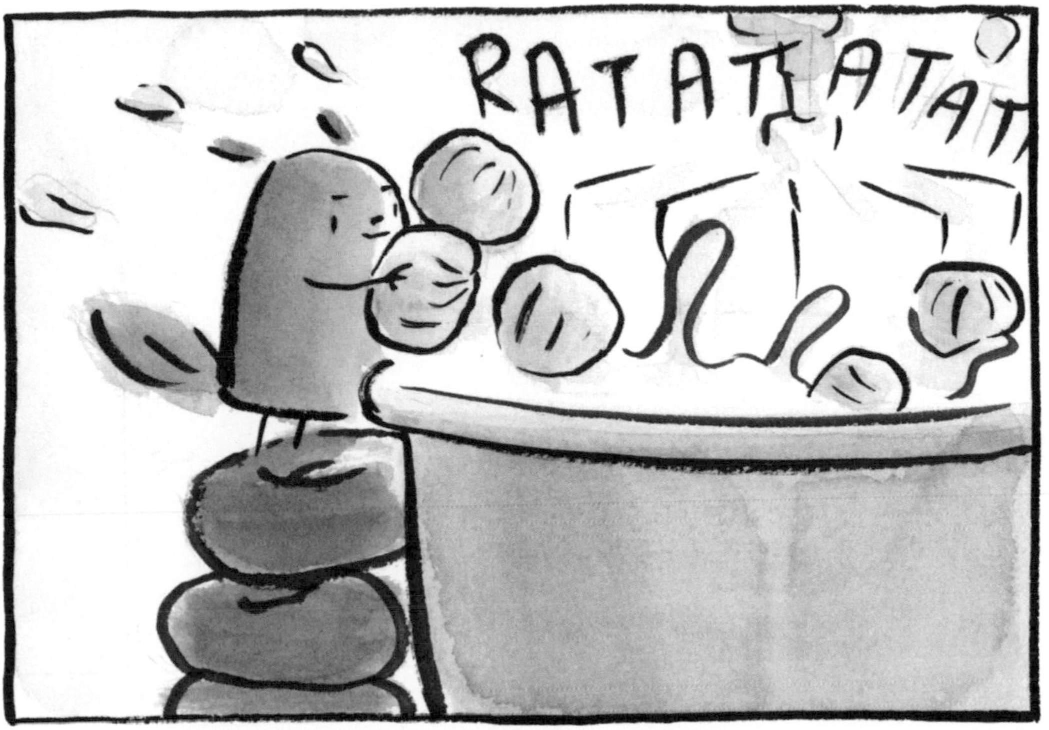
RATATATAT

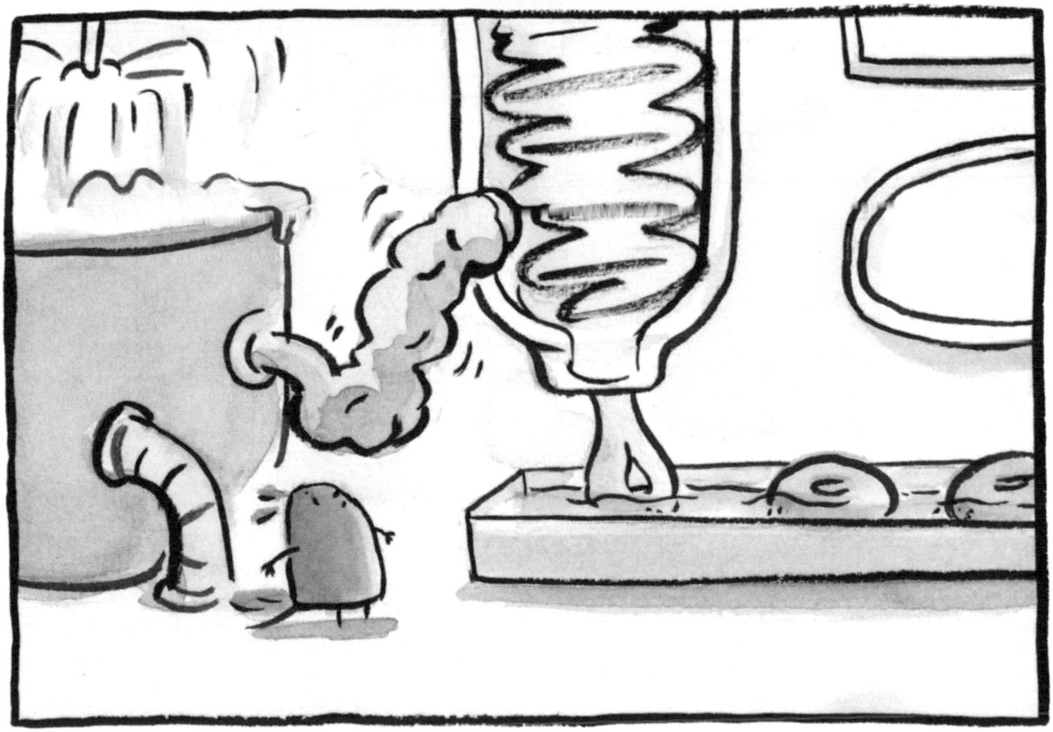

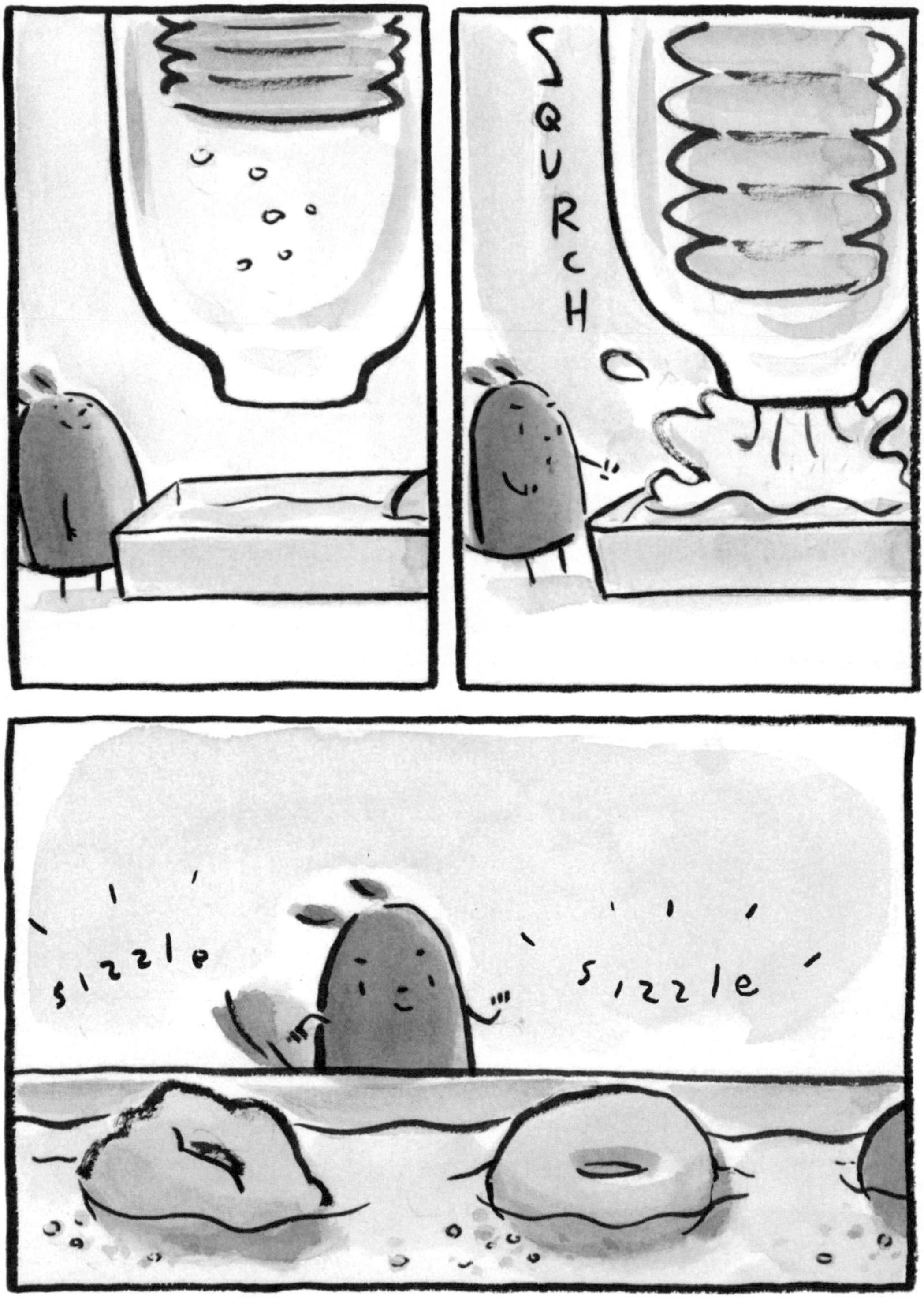
SQURCH
sizzle
sizzle

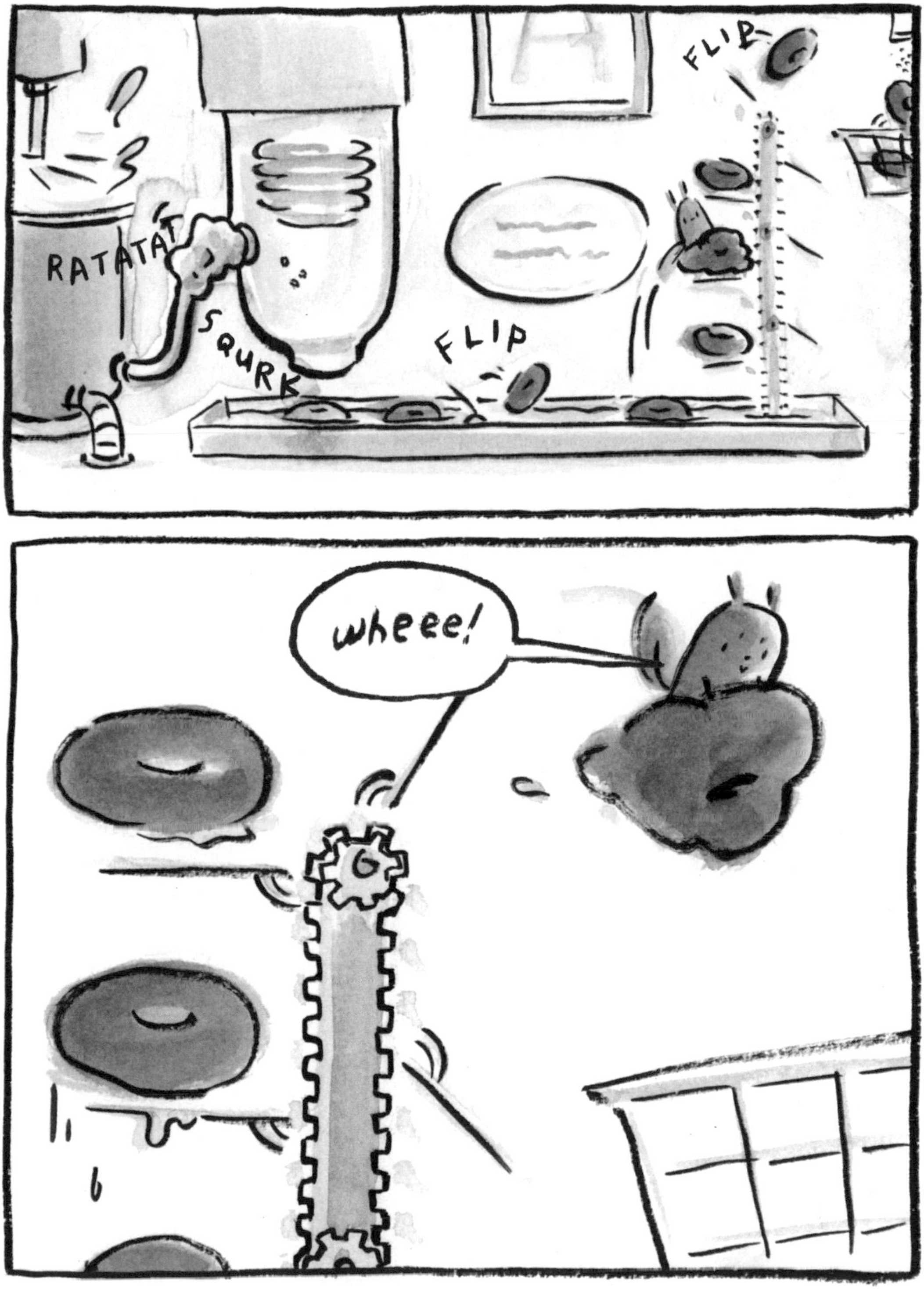
RATATAT
SQURK
FLIP
FLIP
wheee!

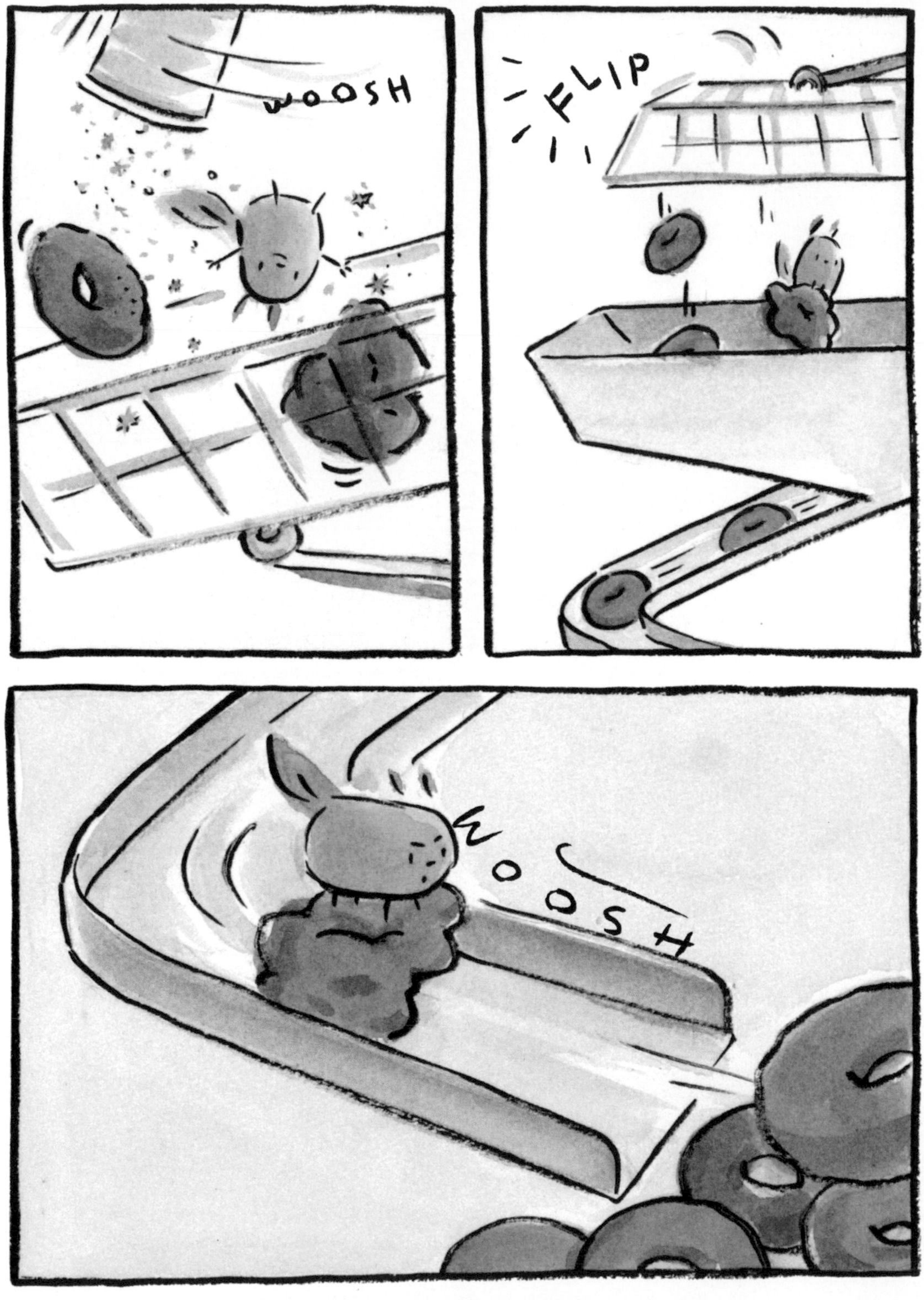
WOOSH
FLIP
WOOSH

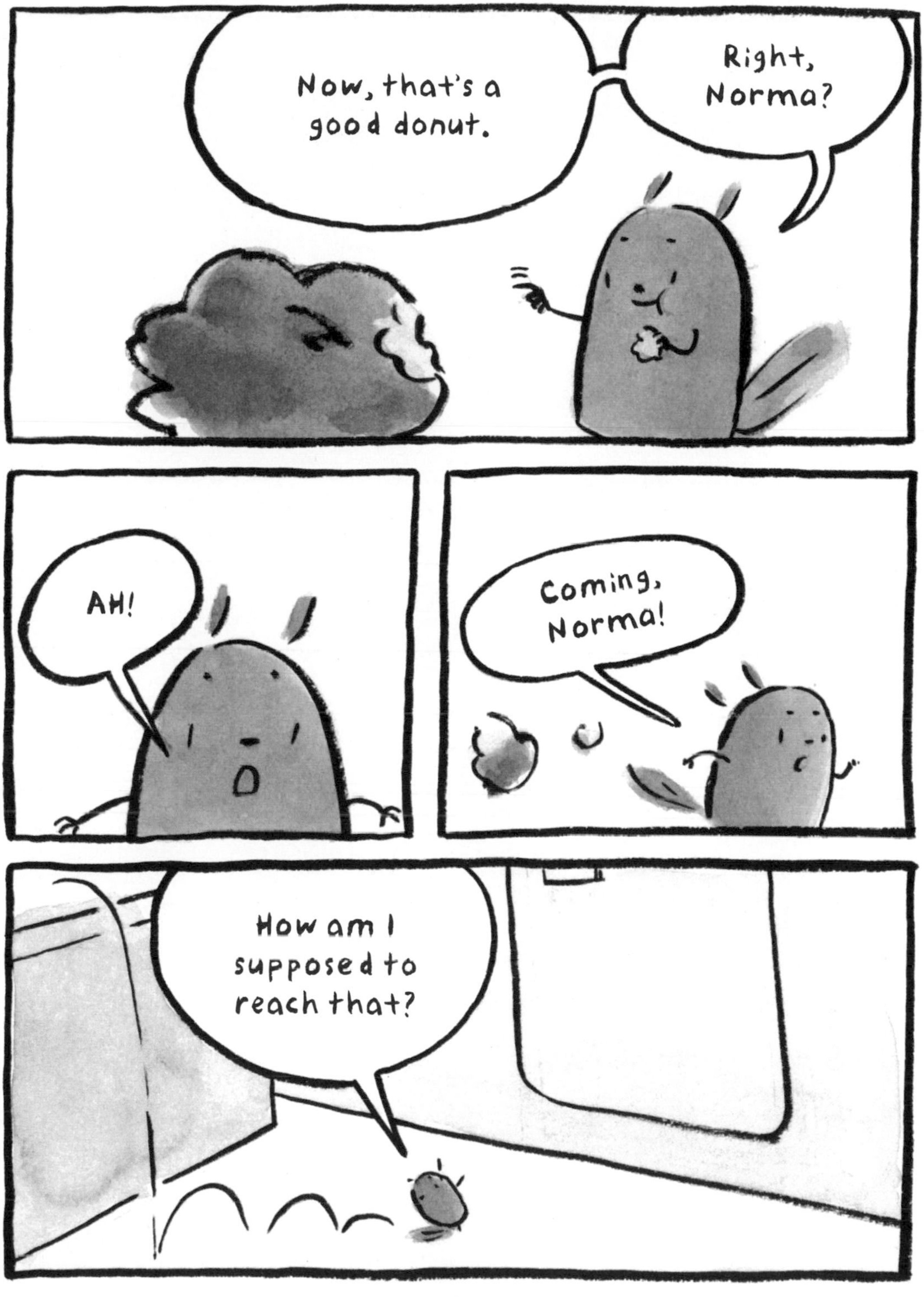
Now, that's a good donut.
Right, Norma?
AH!
Coming, Norma!
How am I supposed to reach that?

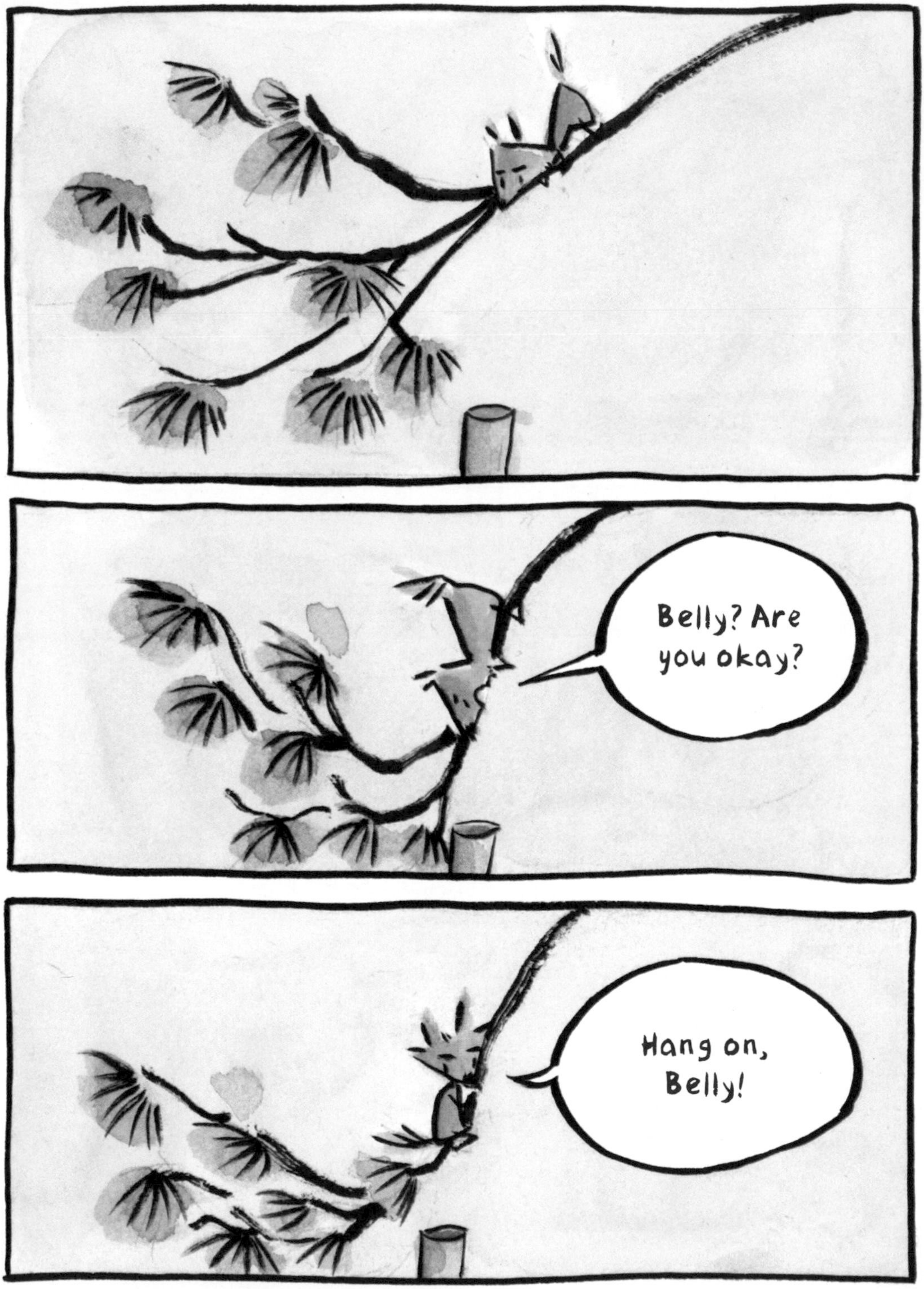
Belly? Are you okay?
Hang on, Belly!

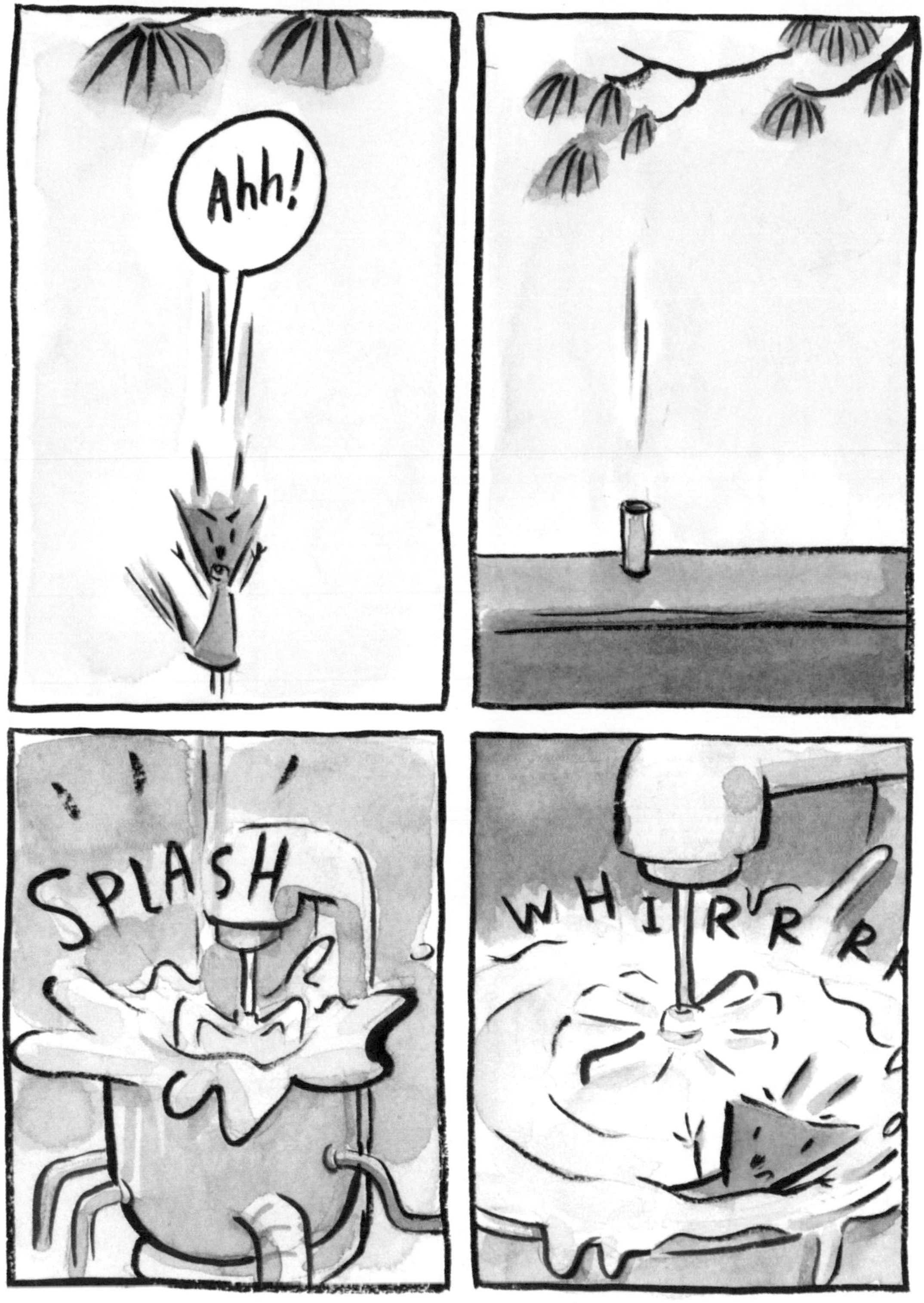
Ahh!
SPLASH
WHIRRRR

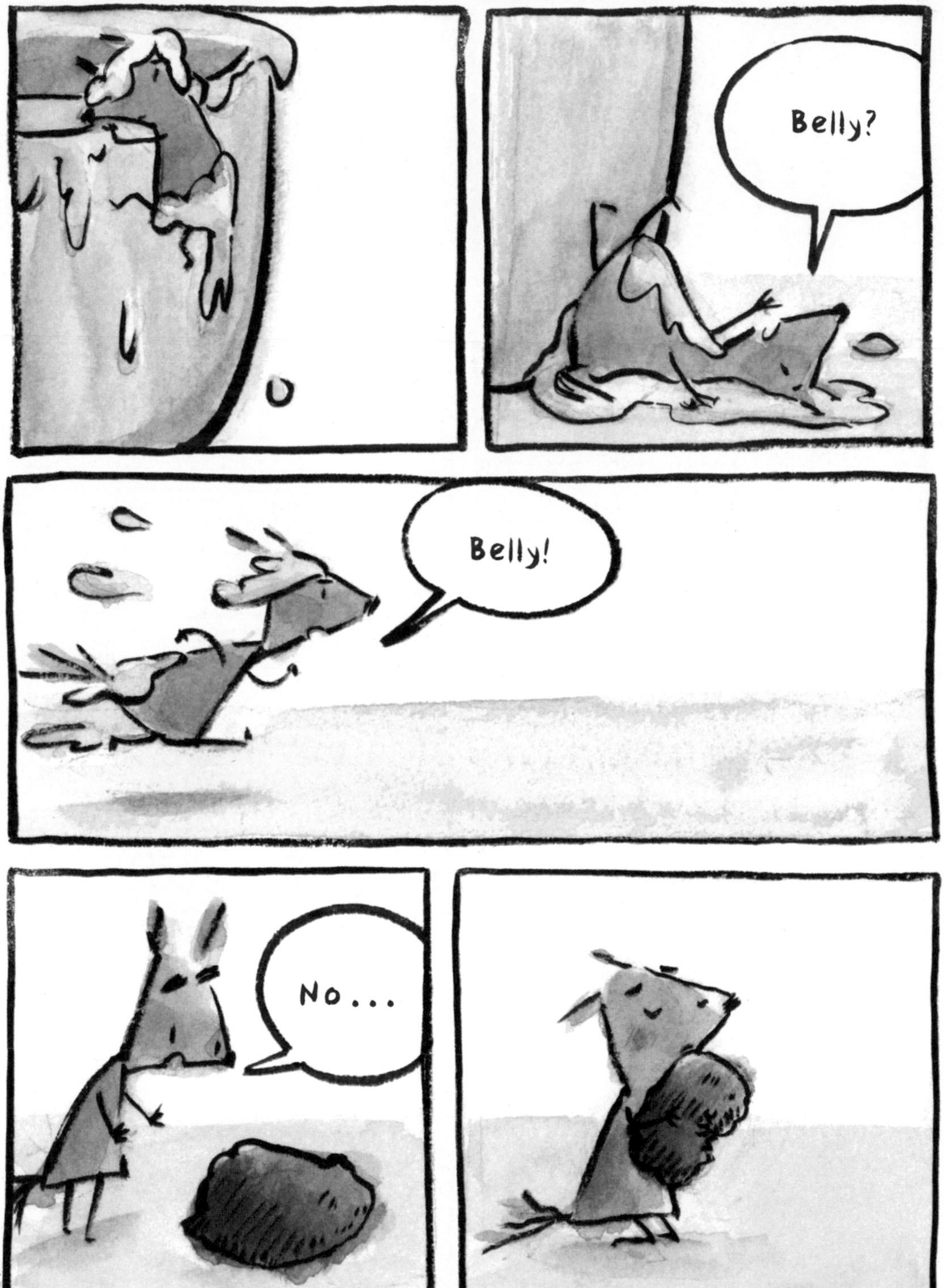
Belly?
Belly!
No...

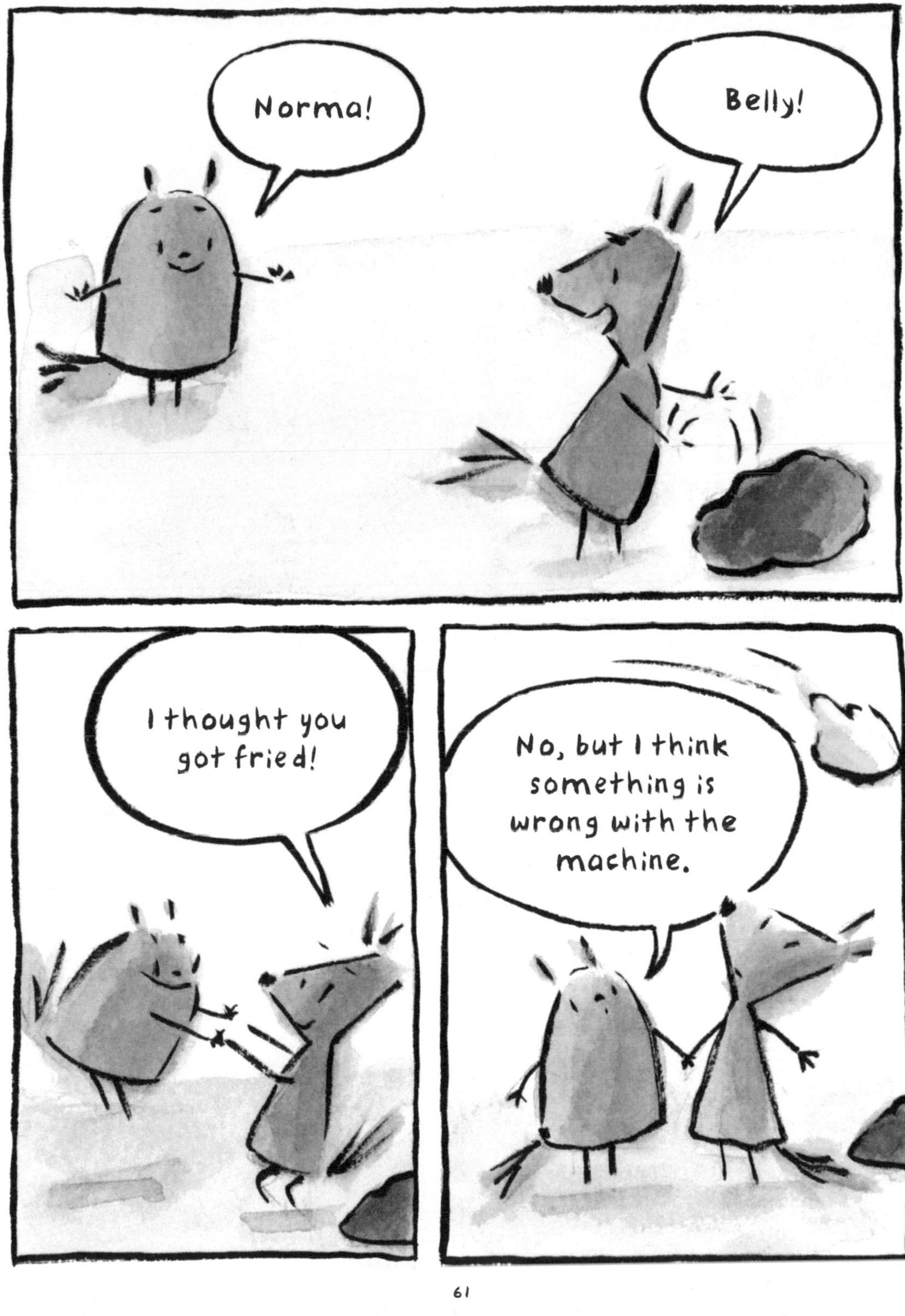
Norma!
Belly!
I thought you got fried!
No, but I think something is wrong with the machine.

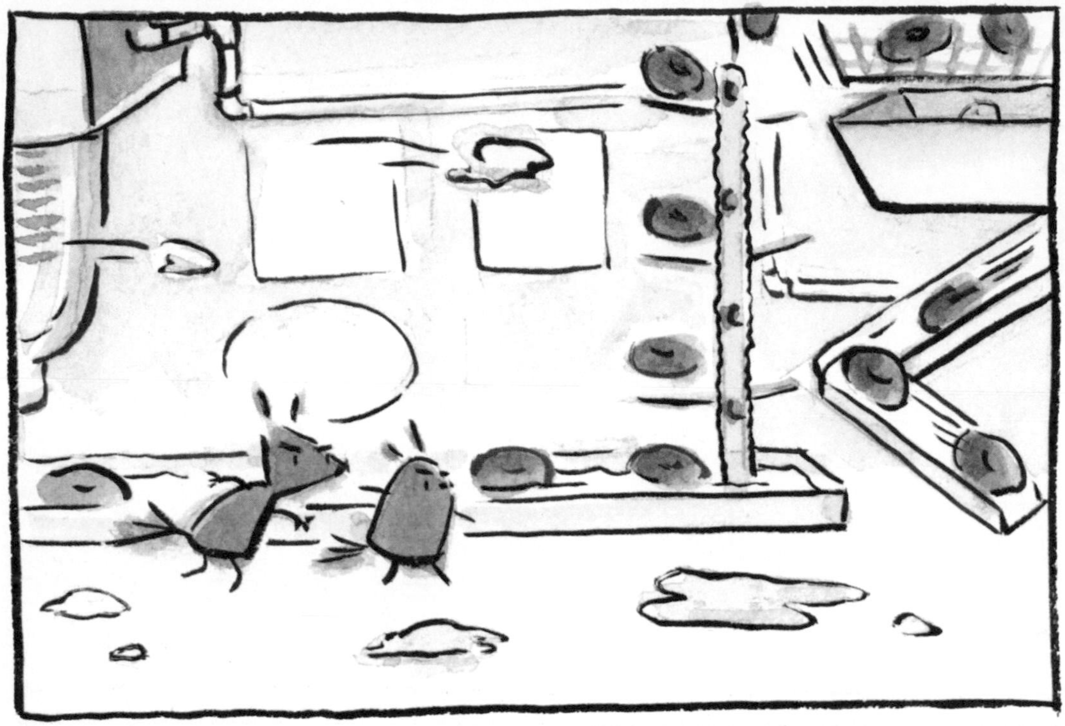

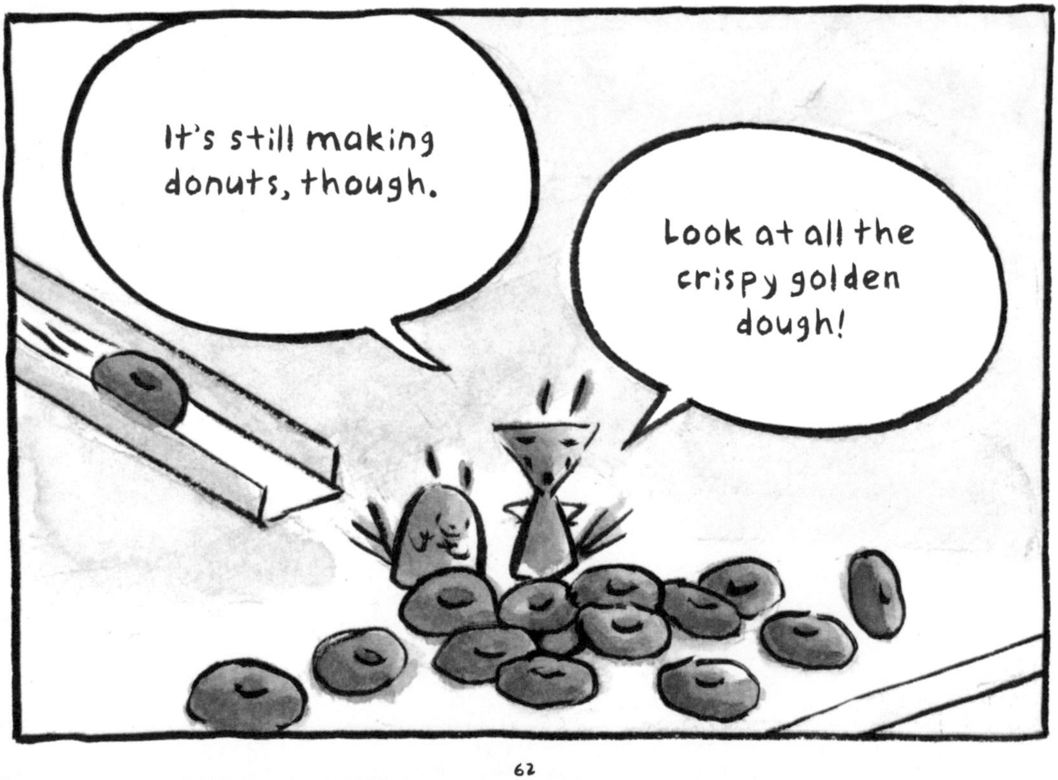

It's still making donuts, though.
Look at all the crispy golden dough!

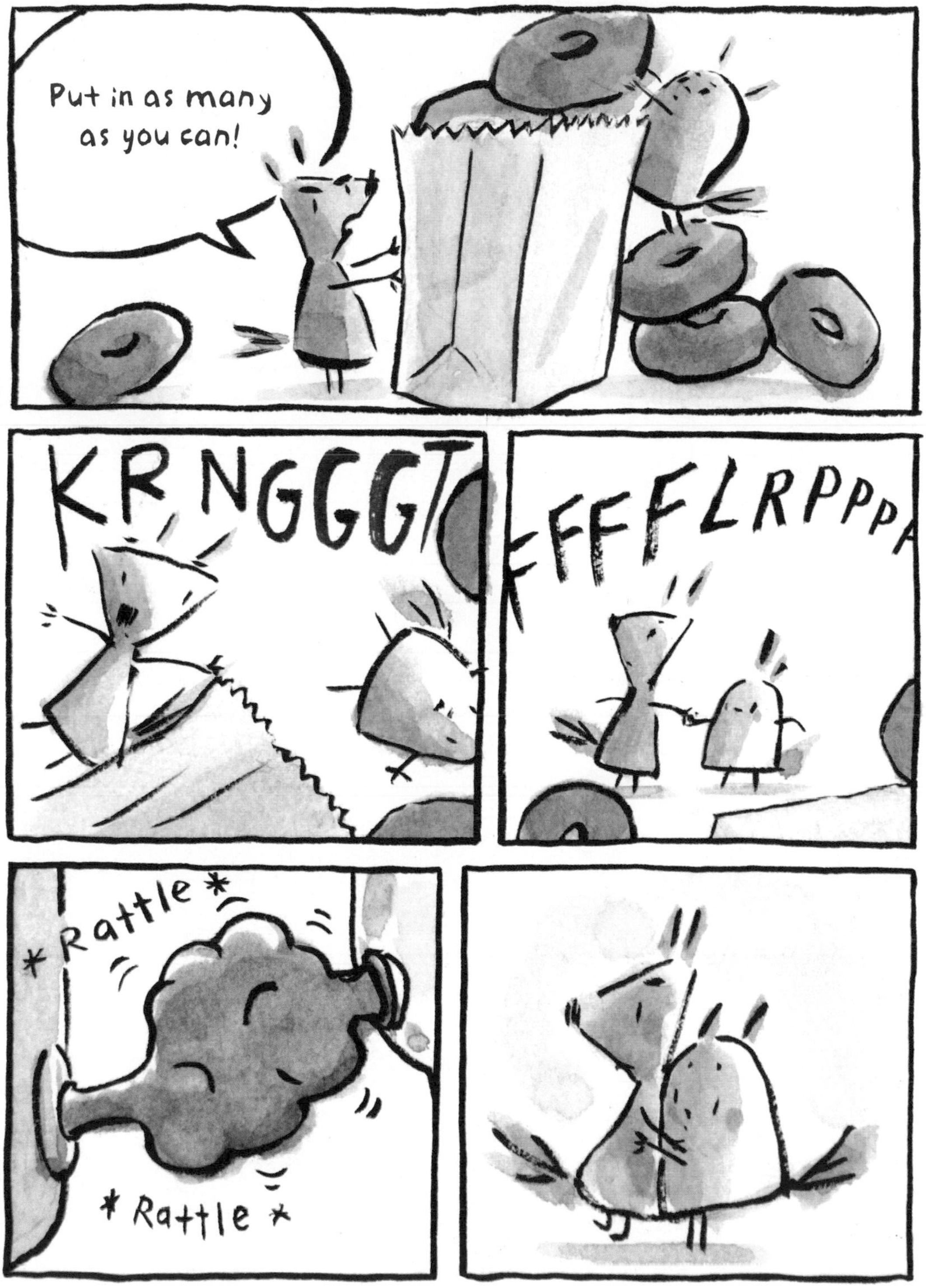
Put in as many as you can!
KRNGGGT
FFFFLRPPPP
Rattle
Rattle

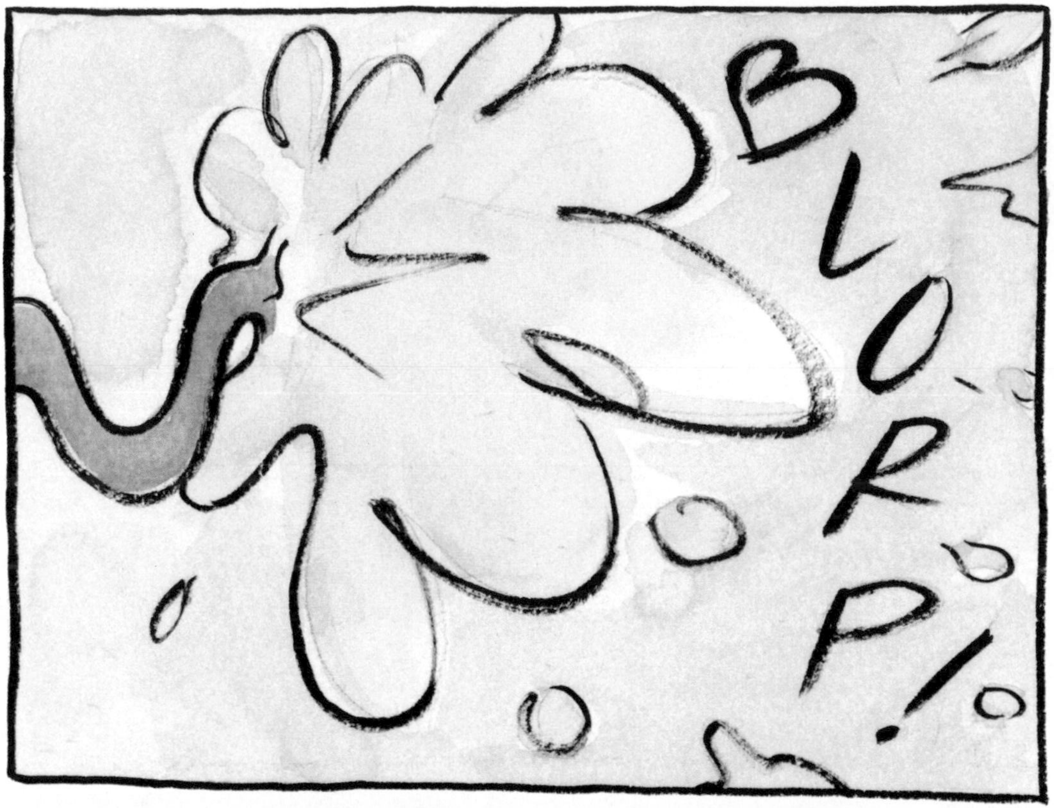
BLORP!

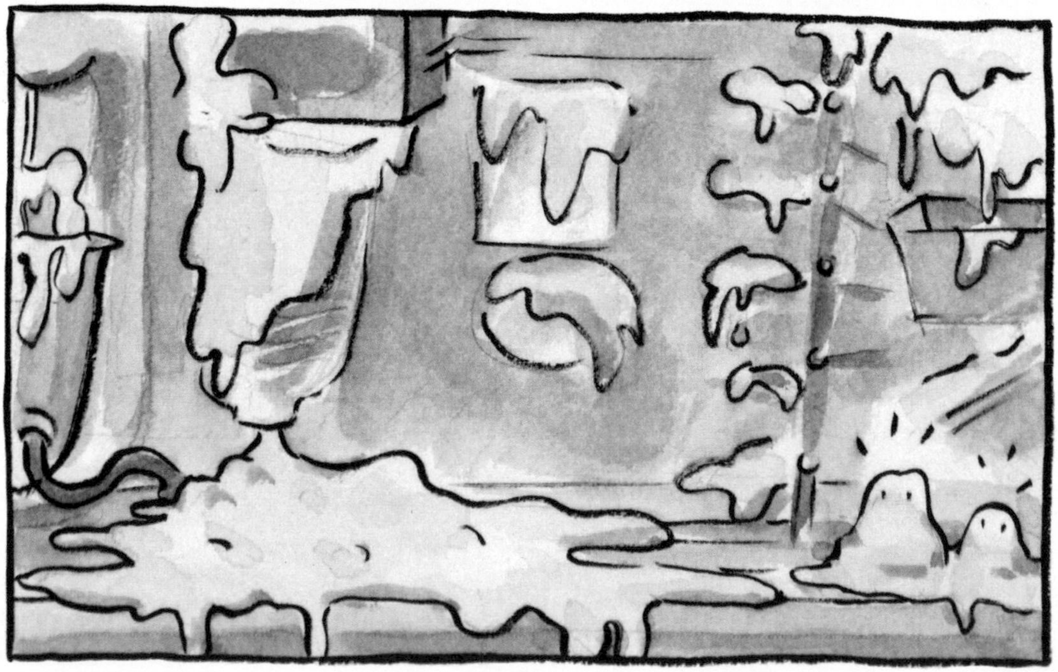

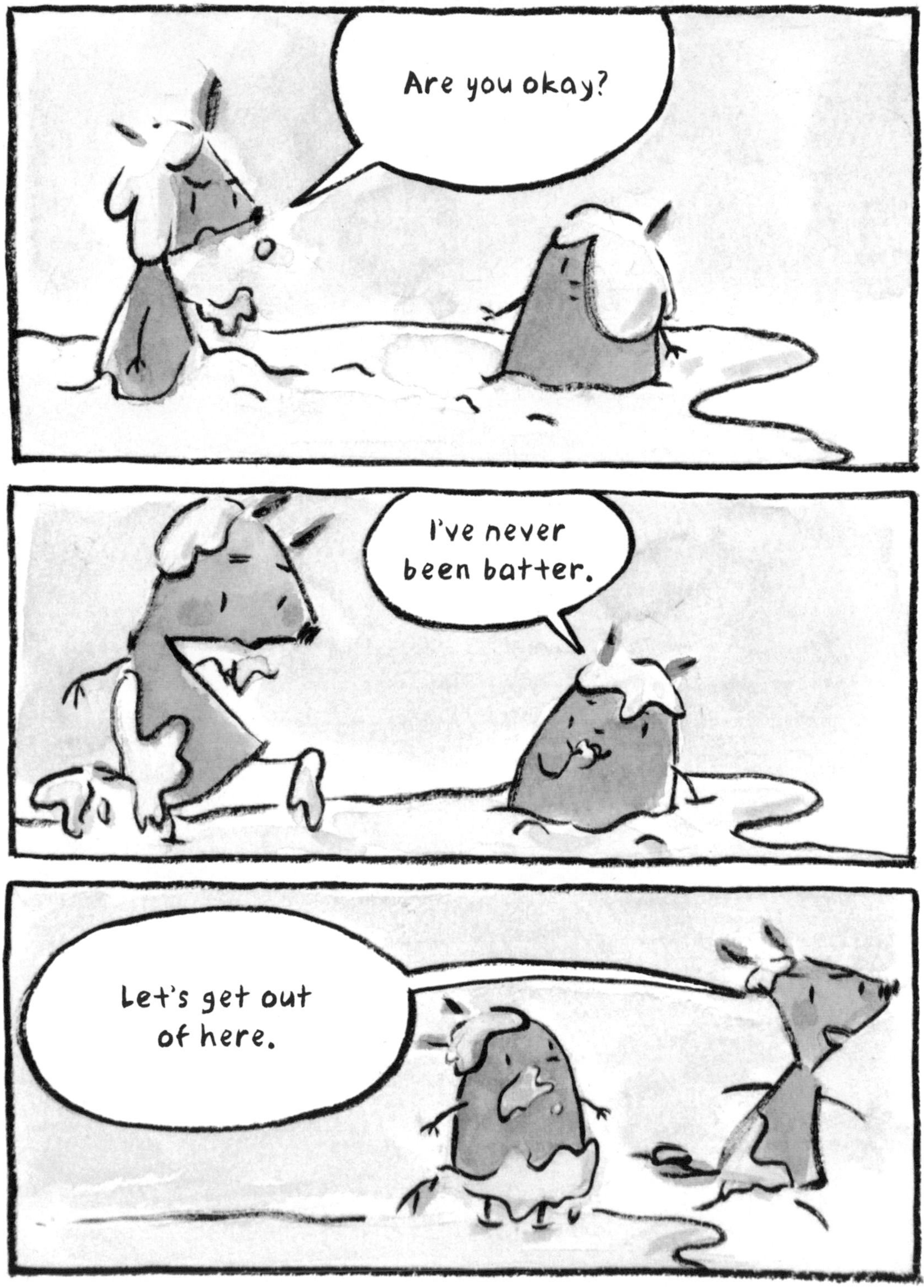
Are you okay?
I've never been batter.
Let's get out of here.

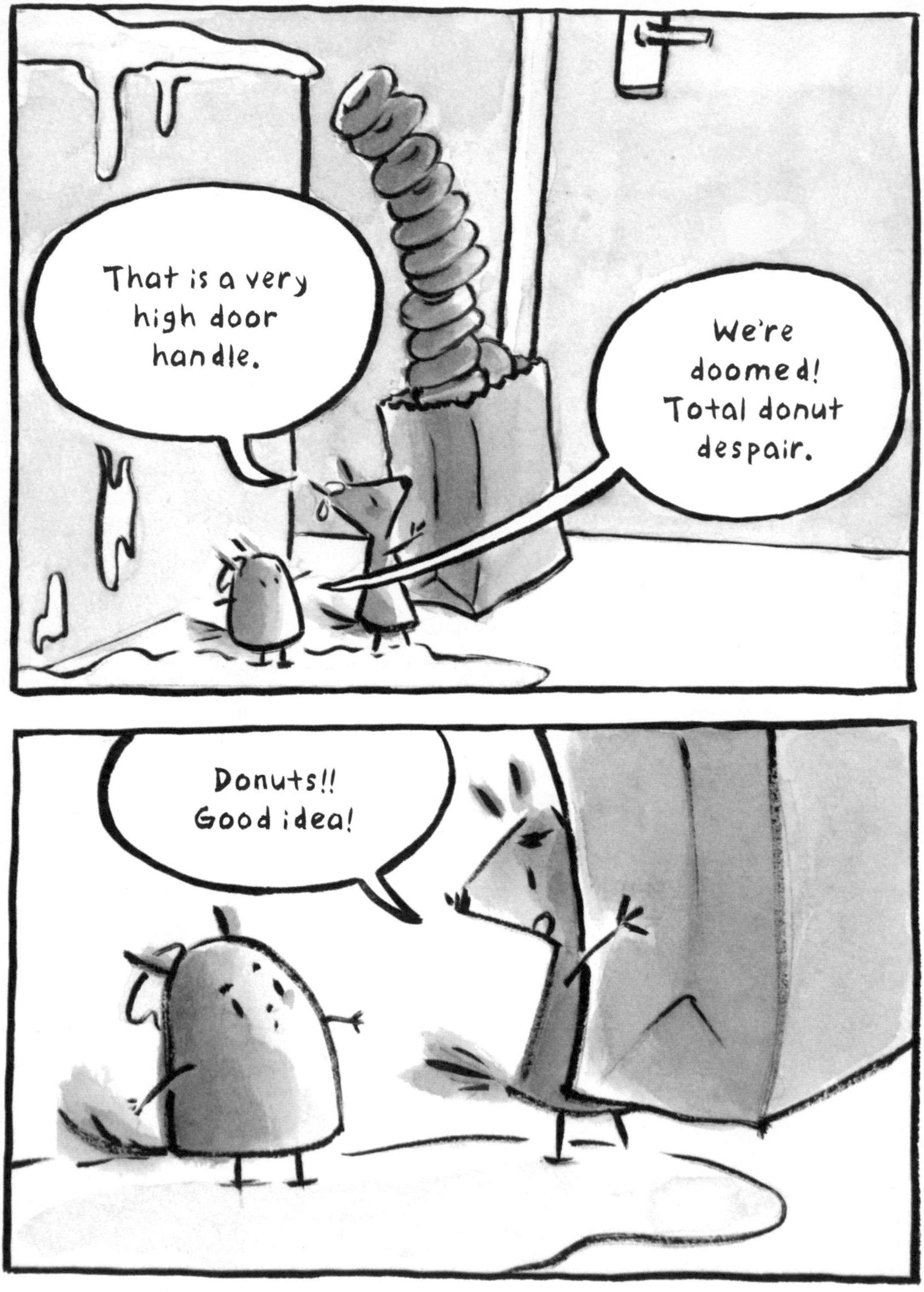

That is a very high door handle.
We're doomed! Total donut despair.
Donuts!! Good idea!

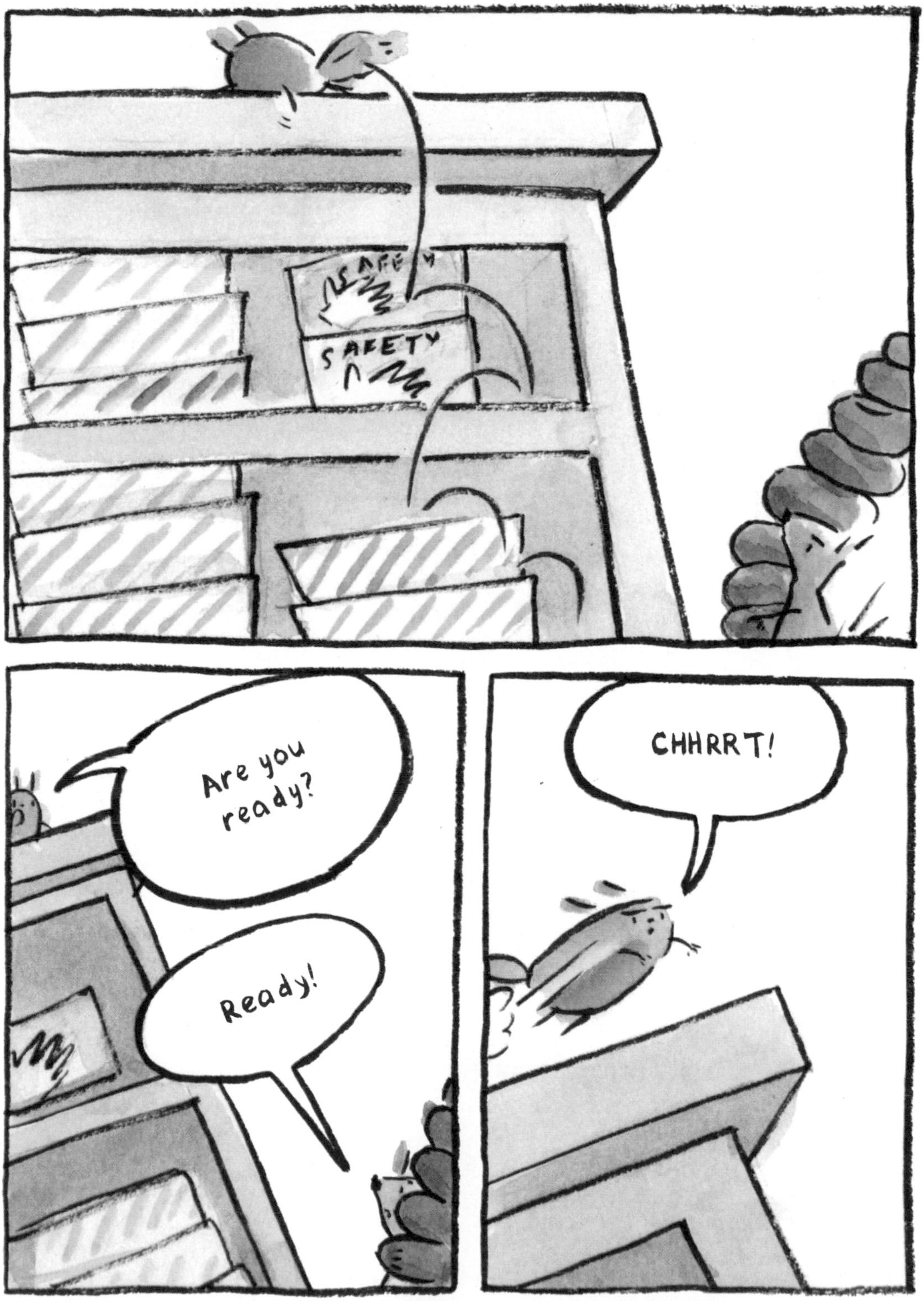
SAFETY
SAFETY
Are you ready?
Ready!
CHHRRT!

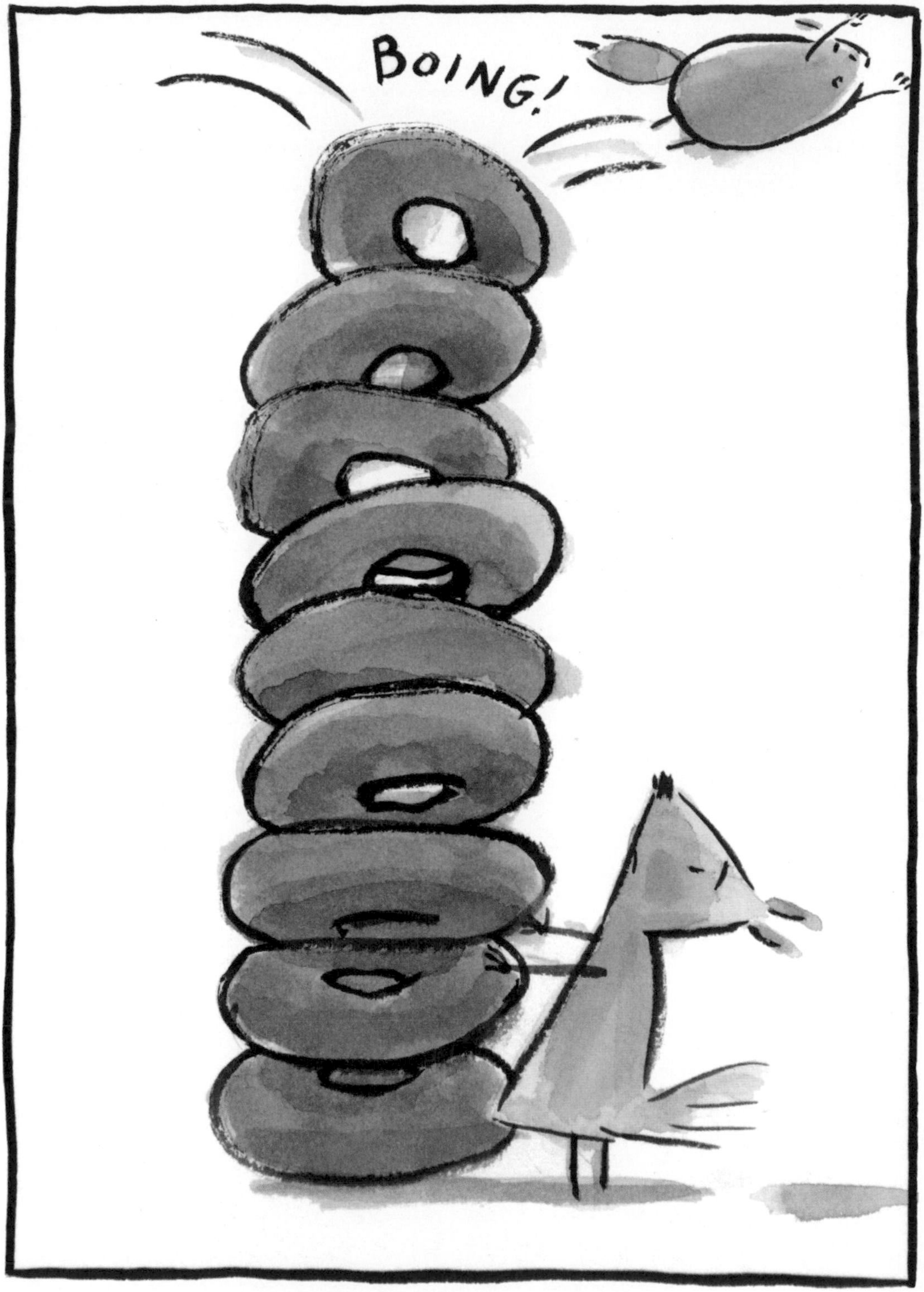
BOING!

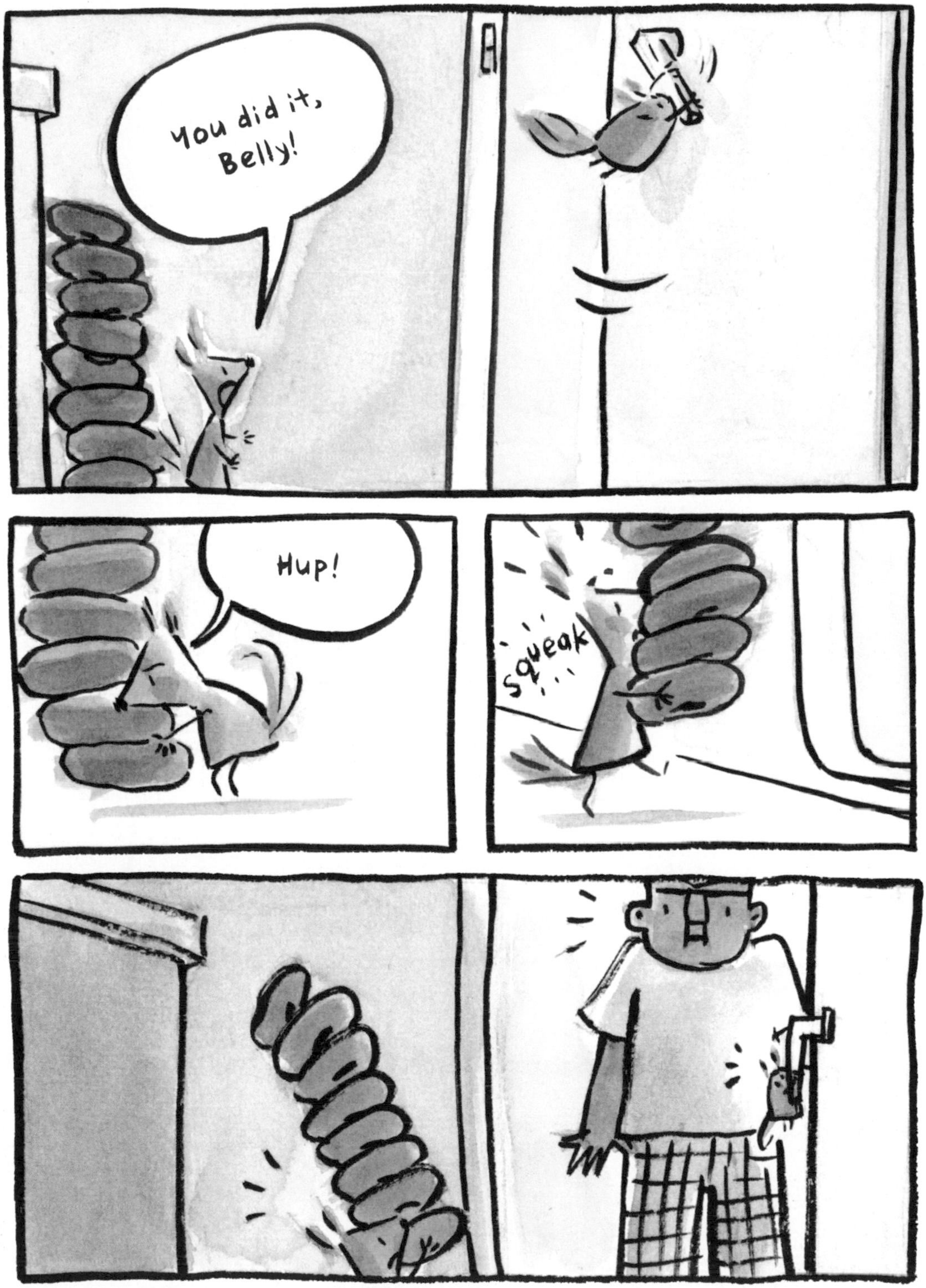
You did it, Belly!
Hup!
squeak

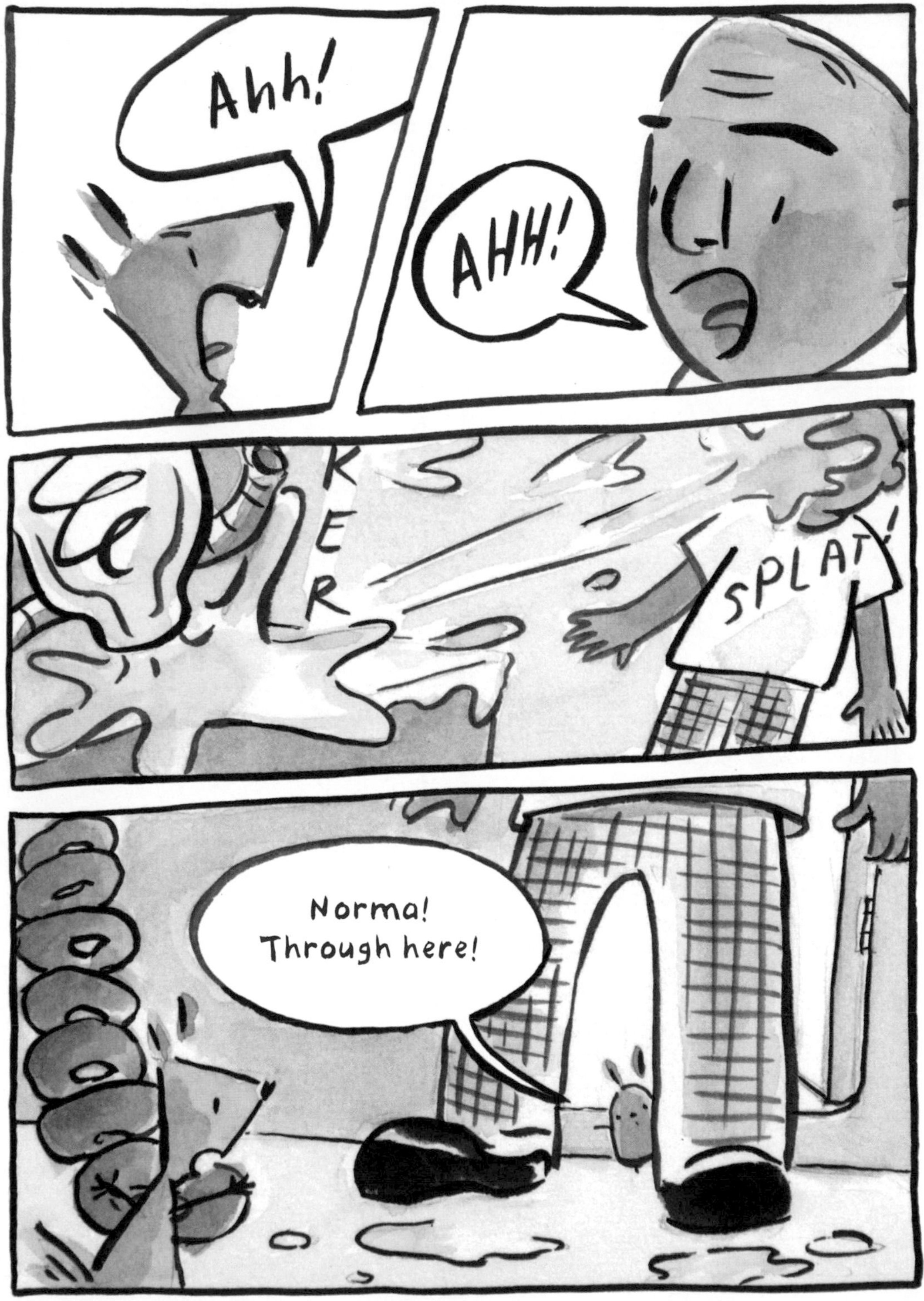
Ahh!
AHH!
KER
SPLAT!
Norma!
Through here!

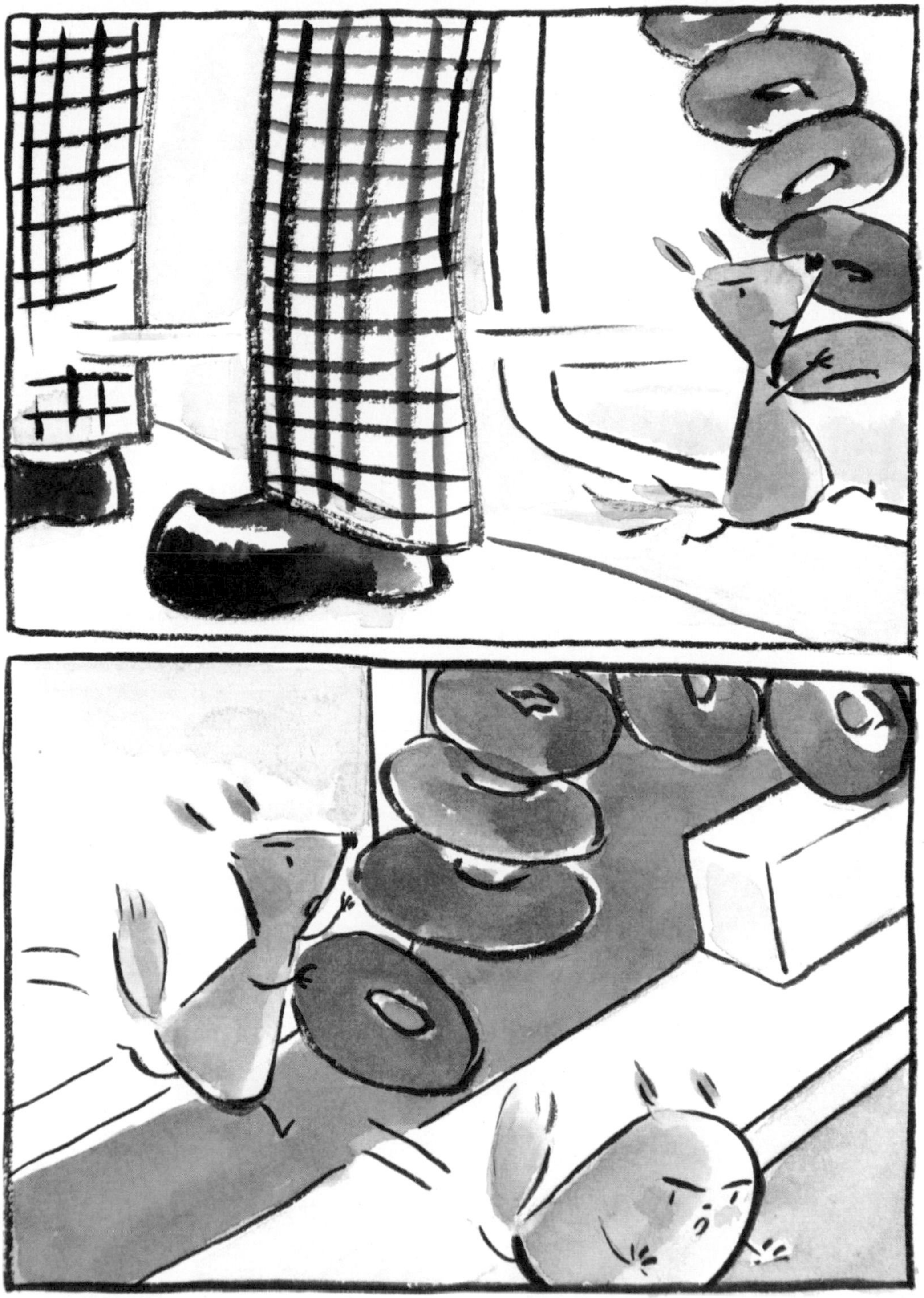

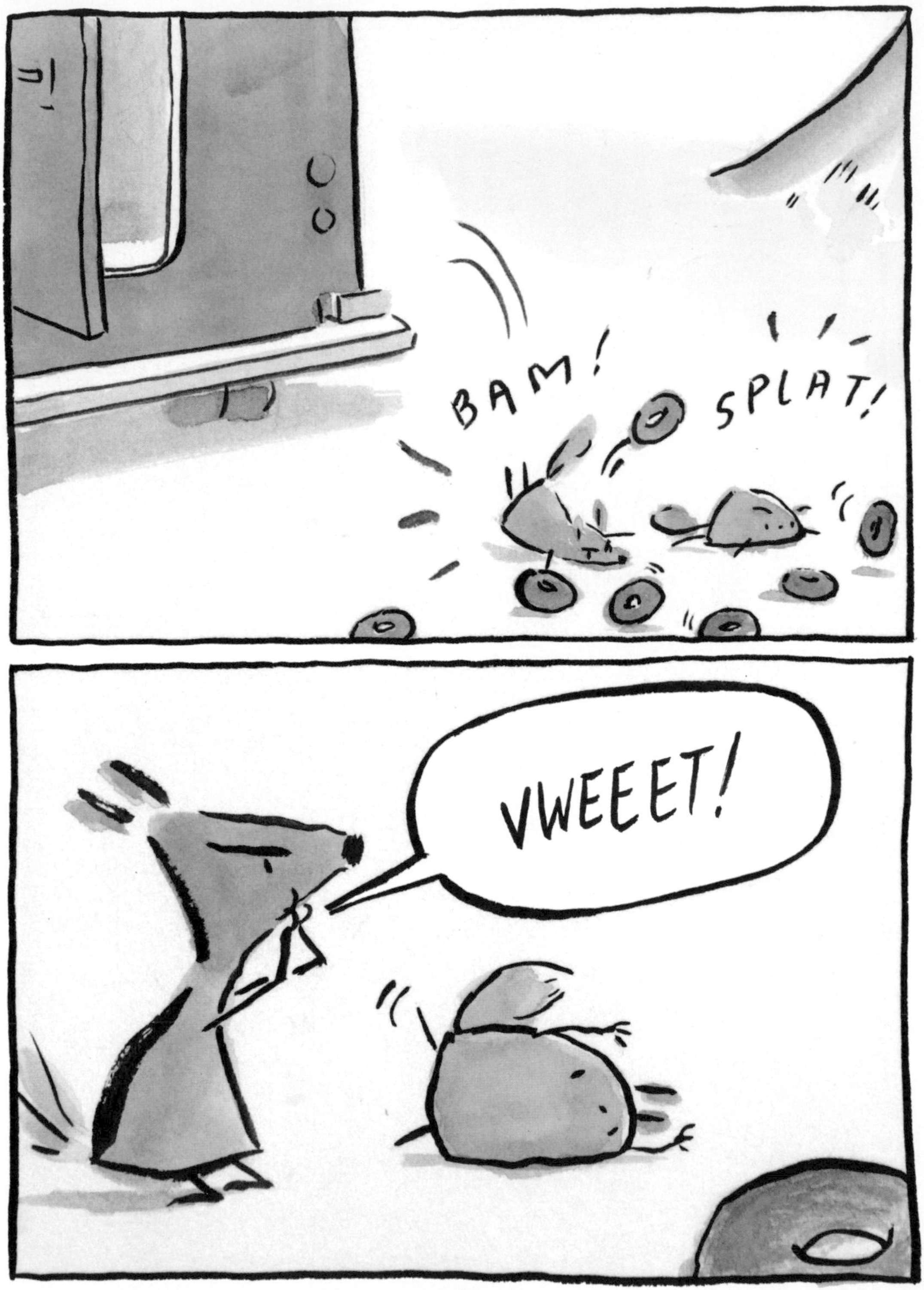
BAM!
SPLAT!
VWEEET!

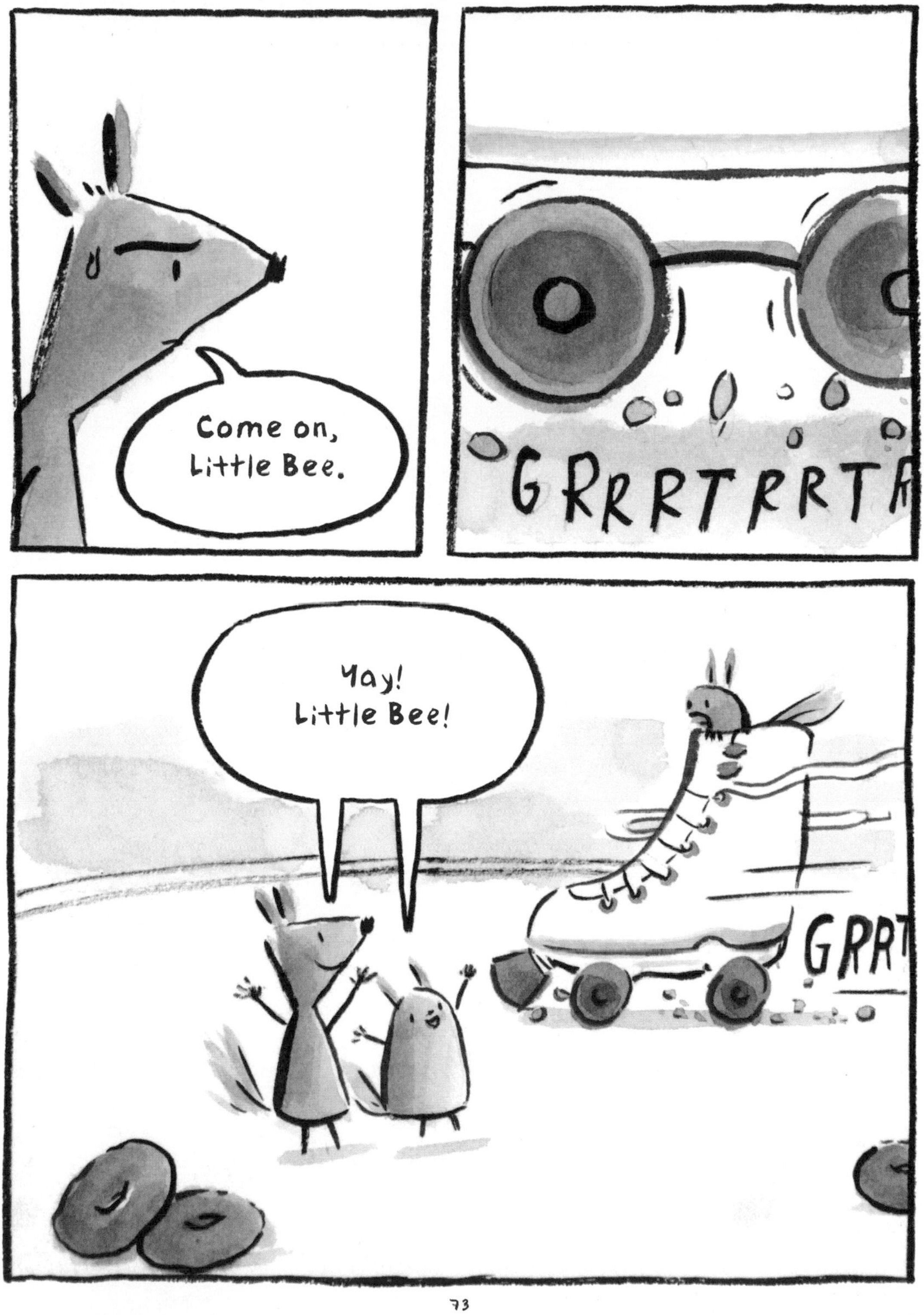
Come on,
Little Bee.
GRRRTRRTR
Yay!
Little Bee!
GRRT

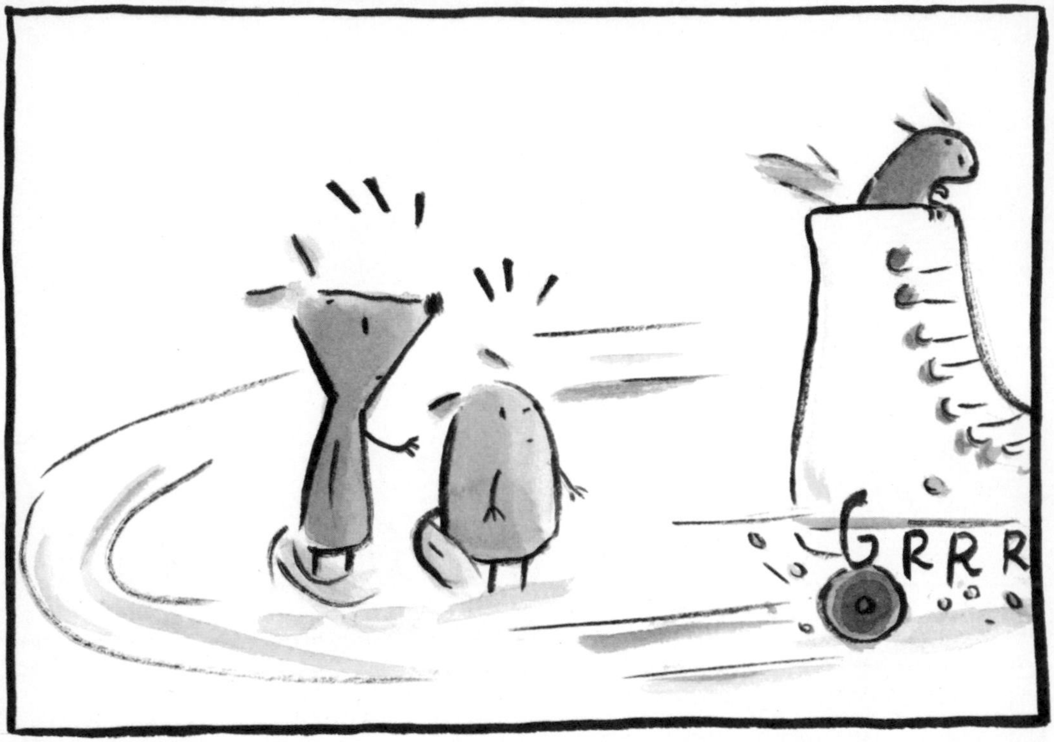
GRRR

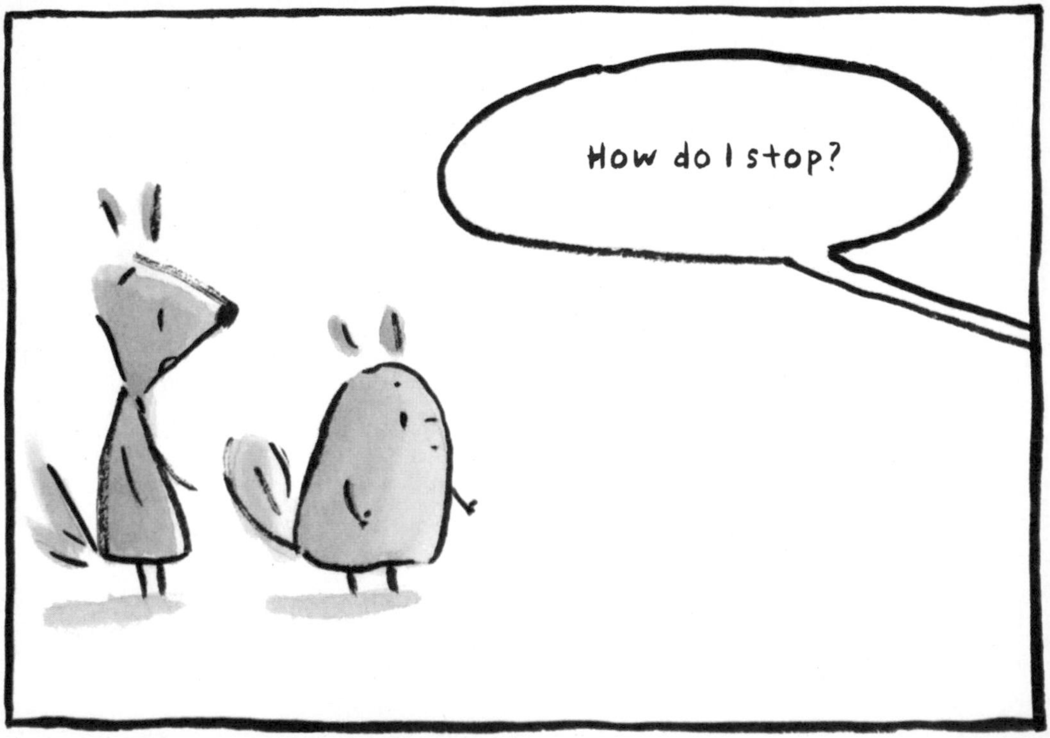
How do I stop?

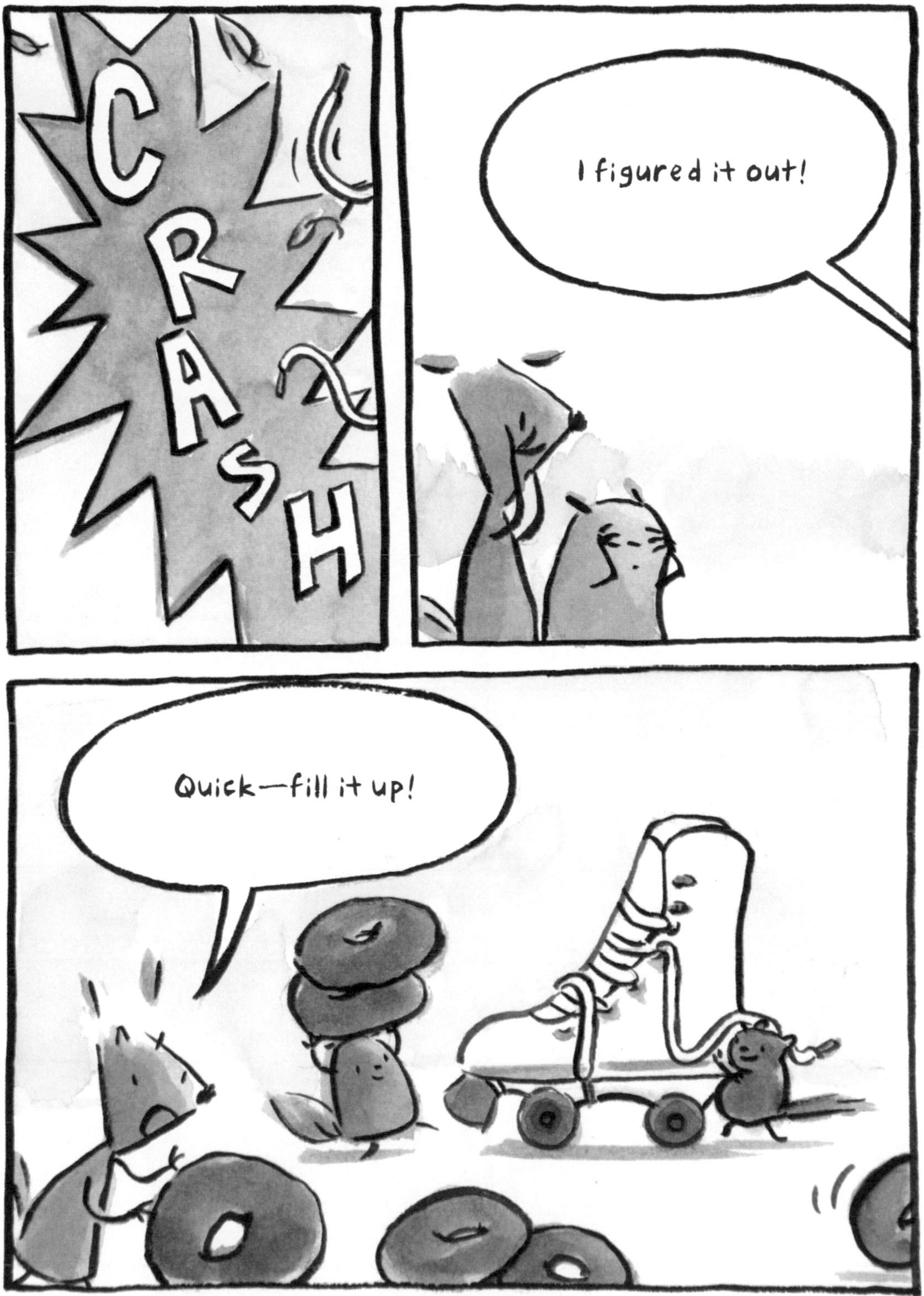
CRASH
I figured it out!
Quick—fill it up!

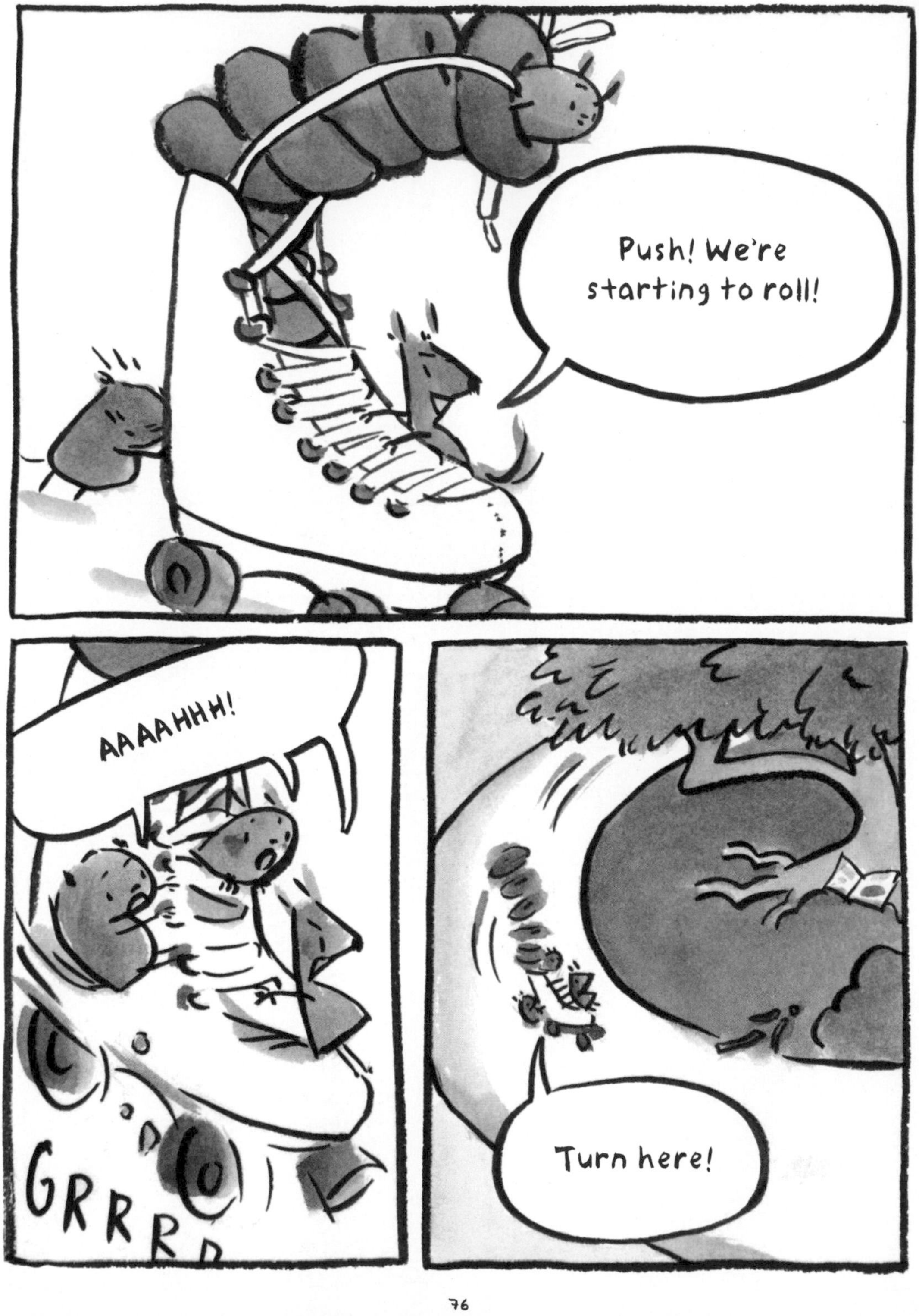
Push! We're starting to roll!
AAAAHHH!
GRRRR
Turn here!

SCREECH
FLAP
WOOSH
FLAP
SHOP SMART

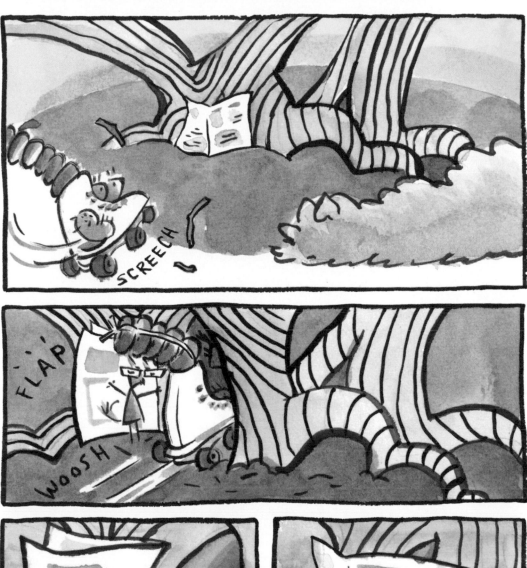

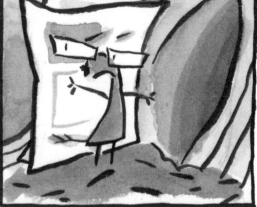

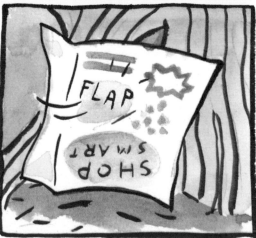

Chapter 4

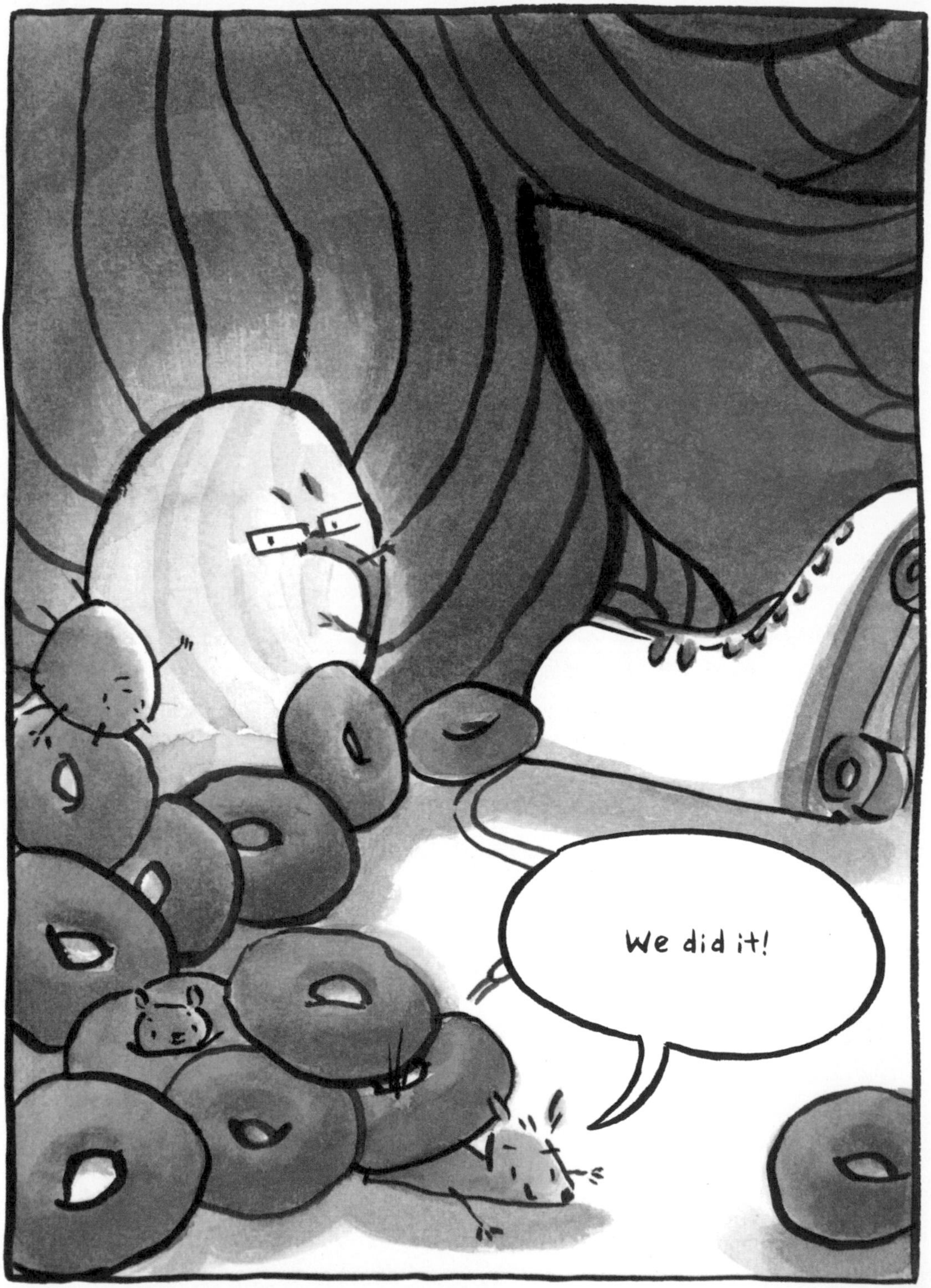
We did it!

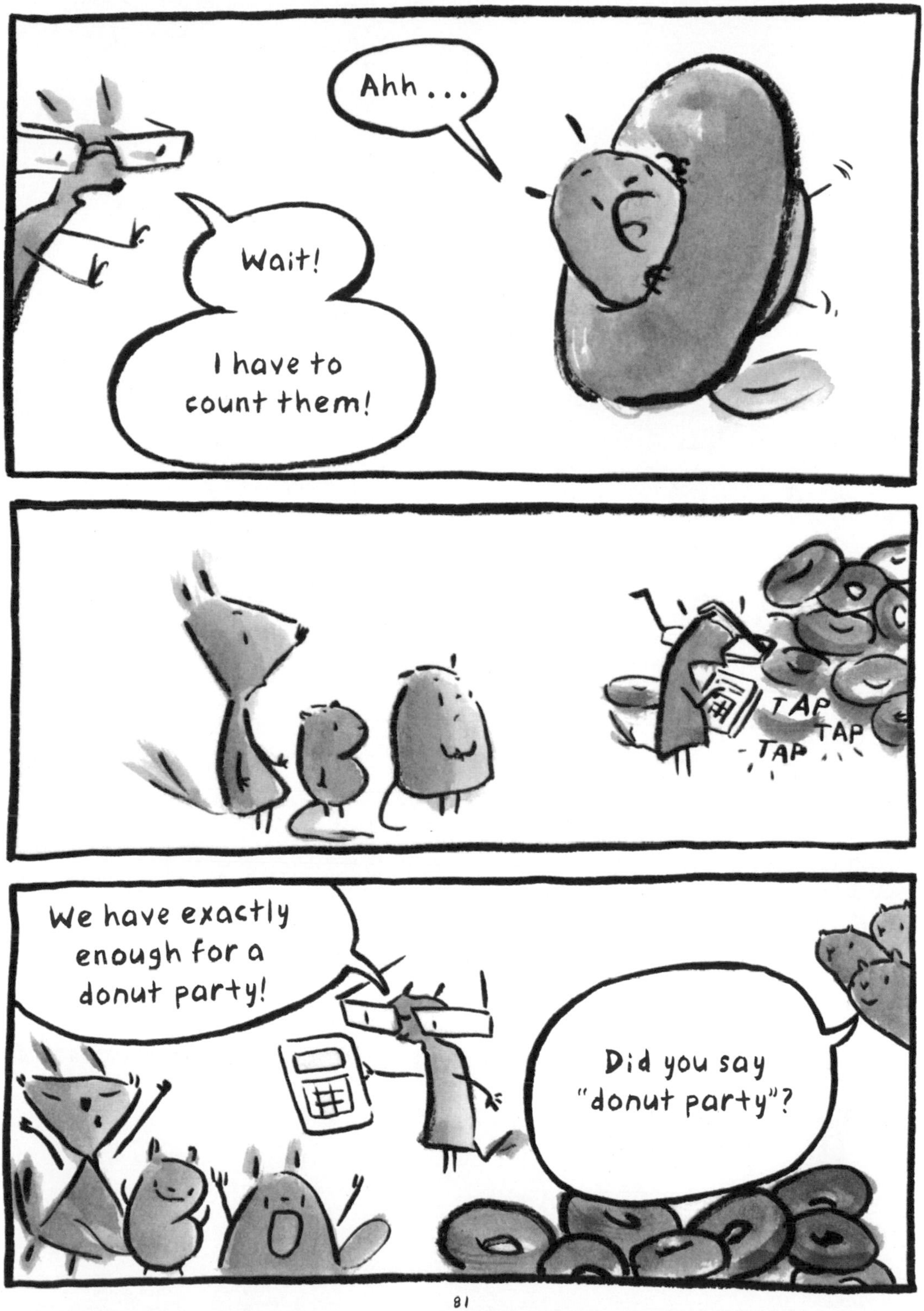
Ahh . . .
Wait!
I have to count them!
TAP
TAP
TAP
We have exactly enough for a donut party!
Did you say "donut party"?

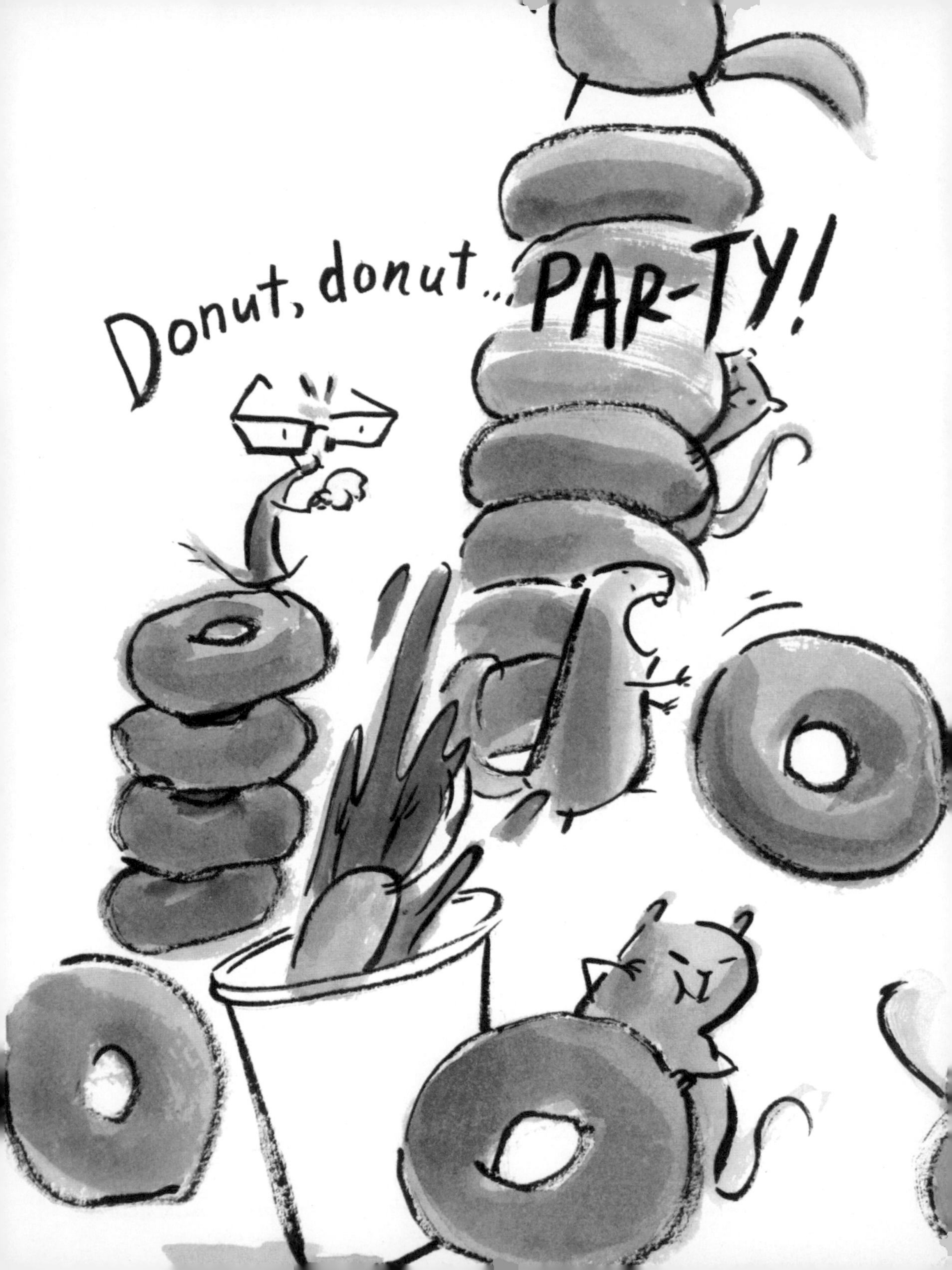
Donut, donut... PAR-TY!

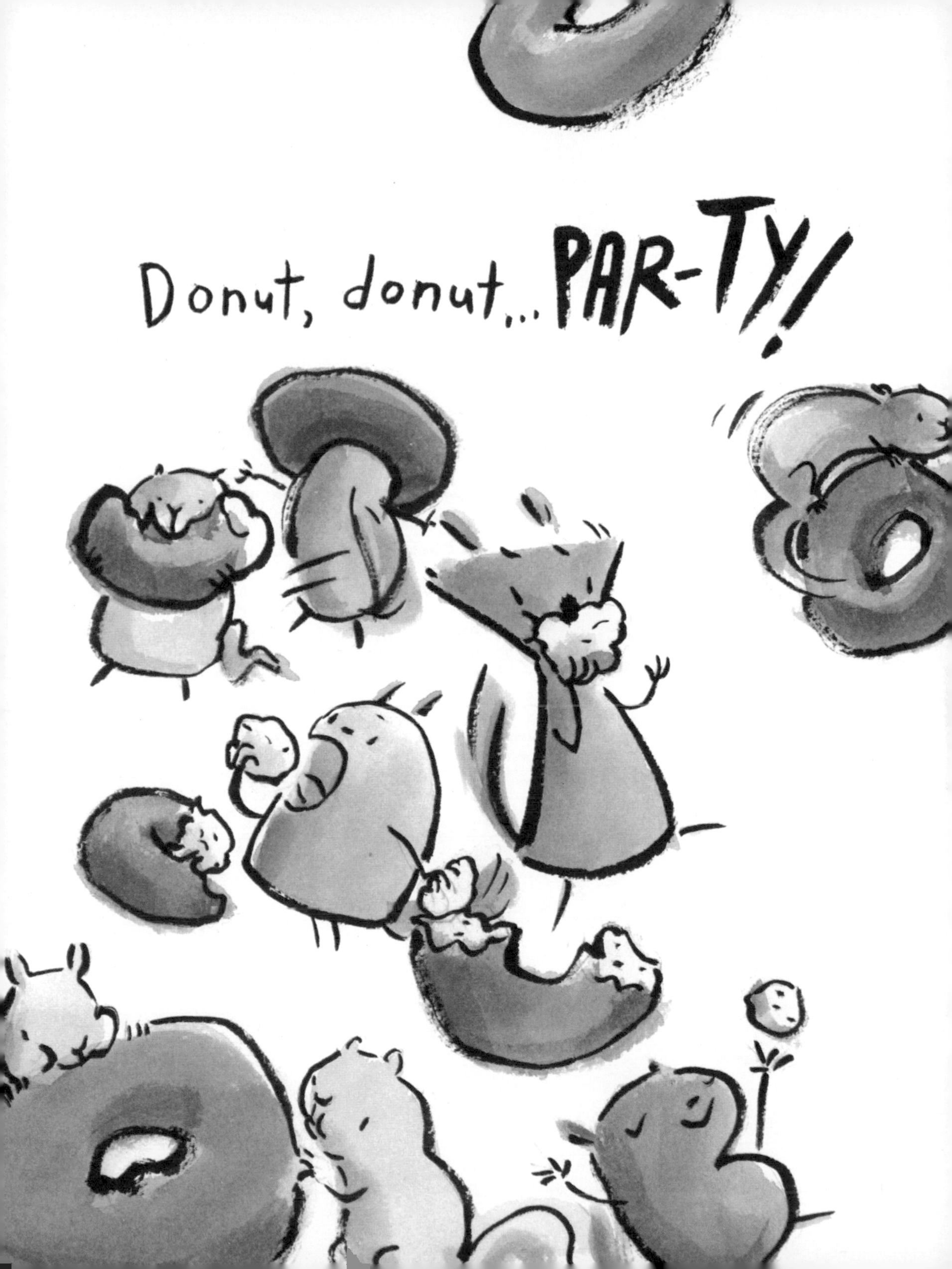
Donut, donut... PAR-TY!

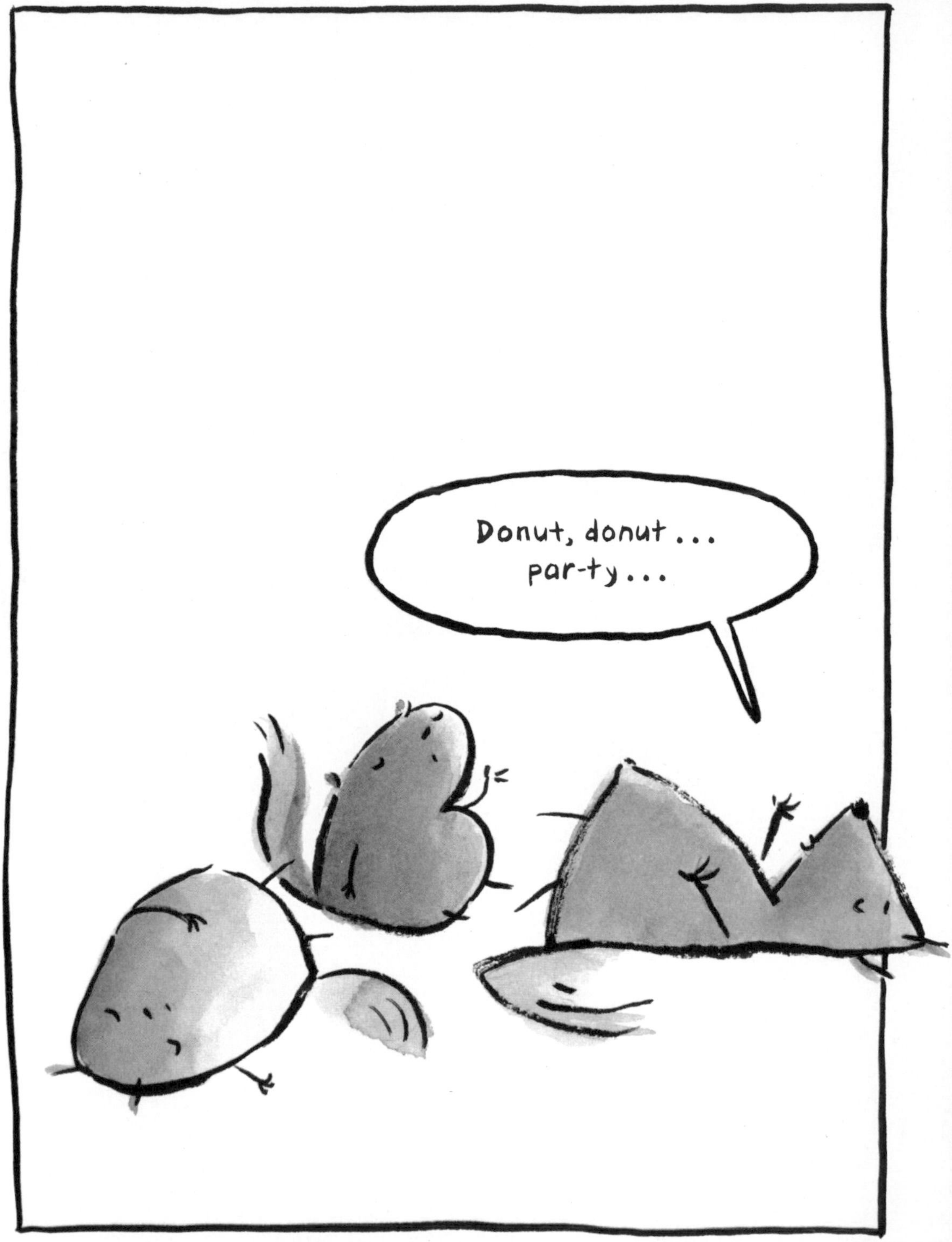
Donut, donut ... par-ty ...

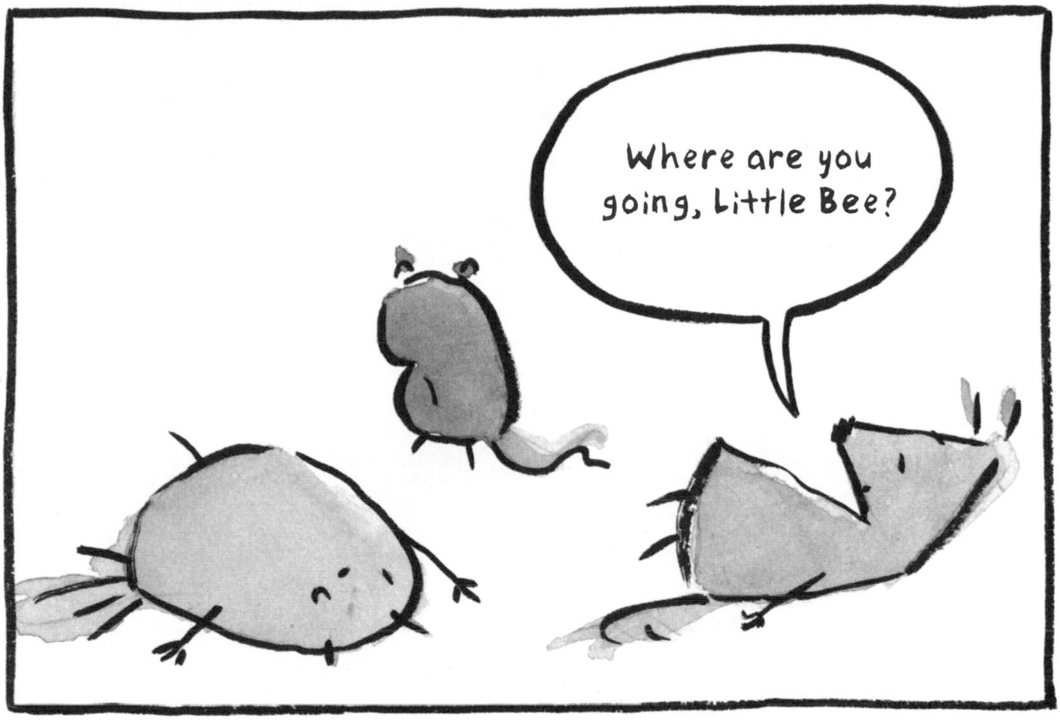
Where are you going, Little Bee?

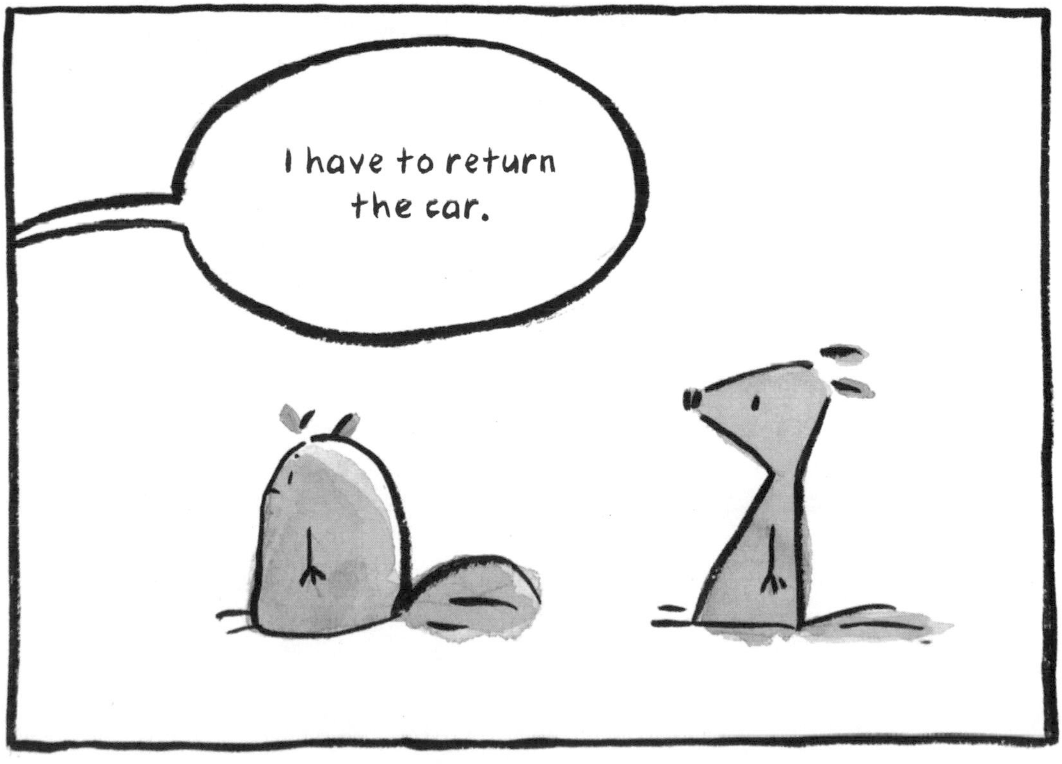
I have to return the car.

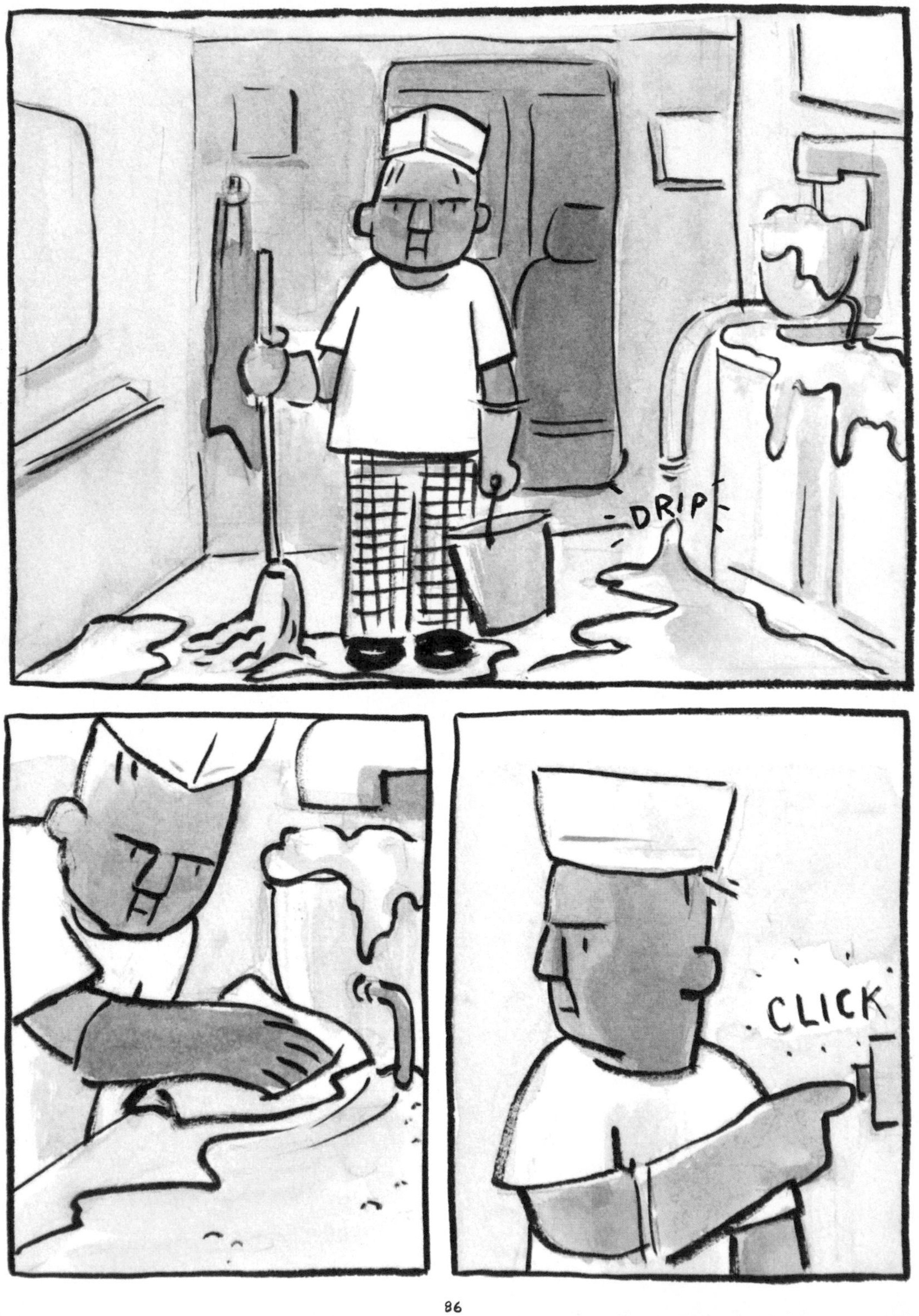
DRIP
CLICK

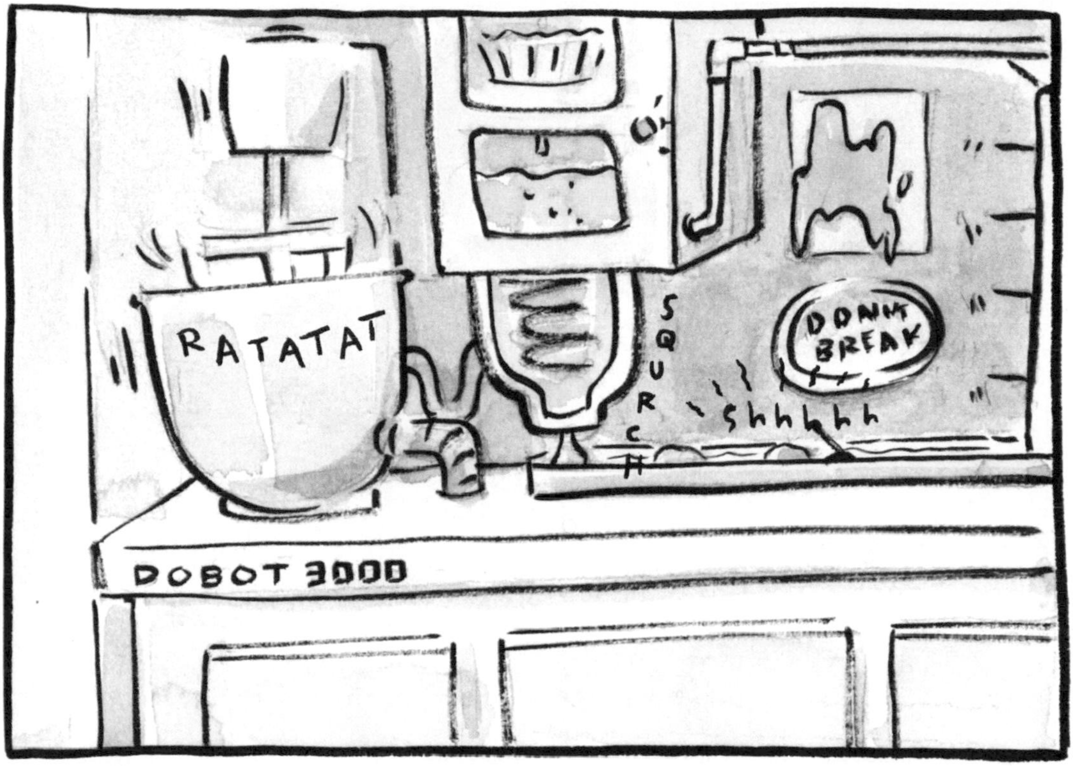
RATATAT
SQURCH
shhhhh
DON'T BREAK
DOBOT 3000

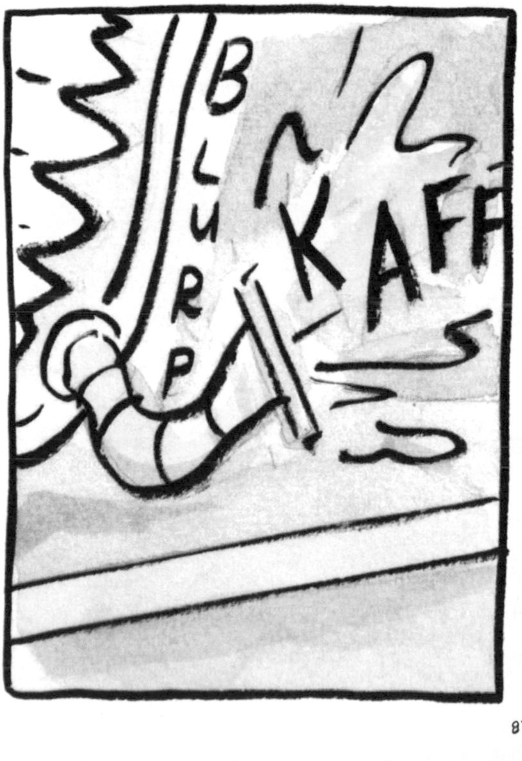
BLURP
KAFF

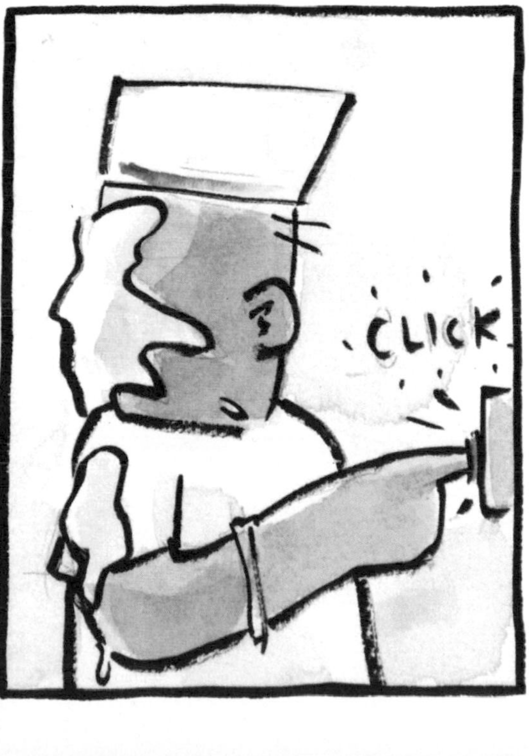
CLICK

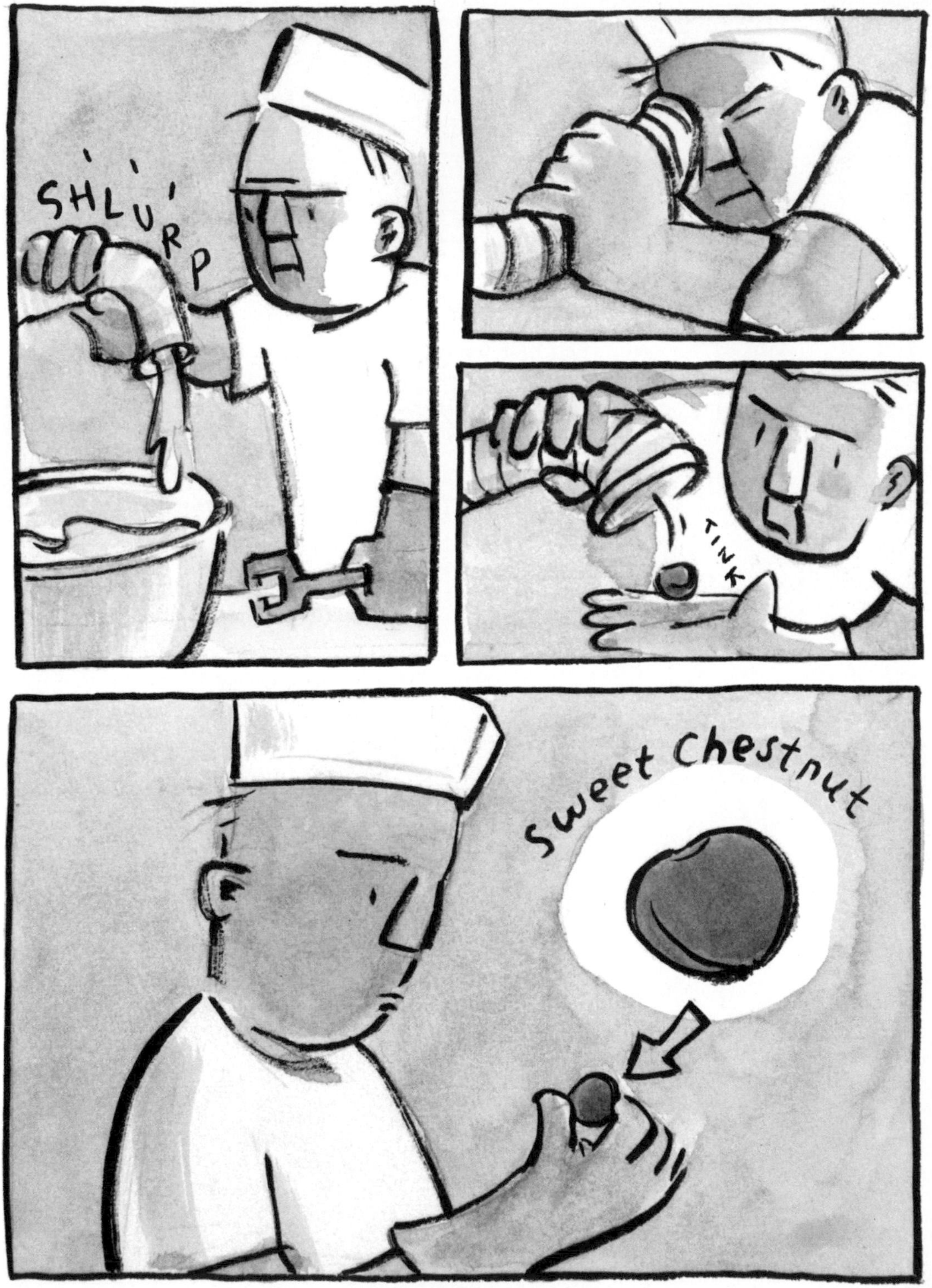
SHLURP
TINK
Sweet Chestnut

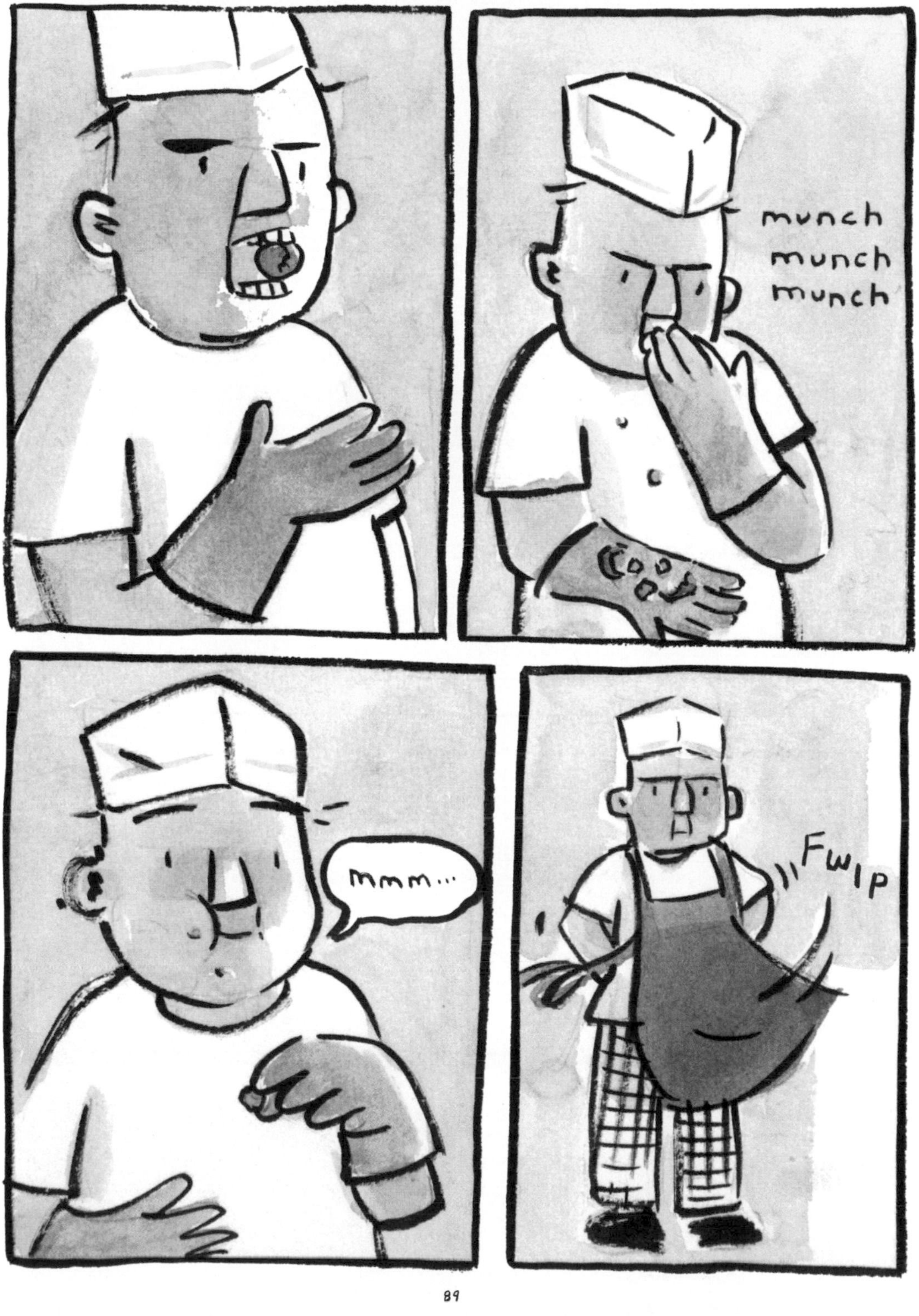
munch
munch
munch
mmm...
FWIP

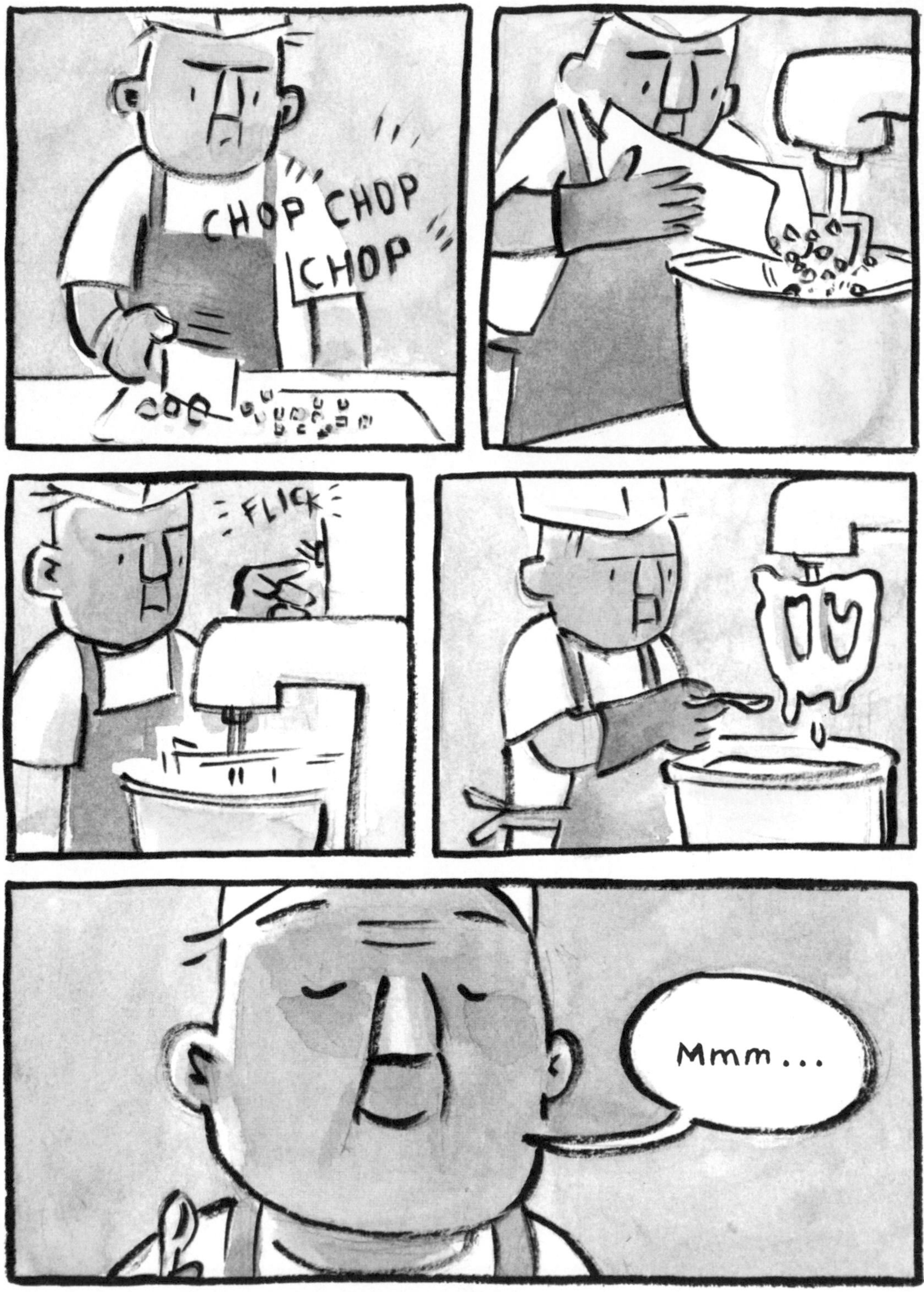
CHOP CHOP
CHOP
FLICK
Mmm...

Chapter 5

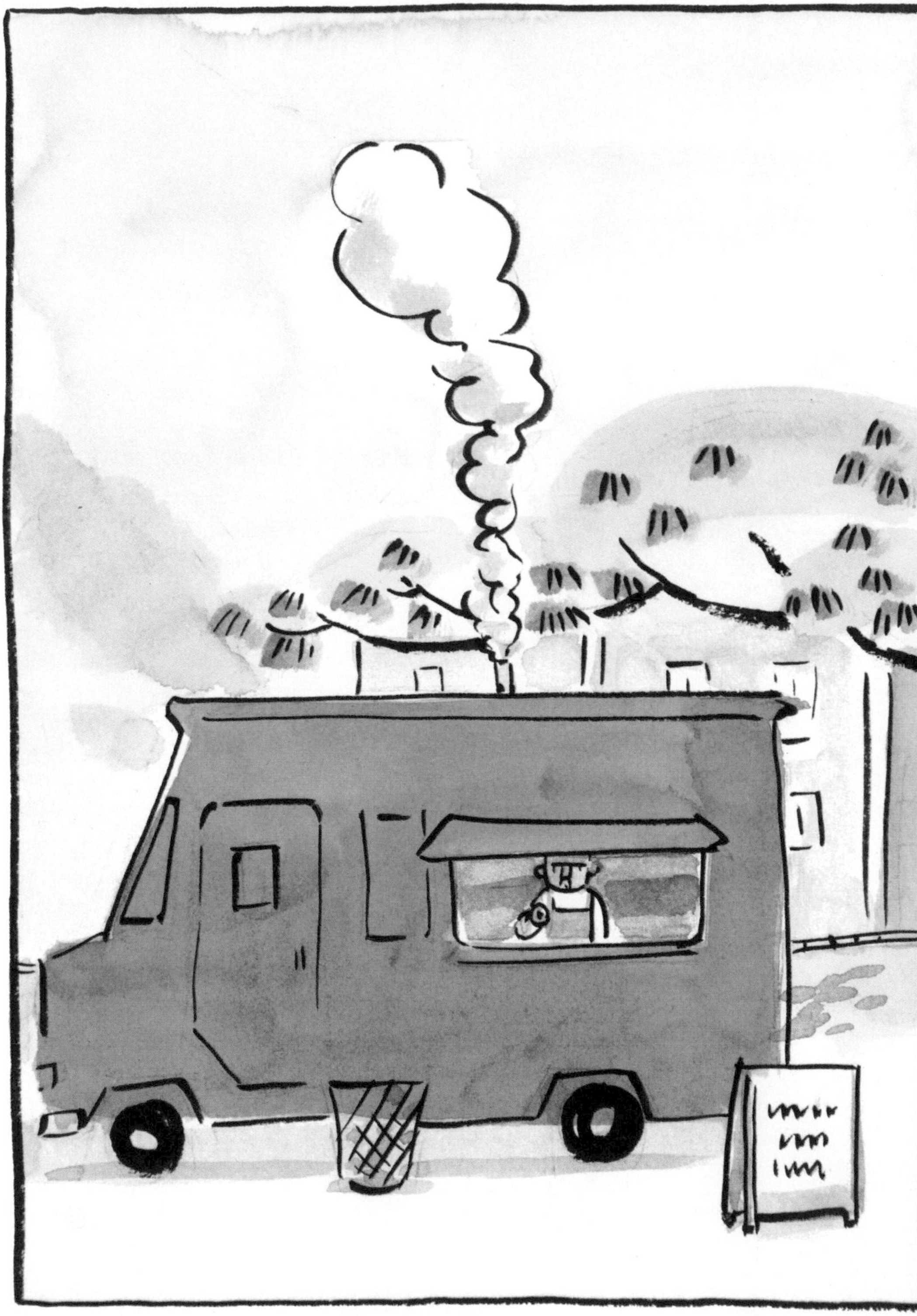

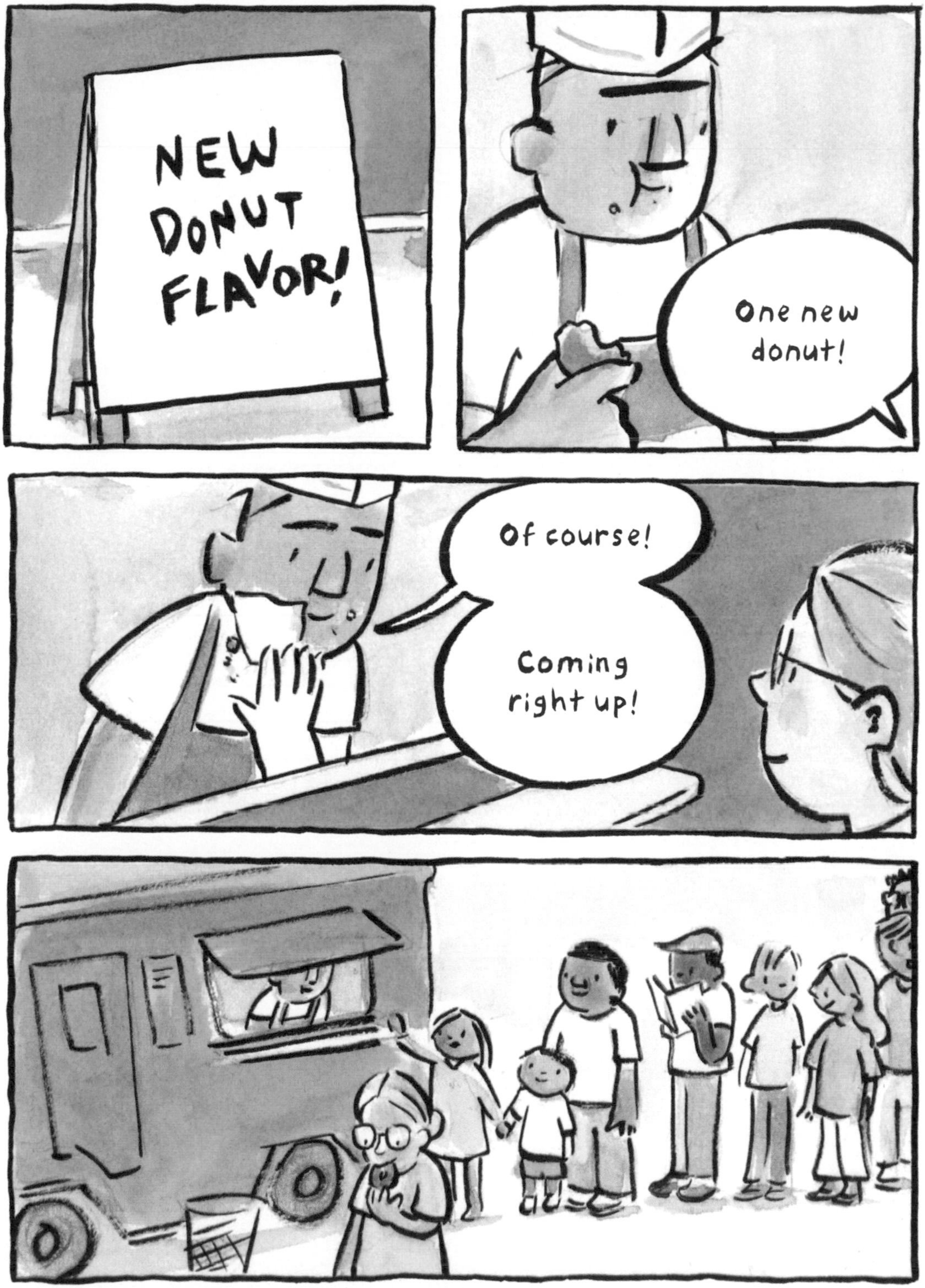
NEW DONUT FLAVOR!
One new donut!
Of course!
Coming right up!

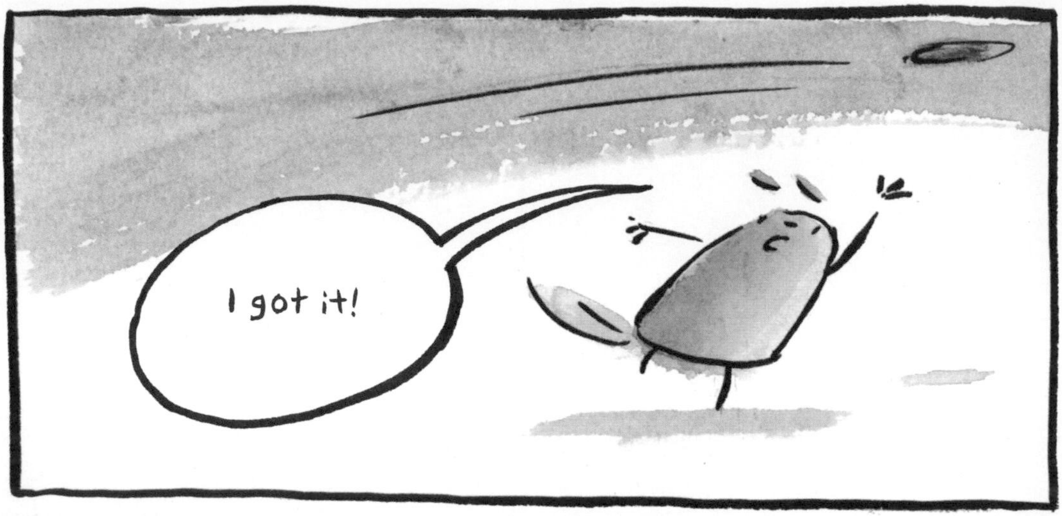
I got it!

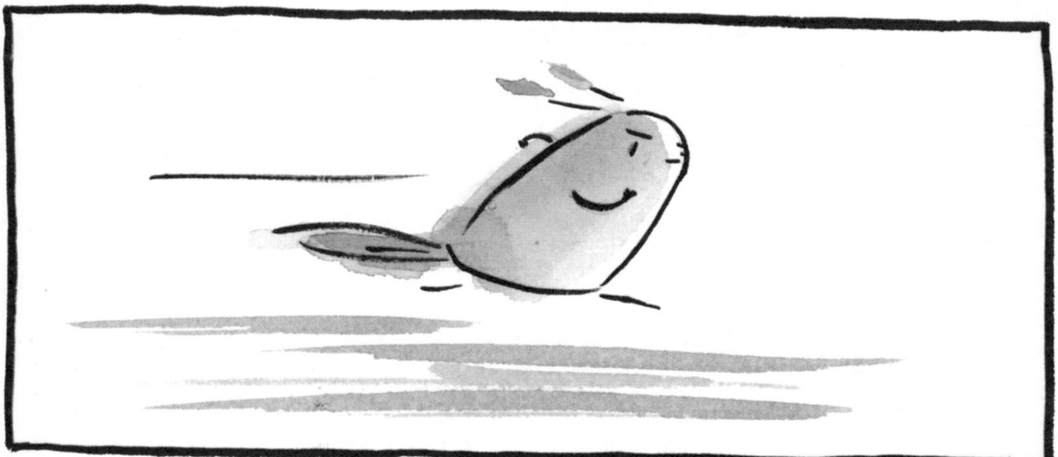

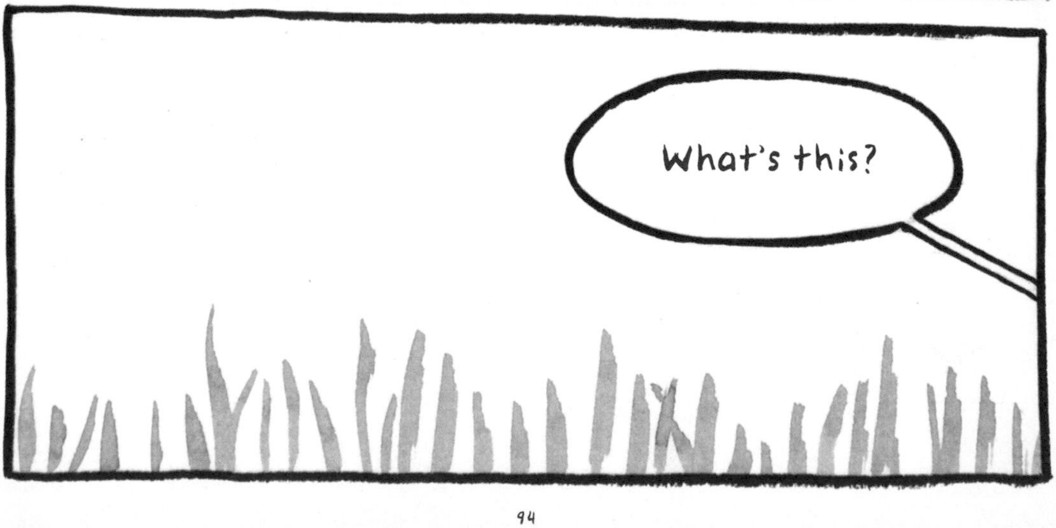
What's this?

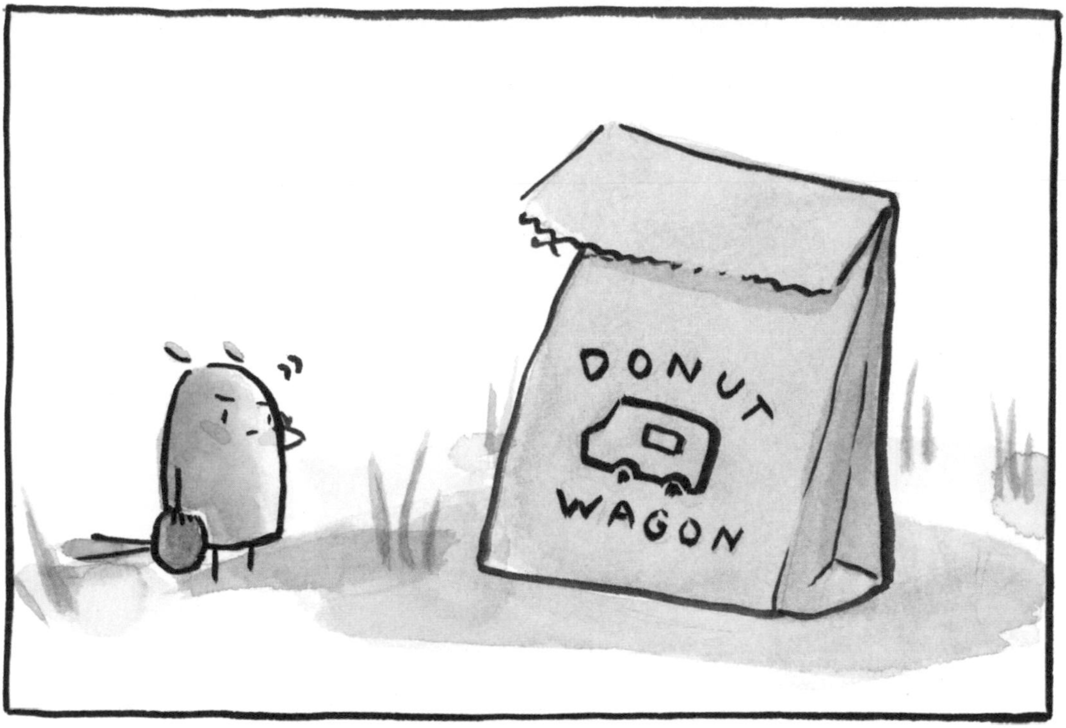
DONUT WAGON

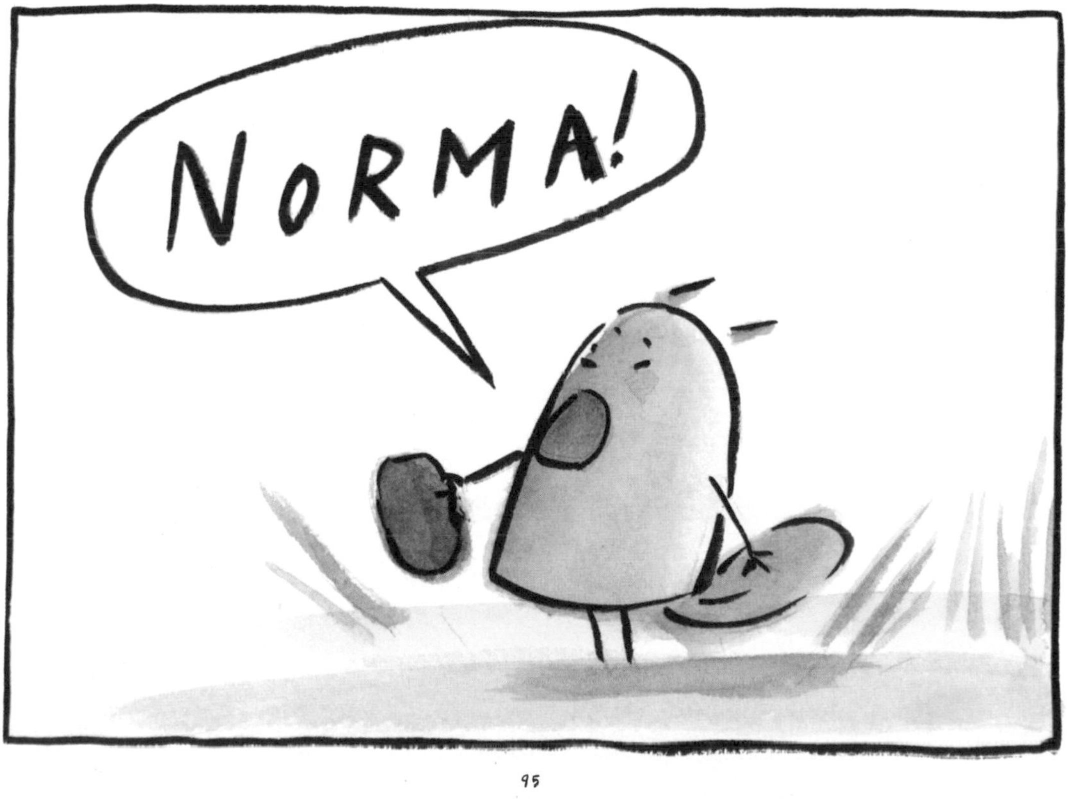
NORMA!

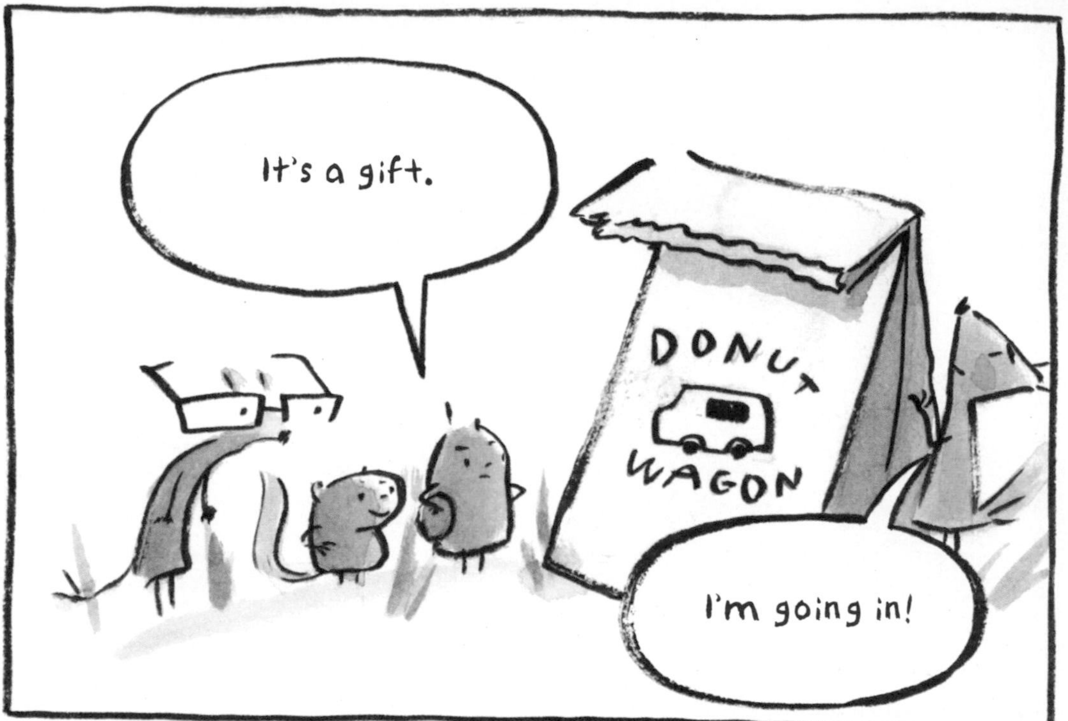
It's a gift.
DONUT WAGON
I'm going in!

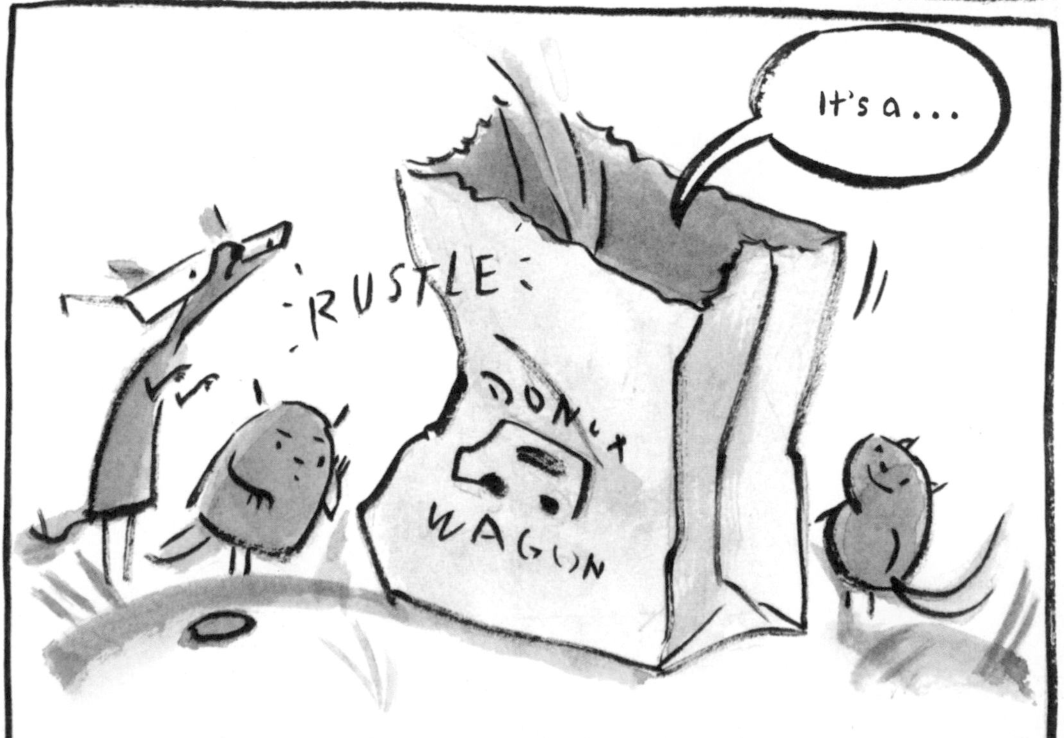
It's a...
RUSTLE
WAGON

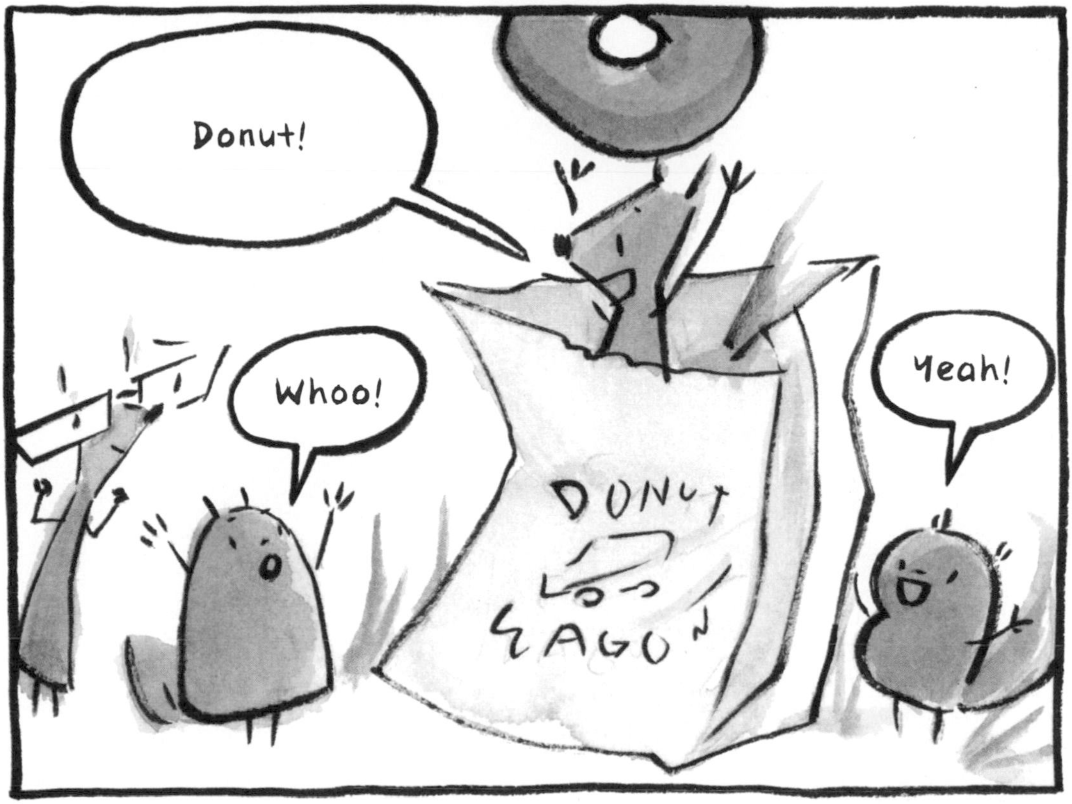
Donut!
Whoo!
Yeah!
DONUT WAGON

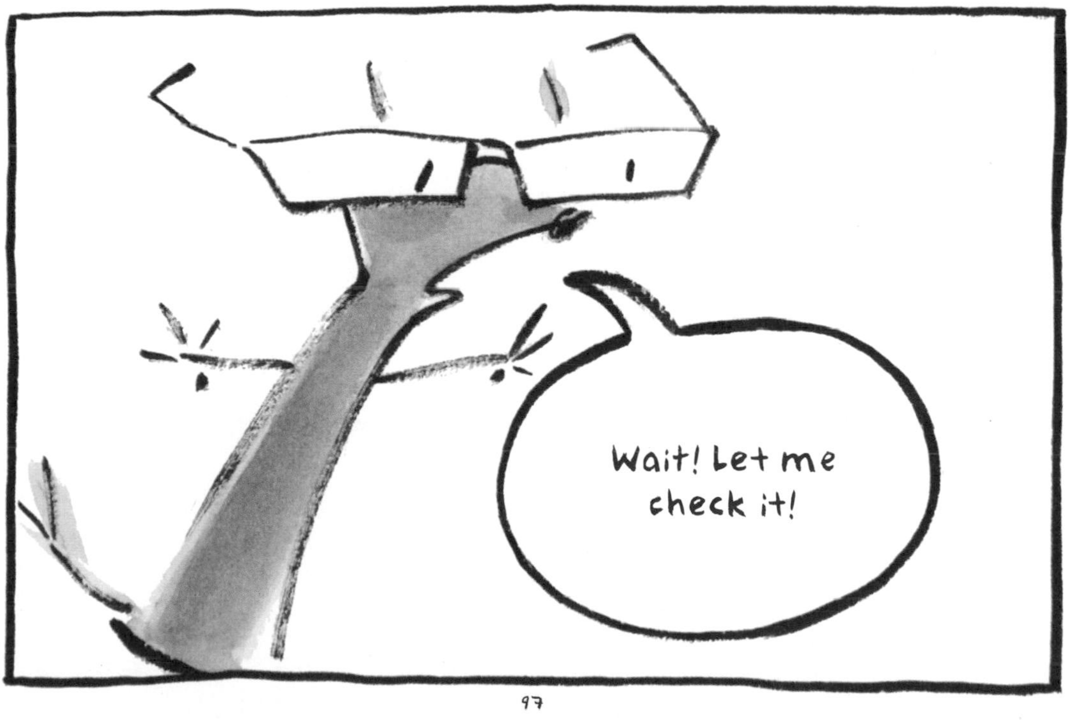
Wait! Let me check it!

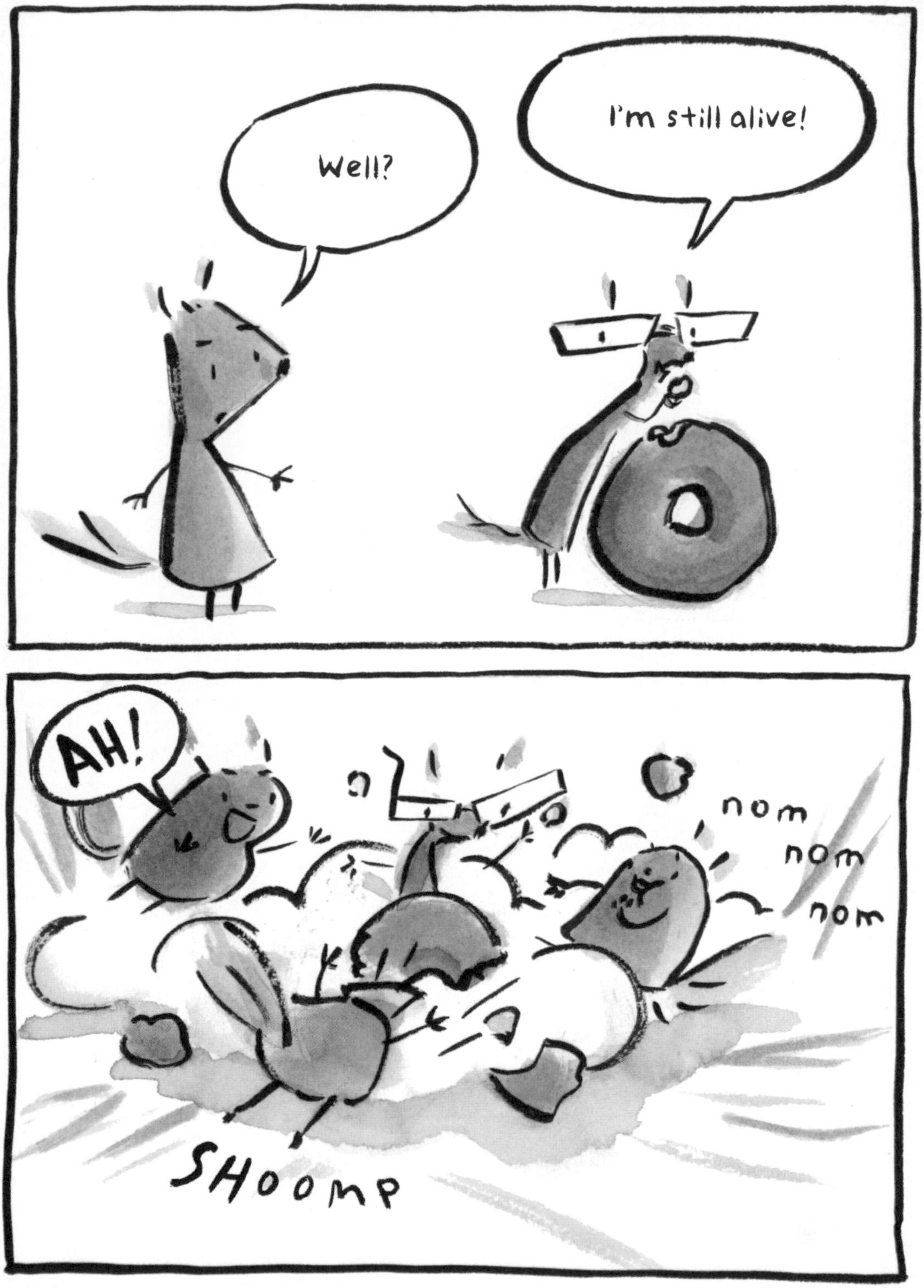
Well?
I'm still alive!
AH!
nom
nom
nom
SHOOMP

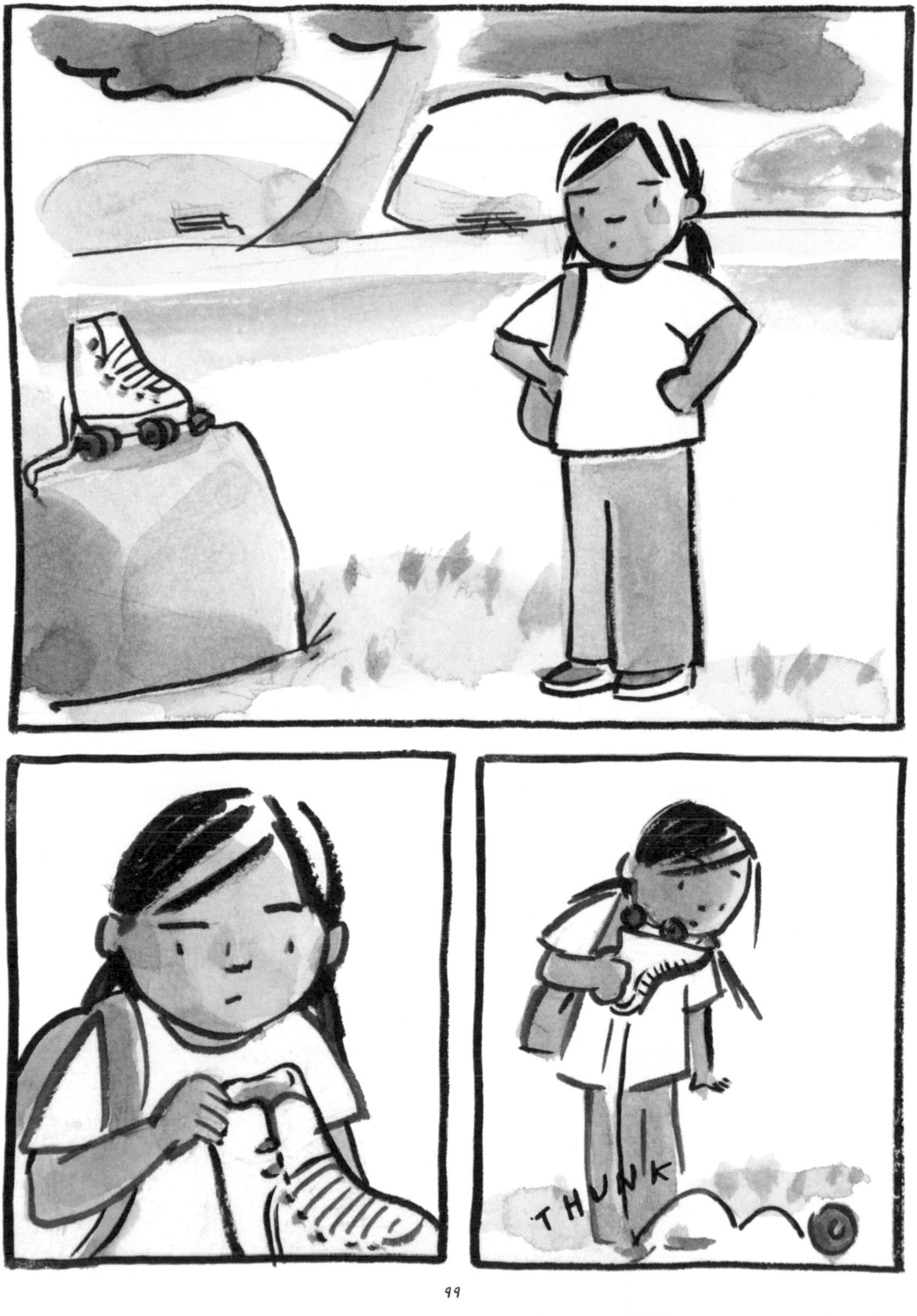
THUNK

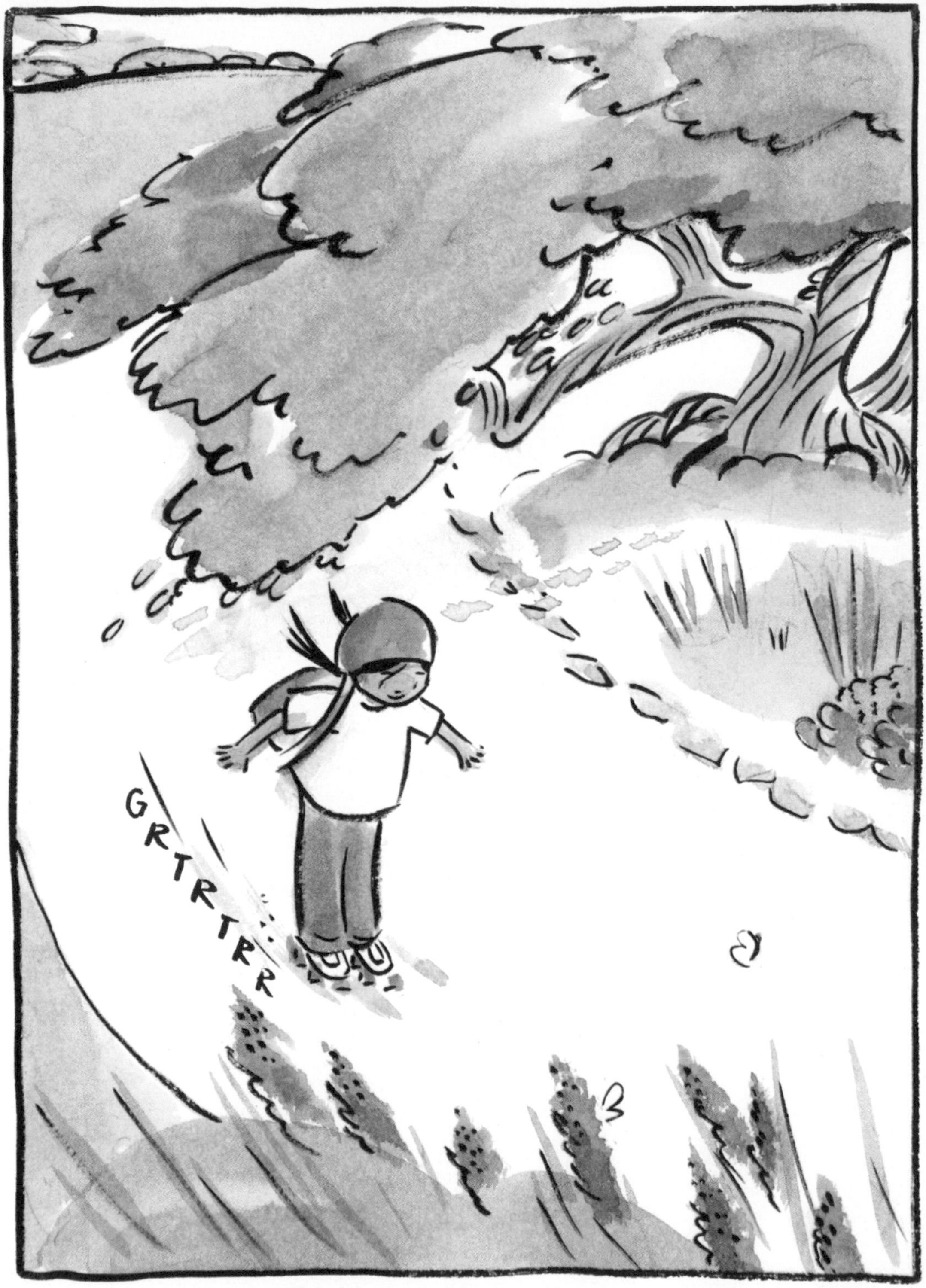
GRTRTRRR

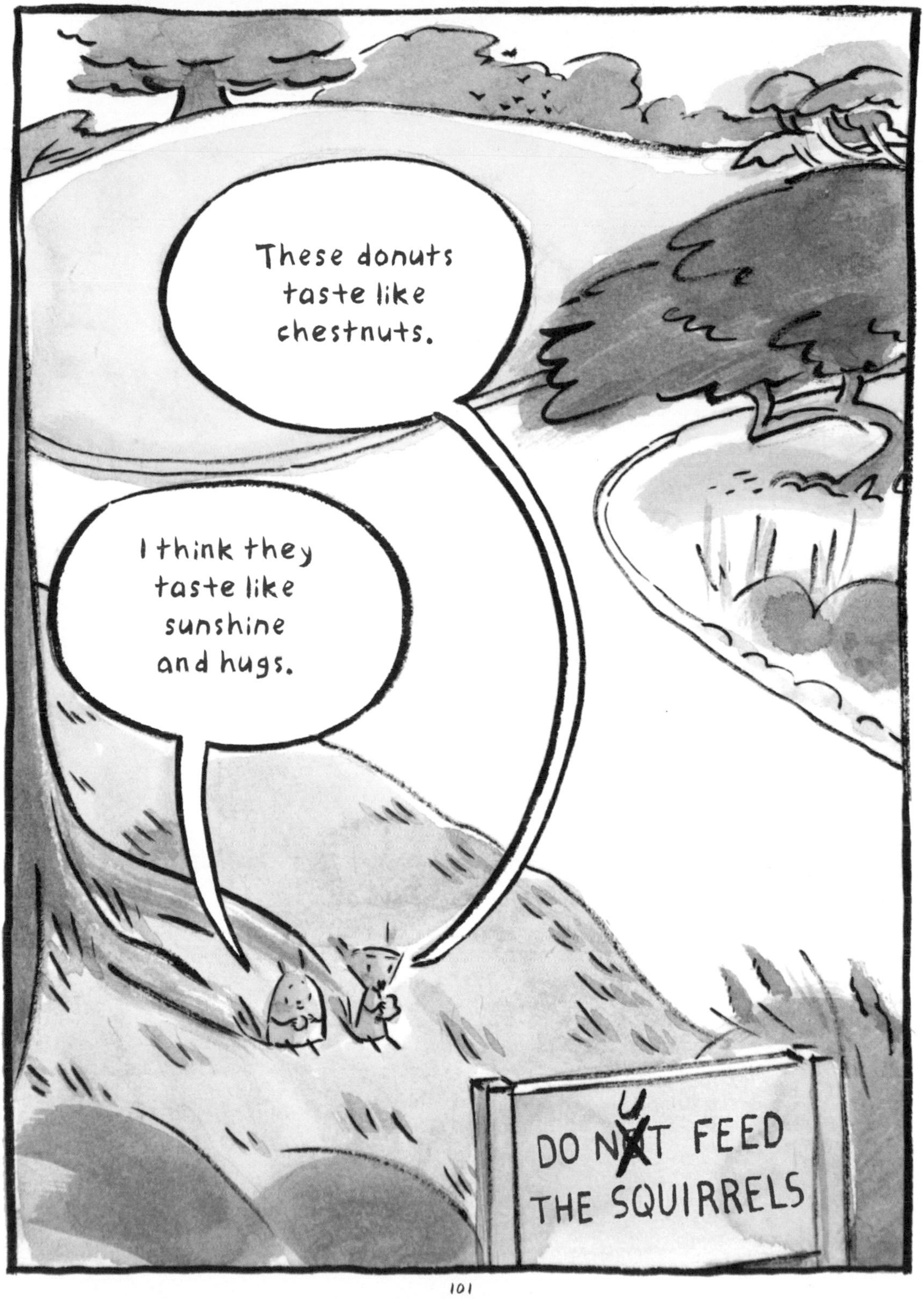
These donuts taste like chestnuts.
I think they taste like sunshine and hugs.
DO NUT FEED THE SQUIRRELS

Acknowledgments

Thank you to Whitney Leopard, Patrick Crotty, and Gina Gagliano at Random House Graphic and Erica Rand Silverman at Stimola Literary Studio, and my critique partners Kenna Weiner, Joelle Jean, and Isabel Roxas.

The story was inspired by the squirrels in Brooklyn's Fort Greene Park.

Mika Song is the author-illustrator of the picture books
Tea with Oliver and the follow-up Picnic with Oliver and has
illustrated several titles, including A Friend for Henry by
Jenn Bailey, winner of a Schneider Family Book Award Honor,
and Hoʻonani: Hula Warrior by Heather Gale. Her books
are inspired by sweetly funny outsiders.

She grew up in Manila and Honolulu and moved to New York
City to attend Pratt Institute. Before picture books, she held
many jobs, most successfully as an animator of children's
educational content. Soon after making the leap, she received
the Portfolio Award at the Society of Children's Book Writers
and Illustrators Winter Conference in NYC.

She lives in New York City with her husband and daughter. She
has always loved making comics. This is her first graphic novel.

🐦 📷 @mikasongdraws
mikasongdraws.com

NORMA AND BELLY RETURN IN A DELICIOUS NEW ADVENTURE

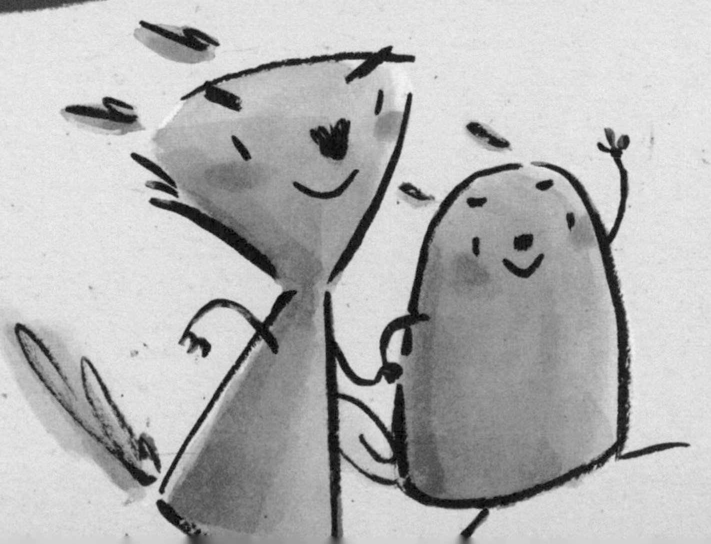

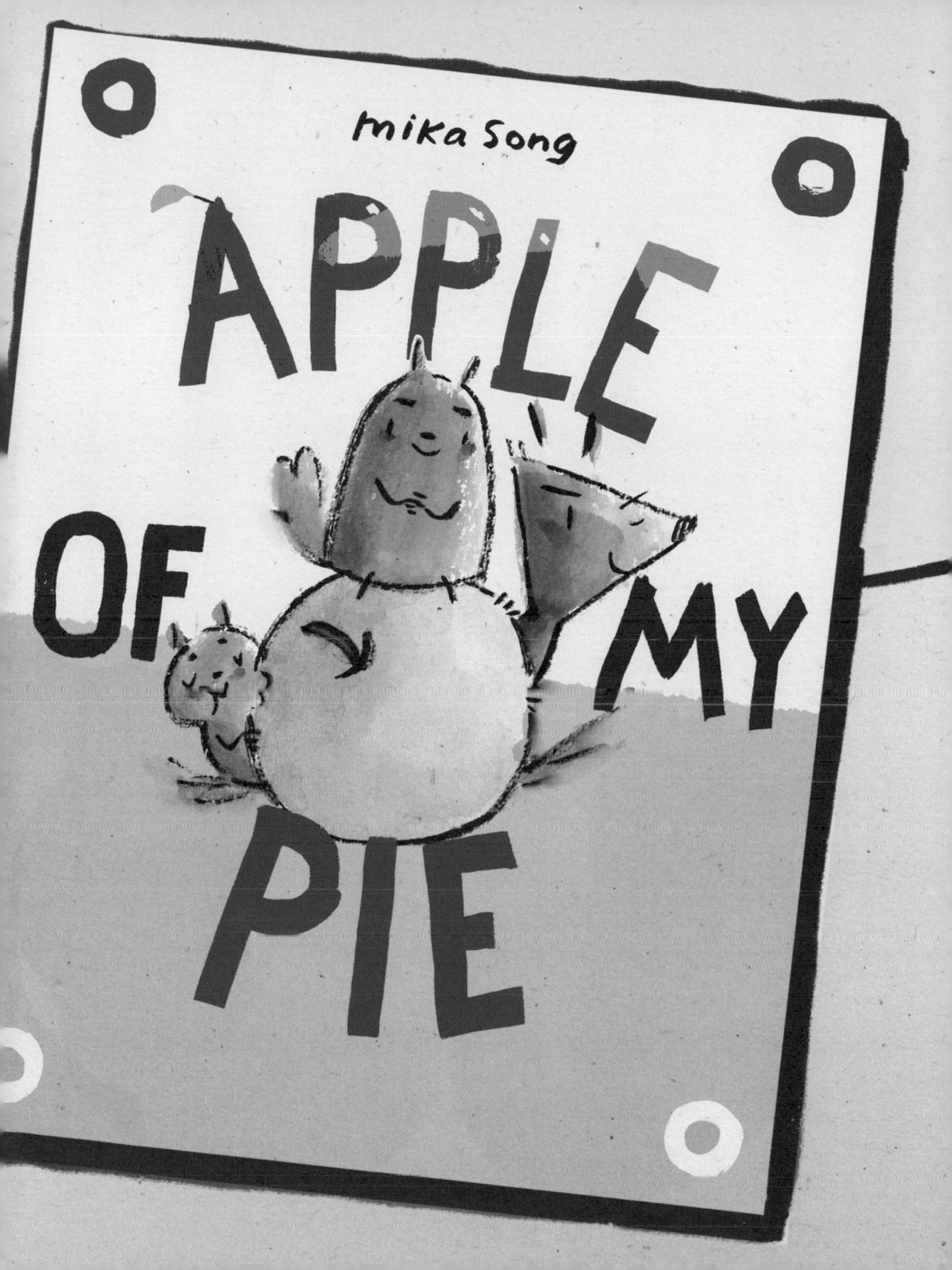
mika Song
APPLE OF MY PIE

AWESOME COMICS FOR AWESOME KIDS.

DONUT FEED THE SQUIRRELS

What will these squirrels do for the chance to eat the perfect donut?

SHARK AND BOT

Will this mismatched pair become best friends forever?

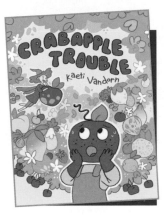

PIZZA AND TACO

Who's the best?
Find out with food, friends, and waterslides.

CRABAPPLE TROUBLE

Join Calla and Thistle as they face their fears in this magical adventure!